Lost American Fiction

Edited by Matthew J. Bruccoli

The title for this series, Lost American Fiction, is unsatisfactory. A more accurate series title would be "Forgotten American Works of Fiction That Deserve a New Public"—which states the rationale for reprinting these titles. No claim is made that we are resuscitating lost masterpieces, although the first work in the series, Edith Summers Kelley's *Weeds*, may qualify. We are reprinting some works that are worth rereading because they are now social documents (*Dry Martini* and *The Cubical City*) or literary documents (*The Professors Like Vodka* and *Predestined*). It isn't that simple, for Southern Illinois University Press is a scholarly publisher; and we have serious ambitions for the series. We expect that these titles will revive some books and authors from undeserved obscurity and that the series will therefore plug some of the holes in American literary history. Of course, we hope to find an occasional lost masterpiece.

At this point six titles have been published in this series, with three more in production. The response has been encouraging. We are gratified that many readers share our conviction that one of the proper functions of a university press is to rescue good writing from oblivion.

M. J. B.

Janet Flanner

The Cubical City

With an Afterword by the Author

SOUTHERN ILLINOIS UNIVERSITY PRESS
Carbondale and Edwardsville

Feffer & Simons, Inc.
London and Amsterdam

Library of Congress Cataloging in Publication Data

Flanner, Janet, 1892–
    The cubical city.

    (Lost American fiction)
    Reprint of the 1926 ed. published by Putnam, New
York.
    I. Title.
PZ3.F6153Cu6   [PS3511.L235]   813'.5'2   74-8655
ISBN 0-8093-0700-6

To

M. H. F.

THE CUBICAL CITY

The Cubical City

PART ONE

I

DELIA sat drawn up in the darkness
on her high stool, waiting for a foot-
step in the distant outer hall. Her
face was turned toward the far end of her big
room where the wall seemed pushed back by
shadows, giving space for her expectations in
the dusk. The sun had gone down and the
dark had sprung up like a balance. The sky
had already weighed out a few grains of stars.
Squared by her window rose her view of the
electric flame and feathers of the colossal cock
on the Heckscher building—neck arched in
space, comb blazing, claws tightened to his nest

of high lights gawdy above Fifth Avenue. Far below from his deep street and hers rose the cackle of horns and the drumming roar of wheels. She stared toward a clock in the shadows but its face was lunar, vague—an undecipherable glow. Then it struck—a collision of five beats muffled by the pomp of gilt and glass.

Her hand reached toward a lamp by her side and from its conical hood a glare aimed down on her long figure and head, leaving the rest of the room untouched and unserved. The brightness faded the blue of her smock with its loose sleeves rolled from bare wrists and its looser folds staining into shadows as they dropped away from her knees. What was left of the color and cotton mass reached down to emerald boots whose equestrian cut had been contented, even worn, by hunting on carpets among chairs. The light bleached her hair to bright chrome, set in thick scrolls about her head. It blazed on her high cheekbones and the redness of their plateaux, lighting the dark fringe of her lashes, as thick about her eyes as bushes around a grey lake.

On the easel before her was a paper smudged with unsettled areas of tentative color and a cluster of inferential black lines. As she stared with drooping lids she saw this flatness already squared in space and hung with painted canvas. Still part of the litter of her room, the sketch had for her the depth of the drafty stage it stimulated and though inert in chalk, lay ready to be peopled and lighted. When she was at work her mind was in Broadway. She co-operated with Times Square's indelicate calcium and flat public colors, respected the spectators, or at least the eager angles where they sat in Goldstein's gilded theater, and as part of its acrid morning air, smelled the odor cast off from early matinal rehearsals and the taint of the owner himself, smoking at her side in the imagined auditorium.

I'll put a door in here, she thought without struggle for the important decision. Her long smudged fingers grasped a stalk of charcoal, her arm lifted toward the paper in the light. I'll have a door, straight center, with a staircase of scarlet spindles and a carpet of white fur leading in honorable retreat from the sultan's tent. A silk tent, inflated. Thus—and with a slit of escape. The chorus girls can trickle out of it like lollypops falling from a torn bag. Red ones. Purple. Lemon. And chocolate for the Abyssinian slave. "Never forget the chorus if you're making sets for my stage," said Goldstein.

He had lolled behind his desk that first day she had seen him, a fat man who seemed the unexcited center of vibrations shaking the silkhung room. Concentrated behind his mahogany desk, he had looked her over with bulging blue eyes, his sluggish mouth emitting limited advice as if, owing to her inexperience, a few phrases were all she could have borne. "The chorus. H'm. They're what I got to sell. The cash getters. I don't know if you know much about theaters, Miss Poole." He had stared at her, confident that handsomeness in a young woman rendered her ignorance ideal. "A theater," he had said, "is a place with seats in it where people on the outside pay to see what you got inside behind the curtain. What we got in our line is mostly girls. In the old days if they was pretty it used to be enough. Now we gotta put 'em across," he had added with regret. "We gotta have expensive lights. We gotta have good music. Beautiful sets. Ideas. They need everything nowadays since life ain't so simple. Since prohibition everybody's got wine and we furnish the women and song." He had stopped talking for so long that she had started to leave. "Beautiful young women. They're a long story." He had lowered his eyes a moment to be alone with the world's great history. "I don't suppose you ever thought much about 'em. I never have nothing else on my mind."

The selected breasts and curried thighs of Goldstein's famous Review had been mere furnishings against space as Delia sat in an empty *loge* those first days, watching rehearsals that whirled like pretentious rounds of housework where polish was put on bright songs or on gestures of powdered flesh. Now after five years the satirists, the singers, the girls with fine bosoms and rolling eyes, the Jewish comics, the Christian *vedettes*—all those creatures of talent decked in sequins or escaping in tulle were like syncopating birds to Delia and the applause of the spectators so much mixed grain they rushed out on schedule to consume each night. The Review had been a special spectacle of the 1920's of New York in which she got fame for gilding the cage and the public spent a fortune for the entertainment of watching the aviary. Theirs was the distraction of seeing velvet, improved chrome lights and pearls flashing among the rare dancing of petulant men, the antics of solemn comedians and the solace of females, finch-pink and gay, hired in large quantities to lift knees in rows, sing on time and be natural in boldness, beauty and eroticism.

At the corridor's end where her door angled

off from the large ill-lit room, she at last heard
voices being raised, both fragile and coarse.
Then hollow high-heeled steps clattered in the
entry, the door opened, closed, and on its ac-
cents Nancy Burke walked into the room. Beneath her small black hat her small white face
hung like a veil with a pattern worked on it of
minute mechanical features. She looked at
Delia. "You've been waiting for this all afternoon, I suppose," she said. Her voice was
lifeless and had an echo of reproach. "If your
friend were used to being in love, he'd learn to
send his letters in the regular mail. Being
postmarked special, the messenger boy has
managed to arrive with this about ten hours
late." She eyed the envelope in her hand.
"Personal and important is written on one corner. And innocence is written all over the inside, Delia. Here." She tossed the letter toward Delia's knees and went on quietly
toward a large gold chair. Her head drooped
as she settled into the cushions, her red lips,
her red-fringed eyes closed. But beneath the

barely visible strands of her apple-colored hair, her ears were cupped for a report. Finally, defrauded by the long silence, she opened her eyes. Beneath the strong solar glow from the lamp, Delia sat pluming her remarkable locks with the ruminant content of a handsome macaw turning in the sun.

"He'll be here about eight. We'll dine someplace. He sails in a week or two." Delia was never loquacious. The letter disappeared into her pocket. "And he says," she added, "to give you his love."

Nancy accepted it in silence. The darkness in the outskirts of the room made a black ring on whose edge she sat, watching with a white face. And in the center of the studio where light gleamed like a core, Delia now turned to her work again. Within the last few minutes her grey eyes had become as warm as ashes in their sooty setting but they were now attentive to her chalk trailing the paper page. Her hand did not waver. Whatever Delia's emotional maladies, they sat up with her before her easel, putting in long days of labor with the rest of her members.

Irresolute before such concentration, Nancy fumbled through some sketches cluttering the ornate table near her chair. "They're good," she admitted. She had never been able to understand how Delia could design costumes. "A woman would know you couldn't. It would take a man to be mad enough to believe. Of course when you get yourself pinned together, you wear your clothes well, but up to that point—" she had once said.

It had taken a coarse man like Goldstein to have faith. Still, no one knew better than Delia his Semitic tastes in orientating color, his homesick passion for importing artistic racial essences from all over Europe and letting them boil again for the public on his Manhattan stages. Swedish ballets, Russian fairs, Spanish singers with high combs and twenty Andalusian lovers to play on their guitars, singing Moscow matrons with boys' hair and adolescent ideas, egg dancers from Algeria with lovely Levantine lips and finally, this latest, the dancer from Siam. Delia had met the banana-colored priestess and though vague as to where Siam might be, had retained from the interview a native impression of brass silks and lovely belled flesh. And for the picked Mississippi Valley chorus which was to surround the foreigner in her canvas temple Delia had invented dresses to hang bare over the barren stomachs of American girls, skirts like Brahman domes, head-dresses high and hierarchical and bodices with bangles.

"One of the series isn't finished," Nancy suddenly protested sharply. She had moments when being both friend and assistant to Delia was more than she could bear. "You know I have to have all six before you go. What'll I do? You could stil' finish it tonight if you only would but I suppose that with Paul coming——"

"I can do it after he leaves at midnight." She dropped back her head with its mane of streaming yellow and beneath this banner

stared at her drawing, lids cloaked, mouth pa
tient and soiled fingers poised in the air.

For a moment Nancy sat in default. Delia
looked quiet and guiltless in the heavy light.
"Oh. I thought since it might be the last time
—I mean—." She stopped. "Isn't he even
going to stay over and see you off at the train
tomorrow? He's still got to go out to the Philippines, he says?" Without gratification she
watched Delia nod.

"He's still got to go to the Philippines and
he's still got to go back to Philadelphia each
night when he comes over here. I daresay his
mother wants to see as much of him as possible
before he sails."

"Though she's helping send him!" Nancy
had no illusion that maternity necessarily in-
cluded logic as one of its pains.

"Why not? It's his chance. Nothing should
interfere with that," said Delia calmly. She
tossed her charcoal on the floor then absent-
mindedly crushing it with a clatter of boot-
heels, promenaded a step and swung into posi-

tion before her easel. One hand held the weight of her chin, the other crossed her thin torso to lift the supporting arm. She looks as if her tooth were aching when she stands that way, Nancy thought.

Delia always drifted to the center of her blatant room, her sensitive fingers with their long clutch cupping her jaw, her body drifting on sagging limbs when the moment came to stare at what she had done and lived by. There was cause for that look of pain her friend noted when Delia viewed her work. Each line of it, each angling scratch of charcoal which, for Delia, would never stay sharp, each blotch of color or tip of sultan's pimpled dome showed the deep volume of her physical talent and demonstrated her inability to draw. After years of success, Delia could not draw a bird or a milk pail without having the models set in a good north light. But she could have designed a palace in which no one could live and everyone would want to. She had a gift for inciting belief in unsubstantial elegance. Had she been a promoter, she could not only have dreamt of but could have handled and created dazzling fortunes for those of faith without herself being able to add two and two or even finding it necessary. She had a twentieth century equipment, ideal for the stage, of imagining color and line in magnificent unschooled unions and she turned out her expensive visions with the energy of an immigrant. "But you can't draw. My God, you can't draw a line. Sure it's grand. It's too grand for any second-rate eye to appreciate. Now it takes a man like me,—" Goldstein always said. A Semitic with a hungry optic.

I suppose that'll have to do, Delia thought and dismissing even the inefficiencies of the sketch, turned to the mate of the chair drawn up at Nancy's side. On the other Nancy sat, as hard as a figurine in black china placed on crocus-colored silk.

"Delia," she said, "I know it's none of my affair but—. What are you going to do about Paul?" she asked with an effort. "With the

others it's never made any difference. I mean
_____"

To what others was she referring? What
was she talking about? Confidences embarrassed Delia. She had never made any. Her
isolated friendship with Nancy had been con-
ducted without Nancy's ever verbally inferring
anything or Delia's ever denying it. Slowly
she crossed her boots placing them like two
green boughs on the flowered carpet. "What
will I do with Paul? Why, what can I do?"
Delia never seemed soiled with responsibility
but met each new question or event in a fresh
rain of surprise.

"You might break his heart." As if to free
herself from constriction, Nancy pulled off her
hat. Her red hair was like another small lamp
in the room. "Paul's not like any one else
you've ever known. Hasn't that occurred to
you?" She leaned forward. Her fingers
tightened, maltreating her hat.

"Yes." Delia spoke uneasily. She added
nothing more. Her eyes looked androgynous,

wide and grey. She would never understand women. "The moment I saw him I knew he was like nobody else on earth."

"Oh. You are in love with him then. Well —" Nancy weakened for a moment. Then with a long breath she revived. "Say it," she insisted, her voice shrill. "After all I've known of you I won't believe it unless l hear it."

"I'll say it." Delia kept on looking at her but her eyes changed. They could take on a porcelain clarity that made them no longer mere organs of sight. They could alter until they looked like two personal inventions set deep in her head, two grey glasses, two microscopes through which she stared collecting her close impression. "I'll put it into words," she said with an effort. "I—I care for someone at last." She had meant to use the word love but she had been unable. Flavored speech always embarrassed her.

Nancy said nothing. "Nothing ever works out right," she said at last. "It'll be his tragedy. He's a stable marrying kind."

Delia sat deaf, undomestic, healthy; even magnificent in her soiled smock and untidy baroque gold hair. "I don't want to marry," she remarked as if in apology. She planted her feet more firmly on her familiar rug. What had once been trees from open spaces were long since turned to beams, gilded and carved, before they had been set up in her rooms and the only visible leaves and flowers were those flattened by her feet on the garden of her rug. Yet in the midst of these falsified forests, these buds from the loom, this air where clouds were stale perfume and a strong lamp was the sun, she sat as if she were suitably settled in some verdant free field. A renter of hired space in New York, still she seemed to be a native of natural seasons whose cosmic burgeoning she carried on in town, thriving like a bigboned blond sapling whose sap and shifting leaves made seasons under a roof.

"You won't marry him then." Nancy persisted. "You love him but——"

"Well, I could hardly marry a man who

hadn't asked me." Delia smiled uneasily. "He hasn't even told me he—he likes me— yet." This was true. Delia's verbal instinct was always for the truth. But he'll tell me tonight, she added to herself. Surely this was no secret. Though she neglected to put it into words, she could feel her unspoken statement spreading in color over her face for Nancy to see. It's our last evening together, Delia went on to herself. He'll say he cares. He'll have to. How could he go away without telling me? "Anyhow," she added a moment later, "even if he had asked me to marry him, why should I want to marry a man who's sailing in a few days for the other end of the earth where he'll stay for a few years?"

"Why did you want to marry Grafton then?" Nancy cried. "Don't forget that when you were in love with him he was going off to war in a few days to be gone perhaps for a few eternities. Had you forgotten that?"

Her nearness dismembered Delia's smile. Nancy's logic and officious memory paralyzed

Delia's tongue. "No, I hadn't forgotten it.
I—" Grafton, she thought—stunned. She had
forgotten him. She hadn't thought of him in
years. And yes, she had wanted to marry him.
Delia had been a person of large appetites.
Big events, faces and seasons had rolled
through her life since she had come to New
York, each heartily received, their passage
leaving her richer if not more recollective.
And in the instance of Grafton along with
love there had been the war. Every drum had
gone through Delia like an orchestra. At
Nancy's words history had begun rolling back.
She saw New York again, gorgeous in its nervous array with flags nailed on its New World
Avenue where each banner seemed permanent,
not merely held in place until European blood
dried. At every street corner there had been
the excitement of huddling crowds of kind
men who, though they believed a little late in
Belgium, once believing, were not afraid to
die. Each male under thirty had seemed heroic. Poor clerks had teaed with the debu-

tante rich and coarse captains had come at
dawn to say goodbye to women and to rooms
they had barely known. Then they had
marched away. Rhythmic boots and the bawl
of bunting conscripted Delia's senses again as
she thought of her past and, scantily clad in
blue linens, sprawling indoors long after the
great bustle was over, still she pulsed in a revival of patriotism as if she were again upright
on a crowded curb, shouting for men on city
streets getting ready for foreign war. One had
been Grafton. Delia was not commonplace.
Except for the flush of profits still circulating
in her America, the war was now long over
but she was unconfused by what had been
called its victory. Stripped of its palliative
pageant and its futile painful results, she persisted in remaining unafraid of death and glory
for herself or even for others. Grafton. She
recalled everything now. "I hadn't thought
of him for years," she said uncomfortably. "I
wonder where he is?"

Nancy shrugged her shoulders. "Or where

the others are, Delia," she said. "In your years
in New York you've made quite a—quite a
collection." She spoke not in malice but as if,
after all her seasons of obstinate friendship
with Delia, at this moment her tongue must
cut a shrill record, incise statistics, which
neither of them would want to see. "Where's
that Russian," she asked sharply. "The one
who said he'd kill you if you didn't see him
again. I remember him, if you don't. There
he sat at dawn, asleep on the curb in front of
your door,—worn out waiting for you to come
back from the Beaux Arts Ball—and be shot.
You never turned a hair. Can't you even remember *that?*" she asked angrily. "And there
was an Italian who followed us back from the
Lido that summer we went abroad. Fulco di
Something—or maybe he was a Sicilian. I saw
him around all that winter. There was Jick
Graves. There was Dick Marquedant. You
were crazy about a blond named Bolton for a
month. What's happened to them, Delia?
Oh, don't you see? It'll be the same story with

Paul. What's happened to Bastian," she added, "and to Guy? Once I couldn't have said this. Now—" She clapped her small hands together. Their smarting sound was as humiliating to Delia as if, nude, she had felt her flesh cheaply slapped. "You were in love with all of those people once."

"No, not in love," Delia murmured. "Only—" She did not want to see Nancy looking at her. She closed her eyes. Faces she hadn't thought of in years appeared in the inner cranial darkness and hung, decapitated by time. All were handsome. Incapable as an artist of perfect line, Delia had always demanded good drawing in the flesh that surrounded her. Yes, all handsome. Weak profiles, soft eyes, susceptible mouths, features, surprising now as she seemed to be noting their similarity and patterned grief. And their kind voices. The helpless tenors of dominated American men. Guy's for instance. She recalled it now as an overtone to saxaphones, moaning and coughing rhythm for their feet along with the wheedling nursing sound of violins. Dick had had eighteenth century eyes, melancholic in the midst of white lights and manufactured palms, orbs that had been turned on her, even to the last, in old-fashioned faithful reproach. These individuals had been figures in a series of slender tall males, following her through bright music into dark dawns during winters of heated night rooms or springs more open beneath trees, summers hung with bold moons, autumns with crisp air and winter falling with soot and snow again. They had all been eager and they had all danced well, failures perhaps at first in their banking, merchanting or whatever was their New York ideal but triumphs by night with Delia when horns drove feet into helpless motion on waxed floors and a pre-Christian African rhythm trembled through Manhattan as the only new invention of the age. "I wasn't —in love with them," she said finally. "You exaggerate. I was young and——"

Young and female, she should have said but

she never had the physical deftness for speech.
She was young and female and they had been
young and male. "But they're of no importance. Now." And probably never had been.
She recalled vaguely Nancy's complaints all
through the brief years. Nancy small, moral,
practical, calling aloud, as if these specimens
who presented themselves were not ripe nor
fine enough for her Delia,—calling aloud in
derision that these were all weak men. Then,
after her outcry, eyeing Delia with jealous dis-
heartened fidelity.

"Are you interested in Paul?" Delia asked
Nancy suddenly.

"What has that to do with it?" Her face
reddened below her red hair, her scarlet mouth
flamed as if painted again. "And if I am, it's
because of pity. It's because he's—he's too
good for you, Delia. And I'm sorry for him.
He's never heard of a person like you," she
cried with contempt and admiration. "He'll
give you everything he's got and then he'll—
he'll be just like me, after Harry left me. I've

been through it. I know." She jerked away from Delia with the same neat strength she had doubtless once used to leap into marriage —a clean fresh athletic jump from school into her husband's arms. "If he tells you he loves you tonight," she said, "it'll probably be the first time he ever said it to anybody. And how many times have you said it? Why you even used to admit to me you'd said it. At first."

True. In her honesty, it had been a principle at first, or at any rate information she had given Nancy that opening night. Or rather morning. In mussed evening clothes, she had walked in and made an embarrassed clumsy matinal announcement to Nancy, alert over breakfast coffee and at the sight of Grafton, entering as part of the explanation at Delia's side. Since then nothing had been said. Delia's emotions had been too vague and complicated for speech. Their differentiations could only have been analyzed by some one with a glib tongue and to some one sympathetic. And Nancy, though victim to her glamorous affection for Delia and though at all times suspicious, was not able to encourage confidence. She had, her Harry had discovered before he fled, the severity that encourages only silence or lies.

Thus she was uninformed. She even exaggerated, it occurred to Delia, about those events she was attempting to guard Paul from now. For what had Nancy ever seen? When years ago both women had been poor, Nancy might have seen kisses snatched under tilting tenement moons. Then as time went on and the scene grew more luxurious, dark figures (one of these always Delia's) turning evasively from topiary gardens to country hillsides as music from big houses died down in fatigue and cocks, fed by the rich, like artists, for their color, took up another noisy rhythm at dawn. In all of that, so much of it inconsequential, what was there to exaggerate or regret?

"Oh, well, go ahead with Paul, then," said

Nancy listlessly. "When you once see someone you like, there's no stopping you. You're
just like a man," she added without flattery.

Delia did not reply. She felt none of her
century's modern antagonisms. All she knew
of life she apprised from the immediate generation surrounding her, offsprings of dom-
inant mothers and fathers respectful of hard
work and the home. Rather ignorant of fem-
inistic history it did not present itself to Delia
as a necessarily bloody trail left by ubiquitous
males who for thousands of years had alternatingly killed unknown women's sons in public
battlefields and privately created sons on their
own unwilling wives. Delia saw men as merely the necessarily opposite sex. Strong herself, to her they were not egotists who had for
centuries left in their conquering wake embittered weak ladies whose existence had been
slow tragedies punctuated by quick births.
Delia was unconscious of all these resentments,
these old truths, these old lives—variants, all
of them, of the mythical brutal Hercules and

his innocent ungirdled Amazon—variants that had been handed down from time immemorial, poeticised in one generation, poisoned in the next, until finally they had become forms of conversation and were practical, even political in a mechanical century where skyscrapers rose as consistently as equal rights. Delia liked few women and made no differentiation against any men. It didn't occur to her to resent being contemptuously likened to what used to be called nature's kings since she conquered them so easily as private citizens.

"Well, if Paul hasn't even told you he loves you, I hope you'll let him sail away in peace. But you won't." Delia did not answer. "You never say ten words yourself but you love to hear the others protest. Oh, I daresay you really don't want to upset him. Then let me talk to him! I could tell him enough to——"

"I—I love him," Delia stammered uneasily. "And I've—I've nothing to be ashamed of. I'm not going to do him any harm. Why do you exaggerate so? You—" Her words gave out as suddenly as they had started. All her emotions had been starting freshly, as if they had never been used, since she had met Paul. Every diversion which had preceded them and which Nancy, unsupplied by accuracy, misrepresented and (Delia wanted to think) magnified was to have been forgotten. "I've never really cared—like this—for any one before. It's for the first and the last time—honestly."

"Don't forget you said that," Nancy cut in. "I'll believe you—for the moment. But if later you ever happen to change your mind, I'll—I'll console Paul," she added. She laughed but it was an effort. "I hope you tell him the truth about—about everything," she said.

Delia did not reply. "Don't go," she said a moment later. She didn't want to hear any more words but she wanted the familiar spectacle of Nancy, efficient, critical and devoted, busying herself about the studio. She didn't want now to be left alone with her thoughts. "I won't see you again for days."

"Do you think you're really going home?"
Nancy paused a moment before extinguishing
her red hair with her black hat. "You're not
going to put it off again?"

"I want to go. I—I want to see mother and
father. I'll take that seven o'clock morning
train. They've been expecting me." After
another night she would start sleeping again
in her old childhood room—hear the trees rattle in the wind and the quiet emptiness of the
suburban road. "I've put them off too many
times."

"You mean Paul has put them off. Paul is
what you've stayed here for."

"This time I'm really going. I've told
Goldstein. I want to go." Her voice died
down as if it were already traveling toward
the distant town and Nancy's pecking kiss that
touched her cheek became the beginning of the
emotions connected with the flight.

"If you go—I say *if* you go—I'll miss you."
Nancy hovered for a moment, looking around
the room. She disliked it when Delia was not

part of its furnishing. Then it seemed dead. Already it looked lacking in its disordered brilliance. "Goodbye." On small plaintive feet she walked rapidly toward the door.

II

THOSE shopkeepers in Sixth Avenue, working between Delia's flat and the edge of the Park, could have set their clocks by her. At a little past six each afternoon she always went by, rain or shine. Today as usual, despite the unrest of Nancy's speech, she made her way along the sidewalk crowded and cold by the fence of the elevated tracks. In the street verdant trams shone like grass among the black flock of evening cabs with their bleating horns and the shepherding call of the police whistle. New York was moving back from work toward those high homes where it lived half way beneath the unseen rock of the island below and the mist hanging in shelter and clouds far over the roofs. Like an anachronous field in the midst of walls and quick traffic, the Park lay undergoing its old inefficient bucolic stages, patient before the façades of noisy streets, watching it for signs of spring.

She entered beneath some tall stale trees that rose from the pressure of shrubbery around their roots like victims of competition, stripped to their branches to survive promiscuous planting and the malady of city air. Day after tomorrow night she would sleep beneath the rattle of boughs if the suburban wind were high in distant Excelsior.

It was a middlewestern town that boasted of its occasional wooded streets though in the outskirts where the Pooles lived, a certain foresting was demanded even without affectation. A long line of catalpa trees fronted the Poole place. As she stood in the Park she thought of them, casting slovenly blossoms onto the new grass in late spring. Catalpas had been blooming before the narrow brick house to which James Poole had taken his wife as bride and he had ever after revived the memory by planting sprouts of the ungainly species before all those dwellings to which the family moved in their early progressive years. In the line before their present home his last planting had had time to mature and settle, growing gross and thick as the seasons rolled on. During the winters they stretched scabrous with naked black crotches and thick twigs lifted toward the drab Ohio sky. In spring they waved their coarse fan-shaped leaves, pulpy and tropical, shadowing a lawn refined with sprouting crocus. By June the tree's blossoming was finished with its sickening ether smell, its sluggish festoons of tubershaped buds lying open-mouthed with greedy centers turned to the warm air. Indolent, the branches fanned the summer atmosphere wherever Mrs. Poole moved outside her house and when October brightened all other herbage with red and frost, the catalpas dropped their leaves in a kind of untidy discontent, uncolored, crumpled and with thick twigs and forking limbs sentineled the winter, their long seedpods hanging dismally in the air.

There had always been something embar-
rassing to Delia in these mementos, circling
each of the neat houses with their ugly fleshly
boughs. Elms or beeches would have trimmed
the small gardens pleasantly but unfortunately
they had not grown beside the brick house
where James Poole first gave himself hurried-
ly to marriage. Even maple trees weren't
utterly unlovely, his daughter thought, staring
at some red-tipped twigs overhead. With the
temerity of its sugary species, here were trunk
and branches already warmed in anticipation
of spring. On hope alone buds now glistened
and swelled, reckless in the late winter mist
with dusk falling in early habit over the city
park.

Idly she listened to the footsteps of some
other wanderer on the gravel behind her, finally turned without reason, then in the silence
smiled. She pulled her hand warm from her
pocket and the man she faced took it with relief.

"I thought it was you." In the depression of

the wet trees, his voice sounded cheerful and loud with surprise. It had a reedy optimistic quality as if its owner, perhaps because of his lively pink face, deprived himself of any morbidity or complaint. In the mist she saw his muscular shoulders stretched in a familiar arc of strength and above them that blond oddly lineless countenance, set like that of a handsome choir boy on a throat thick enough for a sailor. But there were shadows around the pointed nose which she could not recall and the even skin on his high forehead was eating like lacquer into the smooth clump of his yellow hair. The space of the brow looked old. "By jove, I'm glad to see you. Delia. Delia."

His big hand held hers for a moment longer then dropped it without further abuse. An air of obedience settled into his smile as if even there in the dark, had she only spoken, he could be again ordered without protest into loneliness and urged into bravery without turning a blond hair. He stood there while she watched

him and remembered how she had appreciated
his charm.

A smile caused by their meeting, still inflated her mouth. A stirring of flesh set going
by astonishment at unexpected circumstances.
Delia liked drama, co-incidence and other small
acts of God. "You're the last person I expected to see in the Park even though Nancy
and I were speaking of you not an hour ago.
Wondering where you lived. What had happened to you. Once we saw so much of each
other. Now—" She broke off awkwardly.
Her hand moved up to her scarf and stretched
its red across her mouth in shelter as she remembered and wondered at the amiable reck-
lessness of youth. What don't we do, she
thought, where don't we turn our lips and
eyes if the moon is bright or there happens to
be a war or spring? Recollections fell in on
her mind. She stood looking with dispassion-
ate curiosity at a face whose material she had
once accepted, line for fresh line, judging

again the heavy shoulders that had always lacked the selfishness of strength. "You're not much changed, Grafton. After all these years."

"Nothing much has happened to change me. That's all." He laughed. "It's—how many years ago in April since you sat one day by the mirror in that little room of yours in the Square? I know. I doubt if you do."

Her head tilted in slight curiosity.

"You were painting a portrait of yourself. Now do you remember? You kept looking into the glass. Talking. There was sun in the room." A flood of memories drowned his tongue. He laughed again and for a moment said nothing. "I've often thought of that sketch, Delia. It was pretty good. Oh, yes, it was. And you were to keep it for me until after the war—if I ever came back. Well, I came back." He laughed again. "Sometimes I wonder where that canvas is. Probably kicking around your studio somewhere. I'd love to have it. I remember you had a—a green scarf wrapped around your shoulders."

Yes. Bare shoulders, bare arms in the sunlight, she thought to herself, a young woman undressed in green scarf and petticoat. Scarf and bare flesh.

"I'm sure the scarf was green," he said positively as if its color was important. "Do you suppose you could find that portrait? If you don't want it, I'd be—" He broke off, waiting again.

"I don't know where it is. I haven't any idea." Somewhere probably in the crammed untidy cupboards paneling her rooms, tucked away with other articles of discard, her younger face still shining from the dark, squared in the ivory frame which Grafton had squandered his money on. He had always been too generous and too just. She saw his hand wavering and his big fingers creeping toward her arm.

"I'll hunt for it." Her voice sounded hasty

but kind. "It's yours of course, not mine: you should have it. I would try to paint another one for you but——"

"But that you're too successful. I think it's fine." In Grafton's time they had all been poor together. "Well, if you ever do find the sketch, send it to the Harvard Law. It doesn't change nor do I. We'll always be found together, living in the same spot." His lips lifted goodnaturedly. At his smile she suddenly remembered its peculiar trick,—how it lifted the mouth to display his white teeth so that humor and good health were both put on show. His lips were red, for a man, affording him a sense of decoration in a decade where women usually collected all the tints for praise. "I don't change." He shrugged his heavy shoulders. He expected nothing, probably wanted nothing. He merely was making a report.

"I do. I have changed. I'm in love, Grafton. Really. But I mean for the first time, never to—to change again." She did not look at him but stared down the dark path. Of all the people she had known, here was the only one for whom she cared enough to tell her news and here was the one who could be most hurt.

"Good! I always knew you'd do it some-day." His voice was hearty, quick. "You were born to be happy. No one else seems to be." He laughed out loud at her rareness. He wasn't envious. She would manage where he knew he couldn't. "Well," he added more slowly, "I suppose you'll be getting married now."

"That's what Nancy supposed. But I don't think it's occurred to him, the man I love, I mean. In fact," she smiled broadly, "I don't think he knows yet that we're in love. Any-how, marriage would be impossible. He's leaving the country next week to be gone in-definitely." She didn't want to marry. Once she had settled on it. In the first flush of ex-perience she had wanted to ally herself to Grafton and merge passion with patriotism. They were to be in love and he was to go to war. Now the world was at peace and she hadn't seen him for years. "I don't think he's thought of marriage."

"He will if you want him to. Even if you don't, perhaps. Take my advice, Delia. Marry. Being unmarried, my advice is uncontaminated. If you really care, settle down. Oh yes, I'm right. I'm right. That's the only way nowadays to bank one's emotions. Otherwise, a penny here, a penny there and—Marry and send me that portrait as your wedding present." His goodnature had found its outlet again and the sound of it mounted and sifted through the mist that had started gathering in the trees. "Still, if you don't send it, I won't forget what it looks like. If I never see it again, I'll be able to keep it in mind, I dare say." He stepped back. He took his hat from his head, quickly. All his motions were impersonal, classified and deft like a gymnast going through his exercises. "Goodbye." He crushed her hand.

"Goodbye." Her fingers were hurting but she smiled.

"It's a marvelous night, isn't it?" he added and turning, took to the path. His back was straight, his steps long. In a moment he had disappeared. She couldn't even hear him. He was not only swallowed but all report of him was padded in the mist which had descended without her having noticed it.

Now she saw the veils of it hanging around her, smelled the pressure of its moist contact. She stood for a moment motionless, almost thoughtless. She wanted to feel isolated again, unconnected, neither remembering nor even looking forward to anything, merely a lethargic part of the atmosphere's wet touch and soft erasure.

The meeting with Grafton had upset her. Slowly, her animation returned. She started on through the white blurr, facing home again through the uncertain confines of the Park. She looked toward Fifty-ninth Street which

with its bright trams and edifices should have
marked off the ends of the unlighted trees and
rocks. But all rumor of it was walled in by
the fog. Over and behind the hidden street a
mountain of grey dampness had built itself in
the air and on its ascent and height only casual
and topmost lights from the Plaza blazed in
irregular domesticity like the intimacy of cot-
tage lights clinging in pattern as they wound
up a sparse village road.

The wind shifted slowly and other lights
from nearby tall towers flickered and steadied
into view like other evening candles from set-
tlements neighboring on the same high grey
hill. New York in its prosperous grossness
had been wiped out and what was left was a
small feudal town, founded on cliffs and mist
—a petty stronghold, prosperous with little
flambeaux, radiant for a fête with cheap wicks
and free-running oil. And on the peak of
this set of small lights, pricked about by their
halos and cased within the walls of white fog,
rose the colossal cock of the Heckscher for-

tress, the bird flashing like a weathervane mounted in the marketplace.

All Delia's provincial emotional enthusiasm for Manhattan ran through her like quicksilver as she saw the sight. Here, she thought, was the only glamorous city that compensated the western American eye. In her part of the country were to be found only the intestinal states—those organic ones west of the neckbone of the Alleghanies. Here in this city was their head. All else in the land should be covered from sight and shunned as consisting only of incivil torso and vulgar loins. But this, like all capitals, was the country's flaming provoking face. Here one stared. Here was a young male visage, inventive, violent, spoiled, the face of a nervous, handsome and clever only son. Paris had an old girl's countenance, shaded by a trollop's gay wig. London offered the grey phiz of a sour judge, fed on silence, dignity and bad puddings. But here by the Atlantic was a promising Pantagruel, dissipated before he had learned to shave.

The fog gathered, growing denser, more structural. She pushed through bushes that snared and clung, she moved along paths that were wet and ambient with the cold. The lights from the street were now visible bulbs and as she walked on, they turned to clusters, opalescent, frosted, chill.

Once at her corner, expectancy began a swelling process. Her torso felt inflated, light and optimistic as a balloon. It contained no bad humors, no irritations against anything nor any bones. It could have lifted her up dozens of flights of stairs without tiring her members nor wearing out her hope. At the floor on which she lived the hallway, with its flank of bogus arcades, stretched almost with charm as it lead to her door. Paul would be inside. Her hand fumbled at the knob.

A gust of high laughter reached her before the door fell open. The studio was white with lights. Paul was nowhere in sight. Black in the center of the room and baited with sooty silk and fur, sat the worldly handsome figure of Mercy Wellington. She sat in perfect composition. Her elegant ankles were crossed, her fine legs mounted like ebony dividers to her hem. Her sleeves were tight and below her slanting hat and her tawny hair, on her alert mature face little fine lines shadowed embroidery on her skin and seemed to have made a smart loyal toilette on her flesh.

"Ah, you see!" She had a treble voice that was tuneful and triumphant. She bent toward the next chair and vivacity and charm swept toward the one dark man at her side as if he were making on her the stimulating demands of an entire dinner party. "Here she is, as I promised. Of course," she called to Delia, "we've been waiting for you for a full hour, darling. We were just about to cast our nets on the other side of the hall. This is Compton Keith," she went on in her constant crescendo. The feathers on her toque were quivering, great gold chains rattled as she fingered them

on her firm breast and laughed in her deep
lungs beneath. "I've told you about him,
though what was it I said? One can never be
sure afterwards."

Delia nodded to her and to him. He had
a blunt watchful face thatched with adven-
turous black hair. He wore a red tie and was
tall. As big as a pioneer. Yes, Mercy had
spoken about him, she recalled.

From behind the curtains that gave curiosity
and shelter to her bedroom she heard the
rumble of his voice blasting Mercy's mirth and
tried to remember what had been said of him.
Gold mines, Mercy had said he loved, or was
it only coal? Something anyhow of continual
value dug out of western hills in a difficult and
exciting gamble. Whatever it was he hunted,
Delia decided as she moved into her lighter
clothes, he had left part of his youth on the
rocks.

The bell rang.

"Ah, Paul."   He was entering on Mrs.
Wellington's crescendo. "Delia's waiting for

you. And indeed so am I. So is Mr. Keith here without knowing it. Don't deny it, Compton," she said with energy. "If you haven't even been waiting, then you've been doing nothing at all for the past hour. Delia!"

With the effort of facing words and watchful eyes, Delia pushed through the curtains into the large room.

III

DELIA's elbow was planted on the table. Her head grew heavy and rich from her hand. Through a cluster of hyacinths, flowering between her and Paul, her eyes caught extra color and swelled, magnified, as she stared over the bice-colored buds. Her body was hot. All its membered heat hidden by public satin and fur, seemed to be rising to focus privately in her face.

"Paul, don't go back tonight. Why not come up to my studio where we can talk? There's that big couch by the fire."

The bald noble head of their waiter was suddenly laid before her. It lay on a nest of steam rising from the coffee he carried. Below his refined cranial egg she saw Paul's eyes widening, their brown deepening to an astonished black.

She broke off, still gazing at him over the barrier of her high cheek bones. Wrapped in grey furs and gold fabrics, she sat like a richly dressed effigy, swaddled like an ikon stooping for a moment to offer the miracle of common hospitality and to make use of the colloquial vulgar tongue. The waiter moved away. "I'm going home tomorrow. It's the last time we'll see each other for months."

"For years more likely, Delia but—I can't stay." He fumbled slowly over his response, still watching her. Tabled with her luxury, surrounded by the richness of the room, he looked helpless among women and hyacinths, dressed in his shabby tweeds and decorated only by his thick unpetted-looking brown hair. "My mother's ill, Delia. She's always been an invalid, or for years anyway. This time

she's in bed. She sleeps badly and worries.
If I didn't turn up——".

The warmth faded from Delia's eyes and
with concentration they toured the room. Caution and consideration seemed remote from
their table in the Crillon. Behind Paul's head,
filled with duties and the conflict of illusions,
she could see the frescoes of red and blue wom-
en moving nude in their modern civilization
painted on the next room's walls. Ardent
birds and flowers were patterned at liberty on
plaster in the small alcove where they sat.
Tables near at hand flamed with red lobsters
blushing as if they had been abducted rather
than caught and lying now in sauce before rich
men's eyes as a warning to all sweet scavengers
still ignorant in the sea. Trout with numbers
in their tails like registered sailors, had stopped
swimming to lie in copper pans, ending as
motionless delicacies for women too urban to
have bothered with the sound of a brook. All
that she saw was luxurious, caloric. The heat
from it mounted to her primitive mercurial

mind and warmed her senses, forcing their re-action as the flowers on the table had been forced and made to blossom and swell in domi-ciled heat.

"Stay tonight." She spoke in a common-place voice but her fingers, moving in rare promenade among the chill of porcelain, met his and their hands sunk together, locked, be-came braided.

"I can't stay at your place, Delia." The unexpected pressure of each of her fingers was laying a mark on his face. "Men don't stay in women's rooms no matter how much they have to say. Certainly they don't stay when they're—they're in love with the woman as I am and can't think of—of anything except wanting to talk about it and ask if—" The red tint in his face which his first touch with her had laid on his skin was fading to white as if methodically following that slower thera-peutic law by which wounds in the course of time become pale recollective scars.

It seemed to her she had been waiting so

long to hear what he had just said that, having now heard it, it kept repeating itself, each omission he had ever made before, fulfilling itself, all coming at the same moment and coming not once but again and again until the receptiveness of her ears, flooded by the overtone of blood that seemed rushing to them, as suddenly subsided again and she could hear only what had already become memory and her pulse. She wanted to repeat his statement, say "I love you, too," put his admission into her own words but her hands tightened on his with dumb gestures. "Why can't you come to the studio?" she said. "Other people have stayed there. Artists," she added with a certain speed as she watched his face. "Why shouldn't they? Sometimes when one is poor hotels cost too much money. It's my place," she went on with obstinacy. "I'd ask a king to stay all night—if I knew one and thought he was interesting. One gets little enough from paying New York rents. I want you to come." Her hands tightened to his. Her honesty and luxury from which, now that she was well established in life, she seemed to gather such strength, were like a rich endowment from which she drew not only the expensive decoration of her grey furs that gave her grey eyes the value of semi-precious stones but also her special free attitude toward the costly walls that housed her, the sum of all these expenses only being a tithe of what was her fund of resourcefulness and amplitude. "Why shouldn't you come up to—to talk?" she insisted. "Why not at midnight as well as midday? I work all day. Night is the only time I have. I want you to come. If you want to —" She broke off, ill at ease.

His face had on it the shock of an enthusiasm. "You're marvelous. You're what I thought you were the first time I saw you— only more. You're——"

Delia lacked the ego for self-analyzation yet her artistic eye, as impersonally as it might have rolled over a foreign landscape, vaguely informed her of certain truths and shapes of her own life. Her rooms were no habitat for theories of freedom, as Paul's face inferred. She had no doubts nor pretensions. If her door was free, what it led to was merely the luxurious cluttered retreat of someone with a chance but magnificent appetite for healthy liberty. Speech was always difficult for her. Her honesty had been set in motion but it had not reached her tongue when the excitement in his voice arrested, then paralyzed, whatever she had been going to say.

"Yes, I'll go back with you. We'll talk. Oh, you'll never regret having asked me. We have everything in the world to say now. We'll—" He turned dazed to the bald waiter. As if each of his actions was part of this evening she wouldn't forget, she watched Paul, shabby, nervous, his deep chin bent over the flame of his orange tie, his heavy hands fumbling in a worn wallet which finally, in exasperation, he emptied, thrusting it and the grateful employee from sight. "It'll be lonely out in those islands," Paul said, looking now at her.

"Since I've met you, sometimes I've wondered what—what I was going to do with myself out there. I know now." He nodded his head. "I'll remember tonight. Every word we say. You—you wouldn't want to go to the Philippines, would you, Delia?" He leaned nearer.

"Oh, I—" She pulled away from his disappointed face and stood up. She threw her coat about her.

"I didn't really think—I mean I—"

In her preoccupation and discomfort the adjacent room stretched before her only as an indifferent aqueous pool with floating white faces among which there suddenly rose, like a small capped wave, a flickering familiar smile, breaking the surface, catching the eye. Behind the smile a hooknosed young man working with lobsters, dropped the scarlet claws and lifted himself from space. "How're you, Miss Poole? Huh?" As part of his appetite his mouth still hung open, ready to give instead of get pleasure to be localized between his greedy lips. But Delia did not stop. She nodded automatically and went on toward the door. He stared after and as Paul appeared in her wake he sank back without a sound. His mouth that had been ready for speech and was still open under the strain, closed again over a tendron of saccharine pink flesh.

Paul walked close to her side as they started up the privacy of the ill-lit street. "I'm sorry I said what I did," he protested with excitement. "After all," he remarked to himself, "many men must have tried to drag you off to the ends of the earth. It seems to me that Nancy said——"

She did not ask what Nancy had said. Only a few coats were blowing, heels were clicking in the wet February wind that was now rolling quietly up the Avenue. The sidewalk's citizenry was made up of these rare ambulating figures and the row of civic lights marching ahead of them into the palatial distance.

"Love," said Paul, "seems to cost money.

I haven't a cent. From what I can gather, my job is going to take me miles beyond even the civilization of tinned butter. Monkeys and natives will sit on my doorstep. It's certainly no place for a woman even if she wanted to go. And you just said you didn't. I might have known you'd say that. You see, Delia, I have nothing to offer. Though I'd like to know," he added a moment later, a little helplessly, "what any man could offer that would be sufficient for you to change your life." He walked on for a few steps, watching the volcanic sky and beneath it, like the cause of its eruption, the rich lava-colored brownstone of what had once been polite domestic seats and were now turned to ruthless shops in that metropolis he seemed to regard as Delia's bewildering New York. "You earn more than most men I know," he laughed. "And I unfortunately began in the hole somehow. The bottom fell out for us Jarvises when I was ten. You see Delia, if you're in love with me—I say if—" he caught at her arm, laughing still in excited apology, "I'm not much to your credit. Not yet."

They walked on in silence for a moment. She was ignorant of his background, even un-curious about it. Within the last half hour their emotion had become a meeting point from which, with her temperament, the future started vaguely, indefinitely unrolling before her, but it was to Paul a dramatic historical juncture that finished his past. She had no desire to know anything more about him than her eyes could have told her if she had turned them on him for Delia, though without a re-ligious sense, had the loyal indifferent credul-ity that had marked early peoples who had ac-cepted Venus as rising ready-made from the sea, an isolated new arrival without precedent, social ties or childhood, but ranked like Paul because of the emotion she aroused.

"Always to have been without money is terrible—in America," Paul went on. "We had a little once. But my father's eccentric. I dare say you ought to know, Delia, that he's the kind of man who gets wild ideals and then makes wilder sacrifices for them. Including mother and me. He was a lawyer in a small town who decided the public schools there weren't good enough for his son so we sold our house—it had been grandfather's and was nice —and moved to Philadelphia where my schooling was so ideally expensive that father fell into debt, never got out, couldn't find a partner in law and finally became a legal clerk in some big offices there. That was fifteen years ago. He'll finish at that. So here I am, Delia, in New York tonight in love with you and without a sou." He laughed uncomfortably.

Poverty was something Delia approved of, had been familiar with. There had been in her childhood pinching periods for the Pooles. From her bed while her skin chilled with fright she had heard her father patiently explaining the causes of his occasional disasters,—democrats and taxes, slumps in country soil or city land which after he had bought it, he could not sell. Then the encouraging voice of her

mother, the scratching of her father's pen as
he schemed to outrun hard times and, like all
Americans, carry the fortunes of his generation into the flourishing future. And with his
same healthy optimism, years later Delia had
come to New York and nearly starved. But
poverty had developed her sense of selection
and her strength. Poverty was a test. It
threw you a-straddle of life, taught you to
cling to the wild horse. Ride, fool, ride. Or
fall off.

Across the street came to her eye at this moment her favorite rich mansion, Gothic cro-
chetings trimming its sloping local roof,
French carvings mounting from its pinnacles
to stretch themselves like disinterested foreign-
ers into the American sky. If in that house
could be found no old rich grandfather who
had once been poor and who could narrate the
version of his brutal youth,—some one who
had helped stretch railways across the continent's breast as later he would learn, for his
wife, to stretch collars of pearls on women's

throats, then no nimble dining or dancing could make up to his heirs for the dullness of their uneventful wealth.

"Delia," said Paul. "Will you say you love me?"

"Yes."

His fingers tightened on her arm, hunting through the fur for her flesh. "Delia!" he cried excitedly. "Delia! But what am I going to do? Why does everything come at once? For years I've had nothing at all. Now I've got you—and my first chance at a decent job. And I can't choose," he said more slowly. "I'm tied. My father's brother is the one who's giving me my chance. Through all these years my family's heart has been set on—just that. The first Sunday in that new Philadelphia Noah's Ark-house we moved to, I saw a man stroll up the street. I was ten. I'd never seen him before and I never forgot how he looked and the impression he made. I knew he was father's only brother, that they'd quarreled, that he was rich and that he'd lived in the Philippines. That he'd lived all over the world. Sailed in ships. Talked with black natives. I was ten and I'd never been farther than Philadelphia. For years it was my dream to be able to dress in what he wore that day I first saw him. He had on," he said apologetically, "a white linen suit and hat and he had a red silk bandana in his breast pocket. I thought he was grand. The next Sunday he came to dinner again. This time he had on blue serge. And a red bandana. It was September. I found he sent to China for his clothes. White from June till autumn. Blue from autumn till June. The handkerchiefs came from silk looms in the Malay straits. I've known him now for fifteen years and he always wears the same uniform. Sometimes I think they're actually the same clothes. He moves so damned cautiously he'd never wear anything out. Delia, he's—he's amazing. And—mean.

"Well, the second Sunday he began on the Philippines. Natives. Monkeys. Sun. Hemp. And work. Oh, yes quite a lot of work for a white man interested in hemp. Did I know what hemp was? I was ten. Well, he dragged out a geography. Did I know what work was? You bet I did and do. That was the beginning. Father was broke. Old Uncle Boyd was rich and unmarried. We knew he was unmarried but have never known how rich. And so they began breaking me in. Someday, if I lived through it all, I might be made his heir. He never said anything, never gave us any money even when we had hardly enough to eat in the house. But he always gave us hope.

"Whenever I wasn't at school, I worked for him. Warehouse. Clerk. Cordage department. Nine hours a day at half pay. Oh, I always had a job—at half what the other men got. When I left college, we expected I'd be taken into the firm. He came to dinner as usual, began talking about a remarkable opening he knew for a hardworking young man who, (if his health didn't break down and he had the meekness of a Christian slave) could, in a few years, etc., etc. Ah! The young man was me," he laughed, "and the remarkable opening was a clerkship in a suburban bank at $18 a week. But I had a wonderful letter to the president from Uncle Boyd, which made it appear I was so grateful to get the job that I didn't mind the other clerks all getting $20 for the same work. Well, that's about all." He laughed again. "I couldn't afford to go to war when it came. Father had pneumonia and no matter how much you hate the Germans, you can't support your parents on a soldier's dollar a day. Then later Uncle Boyd transferred me to a foreign investment house. Then to a Chinese bank. Oh, he educated me. You should see my mother, though, Delia. She isn't fifty but she looks sixty, my father's age. All these disappointments were too much for her. She caught up with father those years, somehow. Matched his grey hair. Molded her face into wrinkles to suit his. I became— stodgy. Never went anywhere. Nice girls cost money to entertain. The others—Oh, well, I dropped them almost as soon as I'd started with them. Do you believe me, Delia?" He turned to her. She felt his face bending into her own.

"Yes, I believe you," she said faintly. Her hand rose to her throat. She lifted her furs across her mouth to hide it. Why had he to tell her all this? While they walked up the Avenue he had hung it with pictures of his family, his past and his inexperience.

"Well, it's all over with now," he said triumphantly. He held her arm, carried her along in the wake of his disappointments. "The Sunday after I met you the old gentleman came through. Offered to send me to the Philippines, write my name on his letterhead —anything you choose. My mother—and I wonder why, too—wept. My health was drunk in blackberry wine which is all our cellar boasts of. When mother has time to make it. I've been waiting for what's come to me in this last month, for exactly seventeen years. And now I don't want it."

A half hour ago nothing had seemed to her

important except Paul's confession of his love.
Now figures clouded it—the uncle and (perhaps because they carried no red bandana to
guide her pictorial imagination) more faintly
the other two Jarvises. She saw them, two dim
figures standing behind Paul, growing old in
the seclusion of shabby rooms, watching for
their son to save them, making affectionate
gestures to each other while they waited, living qualified lives in Philadelphia side-streets,
in an existence shut off from all active pleasures but those of hope and domestic love.

She turned on the lights in her studio. All
that was in it stood out in a bright and vigor-
ous blaze which she evaded in the shelter of
her bedroom. Through a crack in the mauve
curtains she saw Paul staring about him, motionless in his position on a tawdry rug. Still
strange to her rooms, he stood looking curiously at the unseasoned assortment of furnishings
that made up the background for Delia Poole.
All about him rose that crowd of rich articles
she had herded together with her first savings

and then left on pasture for color and polished line.

At their head was a pair of weak old Pompadour lounges, weighted with an impenitent upholstery of scarlet and mauve, puffing over carved calves. In the doors of a chest near the window glimmered a bright geometry of inlaid woods, squared and starred at a French period when for the first time at a Bourbon court, mistresses' follies no longer mattered, a queen supplying more than enough irritation to inspire the impatient Revolution. Framed in Empire beading and decked with an upstart N, relics of pale Napoleonic needlework lay dying under glass on the walls. In one corner of the studio was a huge ormolu table, regal with polished brass and in another a buhl cabinet where tortoise-shell veins showed bare like scrolls of expensive and skillful dissecting. A final flash of gilt blazed from some low-hung saffron chairs starring the room in a fiery circuit—the last of a crowd of Continental loot rolled into her chambers, as soon

as she could afford them, as ornaments for her
Manhattan empire.

Delia had an elastic suspicion that everything she owned was a fake. None of her
possessions, she opined, had ever inhabited a
gutted palace, as the dealers swore, or had
creaked beneath the weight of a royal mistress.
Still their color and lines were magnificent no
matter how innocent their past. And both
suggested two passionate periods of French
history whose dates she was vague about but
whose drama and force, what she had heard of
them, she passionately admired. Pedanticism
had not spoiled Delia, as her rooms showed.
To her revolutions and kingdoms remained
only grand rumors.

Amidst all this glamorous collection, one
simple article was on view. A clerk's stool sat
before the easel. She had bought it second
hand. Along with a cot it had been her first
New York possession. The cot had been ab-
sorbed years ago by an epileptic landlady who
during her crises, demanded arrears. The

stool was left alone, modest among brilliant frauds.

But if they were all frauds, Delia did not mind. For on only one article had her pictorial imagination settled, hoping that here her Ohio hands touched something authentic from a rich past. There was a tapestry thrown like a priest's cape over the shoulder of the distant piano. The weaving showed young girls to be riding on white jennets through a blue and yellow forest. A greyhound with a scarlet tongue barked at every girl's side. Genuine Beauvais, the shopkeeper had cried, standing on a quai of Paris, contentedly counting her banknotes. Made in the thirteenth century, he had added, at the time of the Courts of Love. Probably hot off the loom, Delia decided later though one corner of the border, New York appraisers said, was probably genuine. She often wondered which corner it was. In her astonishment she had omitted to ask. Still no matter what its partial treachery she loved it. If disaster had threatened the studio and she had had to leave it to sheriff or flames, she would have walked out with the tapestry hung from her shoulder, the painter's stool dragging in her hand. These two diverse articles had satisfied two instincts in her life.

Her hands still tended her yellow hair as she walked back into the room, about her head centering that strong orderly beauty that marked her first moment's flight away from scents and brush. She had exchanged her bright gown for some garment that was sleeveless and black. On long quick steps she roved among the lamps to dim their inquisition then turned toward Paul, her footsteps making the black of her robe tremble like a thin covering cocoon hiding lively forms beneath.

He was sitting in front of the fireplace. She saw his arms lift up in signal from the scarlet divan. "Delia." He reached for her hands.

His fingers, when they touched hers, chained them in a senseless imprisonment of the flesh. His hands and hers felt heavy, too heavy for their arms to support. Her body as she bent toward him was loaded by a weight of attraction that pulled her down. Yet the change in his face arrested her. It had the blurred idealized features of a small mirage whose phenomenon she accepted as part of her own heat. Yet the alteration was not imagined. It was actual. He called her name again, kissed her wrists, lifted his head. On his face she now saw a change of identity. It was as if during the few moments she had left him alone he had, screened by the privacy of her walls, stripped himself of the accumulated egos and cautious considerations he had worn in the street, trusting to the warmth of her fireplace to bare his own nature, to give him the courage to move at first timidly then at ease among his secret desires as though they, like the lounge and pictures in her rooms, made up the domestic furnishings and portraits of his own interior nature, available to him only when he was shut in from the world outside. "You've been wasting all our time in there. It seems to me you've been gone an hour. I've been thinking. I can't leave you. And yet I've got to go away, perhaps for a year." In his excitement he seemed to have the double advantage that comes with fevered delirium when false image and reality both receive an equal focus from the mind. "What can I do? How can I stand it? You've said you care for me. Then Delia—I'm not good enough for you, but will you—will you marry me before I go?"

Because of his face her arms had been delayed. Now they settled over him in a heavy helpless festoon. Even his demand had not been able to check their descent. But her temple against his moved as she shook her head. She heard him let out a quick breath. It was like a sound of mutilation, a sound of escape. The loss of his hope deflated him as if it were air leaving a small balloon. Buoyancy and optimism succumbed with the same mechanical noise.

"I don't want to marry," she murmured. She recalled what Nancy had said. She felt herself sinking with the collapse of this man whom Nancy had with sympathy described as the marrying kind. But the pain she felt she was giving to him and in her generosity giving to herself, began abating as the blood started spurting freshly through her veins. The integrity of her instincts furnished Delia with her only judgments, her bodily strength ornamenting her in a crisis, as now, with a sagacity her arms and lips obeyed, and above their pantomime was her handsome ochred head, towering, immobile and blind. "I don't want to marry." Her hands began to master his with contagious heat.

"You mean you'll never marry?" Weakened by his disappointment, curiosity began reviving him with its faint critical enquiry. He quieted her hands, pinning them down as if he were staking her to the fire-light that aided his observation. The pain of her refusal had wiped her out for the moment as an individual and he began going over the items of her face, her full architectural mouth, her opaque deepset eyes, as if they were the soft evidences of some general phenomenon which, unable to absorb by love, he set his mental faculties on as a last resource. "But of course you'll marry," he cried. The energy of argument and the pleasure of having noted her features at so close a range re-animated him again. The optimism that belonged only to his own love for her aroused in him an animosity, a belligerence that sprang from his recent defeat. "You're a beautiful woman. You'll have to marry." The simple obstinacy with which he had waited half his lifetime to conquer an unlovely uncle animated his voice now, projecting his character and his background with all their limited refinements, establishing themselves like novel importations on Delia's couch before the fire. Youth to Paul was a serious and exciting endowment and love, now that it had come to him, was a domestic ikon he would fight for. His eyes had the fanaticism that blinded him from seeing anything which he wanted as being facile, tender of access or free. "You'll want a home," he added.

She smiled faintly. "I've got one." All her life she had lacked skill in argument. Delia had her face, her quiet resolutions, her freedom and a few facts. Her room was one of these and she nodded toward it without affection or pride, its mottled colors and shadowed gilt furnishing the animation her voice lacked.

"Oh," Paul admitted, "Yes, you have. But a home is some place you live with somebody whom you love." He tried to mingle logic with his insistence but his assurance was weakened. The luxury of her setting was a shock which he had forgotten in the dim light and he gave it a glance now, shivering and coming back to her face. "You've got everything you could want—more than I could offer. I know that. But this isn't a home." He waved his arm at it. "Someday, Delia, you'll want one. You'll want a—a child."

She was surprised by his words. "Yes." With that slow uncalculating thoroughness which was the essence of her nature, she had always reckoned on maternity as one day fur-

nishing her with the most important emotion
of her life. She had in this vague way always
wanted a child, a small animal loveliness she
could harbor among four walls and in this tender imprisonment, watch without ceasing a
creature who answered her profound instinct
even while it ignored her, imitating her silence
with infantile speechlessness. In whatever
served as its cradle it would lie solemnly preparing strength and charm that would live on
after she was dead, by its mere existence ex-
panding her life even after she would have lost
it, thus giving mortal elasticity to her grave.

"Someday I'll want all the things you talk
about—" she said. "But they're for the future," she said with confusion. "Now—this
evening—is for us. Oh, let's not talk, Paul.
I love you. You love me. That's all I want.
It's enough, enough." In a large arc her bare
arms went out over him, circling and cutting
through the dark air. All protests should have
gone down before them yet below the passage
of her hands she saw his hard ruddy face, his

lips parted for their last pantomime of speech.

"If you love me, marry me. Marry me and come to the Philippines for a month anyhow!" The enthusiasm he hoped to arouse in her designated itself on his face, as if in a final effort of optimism and tenderness his body had started acting for hers and what he desired her to feel he already felt for her, exampling her reactions by the pitiable brightness in his eyes. "I know what it would be like out there. Sometimes I've wondered why I listened so much to that old devil. It was to be able to tell you now. The sea is green, darling, and gets purple at dusk but the islands stay green as long as there's any light. There are little boats we would ride the surf in—canoes with outriggers of bamboo. There'd be red dawns after long nights and coconuts to tap and drink milk from if we were thirsty. There'd be—" He came closer. He seemed to be trying to print his words of enticement on the flesh of her face, "There'd be huge forests, speckled with orchids and hummingbirds.

Beautiful ones, Delia. And ricefields with buffaloes wading as we rode past. The women wear red skirts. The babies are naked in the villages." He laughed. "I'm trying to remember all I've heard. And the moons at night are white, white, Delia—oh, whiter than anything—except your face. The nights smell of flowers—jasmin. There'd be everything anyone could want, oh, lovely things, scents, sights,—everything we could want if you'd only come. Oh, oh, think. Think. I love you, Delia, Delia." He looked drugged and drunk with the fright of his own words, his head dropped and his mouth was smothered in the black of her gown.

Her head was dizzy. Unsuspecting, he had worked on a weakness. Delia suffered from an unquenchable curiosity about new lands. A desert in Africa, a gully in New Jersey, a white dogwood tree she had never seen before in childhood Mays when one flowering bush had established the limits of a new territory and a new season. Each of these tracts, foreign

or local, had momentarily eased that optic restlessness which was like a malady seated from
infancy in her heavy grey eyes. She and Nancy, as if to isolate their poverty and new friendship, had once made a grand continental tour,
Nancy protesting, Delia ruddy with excitement, indifferent to the bowels of the boat, to
vermin in Rome, to hunger in Palermo, to
miserable Parisian pensions infested with miserable British virgins, unaffected during the
entire adventure by the gradual loss of all her
small properties including finally her one hat
which she misplaced at Le Havre, contentedly
entering the bay of Manhattan like all the
other immigrants surrounding her, her handsome yellow head wrapped in a striped peasant
scarf. Yes, Europe she knew, but the tropics!
Green seas and jasmin at dawn. "I can't go,"
she muttered. She threw herself into Paul's
arms. With her lethargic clarity she knew his
islands seemed lovely in exaggeration because
he visioned them with their love resting and
bedded upon them. They would be more bear-

able in their native charm when he turned to them at last, leaving Delia not quite unknown behind. "I can't leave," she said. "How could I get away?" she asked as if only he knew.

She looked at his face. Her words started coming more rapidly as she saw the mirage of his Philippines passing from his eyes. His mouth sagged. He stared back at her familiar face with hopeless acceptance, nodding at her persistence, having no energy for any other movement. "I have to work. There's Goldstein. There's Nancy. I have contracts—and things," she insisted vaguely. True, she had once signed some sort of papers in Goldstein's rooms. They would probably prevent her going—unless she were determined. "How could I get away for months?" How could she? She didn't know nor did she try to think. She wanted Paul more than she had ever wanted anything in her life and all her force was rising to take now what might never be the same again. Only to neurasthenics and old people does the future appear with such interest and

fear that it is a certainty. Delia was young
and healthy. Next year, next spring, next
month, even mornings still a day or two away,
she had no contact with, lacking that elasticity
to lasso time that still stretched ahead of her,
unharnessed except by hope or plans. Her
nature and the emotion she felt for Paul
were like the dial of a clock which, despite its
complex mechanism, its experienced permanent air, disregards impending seasons, years,
time itself, announcing only by its internal
tick, clicking like a heart-beat, and its set face
—*now*. "I love you," she whispered.

"But I love you—more. If I were free, from
my family—I wouldn't go to those damned
Philippines. It's their future I'm thinking
of—not mine. Mine's here with you." He
spoke without animation. "I love you more
than you love me. That's as it should be probably. The man, perhaps, should always love
more. And I'm grateful for this night at
least. I thank you. And I won't ask for any
more." He lifted her hand and kissed it,

fumbling awkwardly over the bare wrist. He was defeated.

This was her moment. "You think I don't love you? Oh, what is it you want? Paul, I love you enough for anything. Anything. Don't you understand?"

At last he comprehended. His arms tightened. As part of their strain she heard his long broken breath. Then notation for her ceased. She felt his mouth dropping in disorder on her face. Rare impulses to speak rose in her brain and dropped back. A feeling for syllables and sensations crowded through her mind. The beat of her heart was lifted and stationed in her ears. Faintly above it from between the smother of Paul's arms she heard a regular distant tapping like another heart whose rhythm added to the clamor of senses that seemed to be filling the room. The sound grew louder and ceased. She tried to free her head to listen. She heard it again. She realized at last she lay listening to the vagaries of a knock.

"Someone's at the door."

Only Paul's arms seemed conscious she had spoken.   They listened, tightened over her ears.

The bell rang.   She pulled herself free and with uncertain force stood beside him.   In the faint light that still flickered from the fire she saw her fingers, like implements belonging to someone else, lift from his shoulders and reach thoughtfully for the disorder of her hair, heavy as his arm had been, sagging with its blond mass on her neck.   Over her eyes the hair made a nimbus and in the center of it she saw Paul's head, thrown back, his eyes closed.

She stumbled through the familiar darkness of the corridor.   She opened the door and looked down on a dirty night-blooming boy. His shrunken face was borne up to its last shrewd youthfulness by a tall collar.   He swung a box into her arms.   "Sign here.   It's sort of late.   They give me the wrong address first.   Thank you."

Flowers.   She closed the door.   Flowers

which, making their only voyage, had probably commuted in from Long Island hothouses, had spent their first evening in New York on a motorcycle and at midnight had been brought to die for her. She shivered. She had feared the boy was bringing a message from her home. She would have been embarrassed by that. It would have been like the presence of her father and mother, walking unexpected but expectant into her dim private room. They were waiting for her to come home, as indeed were the parents of Paul— dim law-abiding old lovers, all, makers of Paul's infancy and hers, forming them from modest passions that had flowed through a wedding-ring.

She felt baffled, distracted. Her mood had been lost. "Well?" Paul cried. He stood up by the couch.

"Flowers," she said. She looked at the box without interest. Flowers. They had to be put in water. They were like ships she thought wearily, always needing water. Ships and flowers. The two words started circling in her head. She fumbled at the string on the box.

"Let them go," he cried. "My God, can't you—" He pulled her to the couch.

"Yes," she said. "Let them go. Later though, I'll have to put them in water."

"Oh now, if you want to see whom they're from."

She heard the anger of his voice, his satisfied tearing of paper. Then the quick drift of an acrid scent that floated from the floor. Freesia. She accepted without astonishment their shrill thin smell, rising like a scale of music, mounting like a tonal gamut, note by note, odor by odor, with sweetness for sharps, with the pallid conflicting white sourness for the flattened notes that made a pipe-like perfume, blown from the silent horns of flowers she heard and smelled but could not see. Then, still invisible, she felt their damp metallic chill, the trembling of their little flutes and tight tubes as Paul threw them onto her wrists, her bare shoulders congealing her warm throat with their cold

clamor that mounded to a rim of odor and
noise piled around her chin. "Paul," she
whispered.

"Here's the note that came with them.
That's the most important part of it, isn't it?
Oh I know." He tossed an envelope into her
hands then the edge of the couch creaked with
his weight. She felt its jaded springs give way
to take his young limbs on their lap.

She lay watching him, each new expression
of his face sketching itself into her eyes as if
their pulp and color were thin paper on which
each of its facial gestures made its automatic
and penciled sign. How he has aged, she
thought and for a moment she lay contemplat-
ing the temporary ravages that can be made
by a few minutes' emotion, seeing him older
by anger than when she had left the couch to
go to the door. He had that worn futile look
sometimes to be seen on the faces of new-born
male babies who, struggling to leave their
mothers, arrive in the world to look like
shrunken images of their fathers, already be-

come old men. He had lost the personal muscles that she had seen bolstering his visage with courtesy, with caution, with hope in restaurants, streets and public places. He had only the inherited expression that might belong to all people who had gone before him, suffering with jealousy. Or if it was not their face, at least it was not his own as she had ever seen it.

"You are jealous," she said finally. She wondered how she happened to be speaking of so intimate a characteristic to a man it seemed to her she had never seen before. She only recognized him as the individual she had spent the evening with, since he still wore the same shabby tweeds, still displayed the same orange cravat. He shrugged his shoulders. She opened the envelope. "Compton Keith," she read aloud. She was used to new elements in her career and liked them but this seemed unneeded and spectacular. White flowers at midnight from a man with black hair. That was all she recalled of him. What else had

been Mr. Keith's characteristic as he stared at
her in her room that afternoon when she was
waiting for Paul?

"Yes, I'm jealous," Paul suddenly said. "I
—I never was jealous before. I was never in
love before. I wanted you to marry me.
What have I got to give? Myself." He
laughed. "This man," he pointed to the card,
"has that much. And a great deal more. As
rich as Midas and a great deal more modern,
that's what your friend Mrs. Wellington said.
Well, he only met you this afternoon. Why is
he already sending you flowers? Delia! Answer!" He jerked her hand, gripped it.

She had thought that between her and Paul
there would never be any intimacy again. And
yet the touch of their fingers, those menial
degraded digits, trained to clean, to cling, to
slave at menial undignified tasks for the helpless brain and body and also to inform it of the
approach of ecstacy, as now—at once re-es-
tablished a new and trembling union which
Paul fought against. He tried to draw away.

"You won't marry me. You never met this man before and yet he sends you flowers. Why?" he cried.

"Why shouldn't he?"

"Because—because I don't want him to," he muttered. "Because you shouldn't want him to if you love me. Oh, how can I stand it." He threw his arms around his head. "There I'll be buried in a jungle thousands of miles, thousands of hours away from you and what'll be happening to you? What'll all the men here be trying to do? How will they know you love me? If you'd only——"

"Even if I did marry you, would that keep them away?" she said. "A marriage license isn't like a poison sign on a bottle. Not nowadays anyhow. Mrs. Wellington's married. There's still a Mr. Wellington somewhere. But that doesn't keep Compton Keith away."

"Oh. Is Mr. Keith—?" He stopped. "I mean is Mrs. Wellington—" He clung to the idea he had gained. For an instant it saved and shocked him.

"I didn't mean that, exactly." She hadn't meant to describe Mercy's private life. She knew nothing of it. She had merely meant to use its public facets as an example. "Whether you live far away or around the corner, you'll have to—trust me. As I'll have to trust you," she added with inspiration.

"Oh, me!" He laughed abruptly. "Yes, you'll have to worry about me a lot," he said angrily. "No one will be sending me flowers! And if anyone did, I mean if any woman looked at me, I'd—I'd look the other way. Oh I would. I'm like that. I'm a fool, a fool. Oh, Delia, there never has been anyone else, has there?" He threw himself into her arms.

"I mean you never cared for another man as you—as you care for me?"

"No. Oh, no," she cried. She felt she was telling him only the truth. Those dim women Paul had known in his youth and Delia had never seen seemed no dimmer now than men she had once known.

"It's not just for tonight," he whispered.

His hand shook her shoulder. With his violence the tremors of the flowers she had forgotten rattled perfume against her nostrils.

"For tonight, tomorrow. I'll not leave town. I'll stay with you. Oh, say you love me. Say it, Paul." He moved and the smell of the freesia jetted into her face. Their juice was being flattened onto her flesh. They were being crushed into a girdle that circled her. She thought of them for a moment with regret then recollection of their destruction slipped from her mind.

IV

THE bedroom was littered with the disorder of haste and intimacy. While Paul waited Delia hurried into her clothes then bent before the dressing-table, seeing her three faces in its three mirorrs whose triptych she began to paint. She sketched in color on her skin as if it had been a canvas, here the resurrection of the red mouth and on either side the waiting pink figures of her cheeks.

"That's as good as it'll ever be, I daresay." She closed a drawer, caught at her gloves, pulling loose their mussed napkin-like fragility from the cluttered composition they rested among—chalices of scents, gold boxes, rings, and over all of them, resting like the bright minute cracks netting the lacquer of some ancient painted placque, a cross-work of occasional thin blond hairs.

"I never saw another woman wear and have such odd things." Paul pulled her to her feet against him and looked at her, looked at her possessions and her room. "Women always seem luxurious to a man. Any woman to all men." From the night of one day to the night of the next and all spent with Delia shut up in these limited rooms seemed to have driven Paul back to troubling fundamentals; the flat had finally grown empty to him of any furnishings except those he and she made in their character of blonde and brunette, of male and female, original as if they were the first and last examples and prisoned under glass in this specimen room. "I don't want to go out of that door." He pointed to it. It was no longer a commonplace architectural method of escape. It was an aperture which, once he walked through it, he seemed to feel would disappear. "Delia. What if something should happen and I won't see you again Saturday." As if love were a weakness, it brought out an intimate timidity in his features. The face his parents knew or a casual photographer, had been scraped of the habitual expressions that made up his identification: fear, distrust, lassitude, humbleness and obstinacy made a bewildering physiognomy for him above which his eyes peered out, disconcerted and soft as if they knew they looked out over a new front.

"Nothing can happen. I've sent word that I won't go home to see my family until next week. You'll come over again. We'll have two days." She drew from these plans some means of fortifying herself, leaning with weariness against Paul, but her voice sounded apprehensive.

"How can you be sure? Why did Goldstein send that note about your vacation ending at midnight? You said he thought you
left this morning."

"He did think it. He was supposed to
anyhow." She wondered how he knew. As
an undercurrent to friendship, business,
money-making, love, ran always this wire of
curiosity, spiralling out from the brain or heart
of all those who surrounded one in life. How
had Goldstein found out she had not left? And
why? He was waiting for her. She would
soon know.

"Is he in love with you, too?" Paul demanded. His arms tightened. Every question,
answer, every phrase or protest directed toward her since last night, Paul had punctuated with some constriction of his inexperi-
enced flesh: all this force expended by love in
isolated embraces, lifting arms, clutching
hands, would make up, if delivered in one overwhelming blow, a pressure that could kill one,
she thought.

"No. He's not." Slowly her mind settled
on his question and she smiled. "You should
see him." Appearances influenced everyone's
reactions, Delia's perhaps more bluntly than
most. To her Goldstein's paunch and face cut
him off from the occupation of love, Delia
making use of those primitive sensuous convic-
tions which led her to regard passion as an
exalted profession for which Goldstein was
not fit. "We're friends," she admitted. Despite
his tyrannies, she thought of him with mute
loyal warmth for he was, in many ways, an
oriental after her own heart. His pasha eyes,
bloated and wrongly blue, that had come from
the slavery of an East Side apple-cart to set
up their final magnificence on Broadway, his
belligerent will, his passion for beautiful tex-
tiles and pageants whose gratification was like
a financial vice, these made him a bulky, pow-
erful arrivist, dominating the peacock-eyed
lights of Times Square, a man to whom she
offered an amity neither of them understood,
their mutual success in his harem-like theaters

furnishing the common emotion both clung to without analyzation. "He's my best friend in the world next to Nancy," Delia added. She always classified individuals in this simple arithmetical routine: first, second and third, up to ten when they became a pleasant mass. "And he'll be the angriest if I don't hurry. He hates to be kept waiting. Darling." She smiled again at Paul and took his face in her hands. Separated from each other by their final withdrawal from the embraces of love, both of them in this exhaustion and quiet that preceded their parting, had been sending to each other small hard questions, little faint demands, words from Paul's mouth hurrying to her ears, and syllables from her lips passaging in return to his brain, in an attempt of communication both knew was empty, irresistible, hopeless, but both accepted like some civil chattering reflex following on the silent thoughtless absorption that had been their love. "We must go," she whispered.

"I'm the one who's really going. I'm leav-

ing this country for another. Yet you're the
one who always seems to have the air of
flight." He kissed her with helpless final fer-
vor. He looked at her a moment. She walked
to the door. In the corridor outside the dim
lighted walls stretched out in chilly nocturnal
arcades where only thin shadows could hide.

They climbed in the waiting cab which had
the same air of stationary trance as its chauffeur, resting and dreaming dreams for which
each click of the meter added sweetness and
paid. Paul shook his shoulder and slammed
the door. The visioning was over. The filthy
odor of carbonizing gasoline was real.

"Do you mind if I tell my mother—about
you, about us, I mean?" Already several
cross-streets had shed their vista into the dark
moving cab window. Neither Delia nor Paul
had spoken, silently clasping each other's
hands, clinging to muscles, bones and flesh to
bridge the speechless void their descent into
the city had set up. "She has very little in her

life," he explained with patience. "Only me, mostly. And I'm going away."

"Yes. Tell her if you wish. I—" She checked her words. Love did not unite people once they were out from the privacy of the alcove retreat where for long hours two individuals seemed honestly to share ideas and theories, the members of the mind seeming like members of the body over which agreement was part of passion, contact with streets, house fronts, pedestrians, public lights, disengaged the individual brains again as actively as it disengaged lips and knees and if indeed no struggle resulted, there came at any rate a feeling of isolation which nurtured either generosity or retreat. "Tell her," Delia repeated more quickly. She had not thought of the necessity of communicating to anyone their love. She and Paul had exchanged their confessions, made their report which she felt would affect her for the rest of her life. And now his mother must know and perhaps hers, and Nancy and Goldstein. The fathers too would have to know. And who else? A sense of uneasiness began permeating her body and mind. What had been unique and secret was undergoing an intangible subtle dissipation because it was being exposed to eyes and air.

"Mother'll see you as a blushing bride," Paul laughed in embarrassment. He lifted his head and laughed again.

"I'd blush," said Delia. "I'd get red as fire. I hate being stared at and no one saying a word." Here comes the bride. She had seen them in Excelsior. Chopin, white tulle, the Baptist aisle and brides who were going to be happy forever, as indeed often some of them were. Thinking of their blushes, she blushed, she did not know why.

"If you hate being stared at, I hate four o'clock in the morning. Or five. Or whatever hour I'll be forced to sneak from your rooms when I come back from those islands. I wonder if I'll be able to stand that, Delia? I'll love you for the rest of my life. I'm that kind of man. Once caught," he said, "and—and I'll never be able to change. I'll love you until my love finally wears out, hiding and cheating and sneaking out of whatever flat you live in at dawn."

She was silent. There he was, plucking at their future again. "Dawn," she murmured. The pale streets of New York which Paul was already fearing, though they were months and even years ahead of him, she had also seen and without repulsion, walking through them in the chill dawn light. Long dead avenues, they had appeared to be as she had crept out on them from this room or that, alleys they had seemed, despite their breadth, paths pointed and cypress-shaped like the walks in cemeteries with early workmen stumbling through them like hired mourners and behind them the trestle of the Elevated straddling Sixth which it hung over like a coffin. Then as the deadly quiet minutes and the soft growing light grew sustained, the tops of distant buildings would appear visible with the break of day, sky-scrapers as flat, erect and faceless as tombstones but the first sights to be saved by brightness as another day spread slowly over the city and New York had its routine resurrection. Delia had never disliked dawn. The isolation of its spectre, rising from night, had always visited her with stimulation and strong excitement.

The cab slowed down. She glanced through its glass. Already she and Paul had arrived at her nocturnal oasis of Times Square. Its minted glare rose and spread with a tint of candid avarice into the tainted sky overhead. Money-colored lights dappled walls of surrounding buildings—lights shining like coined planets, like constellations of gold-pieces strung on invisible wires. Erect on the roofs angling the Square and bright in lively legends of electricity, a bull, a cat and two peacocks, all their parts gleaming, shone like emblems of a new spiritual faith placed visibly this time in the heavens close above the faces of credulous humanity. Everything within sight was close enough to shout to—animals, huge stars of red, bars bright as lightning and flashing in a cold sky without sign of a summer storm, and from a corner of the Square, rings like Saturn's own, of gold, all of them flickering on their little height in set financial pattern and without mystery, twinkling above New York's crowds in a steady nocturnal voltage.

The cab halted, the door swung open. Paul got out and stood waiting on the curb. His arm caught at her elbow. "Kiss me goodbye," she said. "No one will see. Kiss me, Paul."

They had the isolation of being in a large crowd. The stream of bodies shuffling on the sidewalk walled them in. She smelled from their movement the odor of cold dangerous winter dust and the scent of women's furs and their men. His face descended, felt warm: there was no other contact except that of fleshly heat. Then it drew away. He said something, she did not know what and with his eyes on her, withdrew into the cab. His arm reached out to catch at the door and the cab rolled away.

She stood a moment, looking at the place where the cab had been. Another took its place, another hired vehicle of cheap luxury with a man who was no one's servant in livery at the wheel. She turned and pushed through the tide of the crowd. Shoulders came before her like floating timbers, cluttered with the light froth of blank faces—unfamiliar eyes floated on a level with hers. Then she saw standing on the steps of his theater the unmistakable figure of Goldstein. He was watching her.

After a long stare his hand lifted to twitch his hat as she came near. Beneath its shadows his blue eyes had the effect of being shaded behind dirty glass but still visibly mounted on their swelling metallic lids.

"That was a pretty little love scene. I been watching shows on Broadway for years. But that was—good." He watched her but his hand fished for his watch, hiding in the tidal swell of his belt. He glanced at it. "You're late."

He wheeled and started for the door. The crush of the entr'acte clustered the portal. Between three mosaic walls and the rim of the sidewalk rose the turning heads of his audience come out to raise a cloud of smoke while they got a breath of fresh air. Their bodies made a thicket of thighs, an underbrush of skirts, clinging coats and gowns, garments and bones all blooming overhead with smiling faces, perfumed with dinner breath and nodding passionately. She left them behind, turned through a large door, went down an empty hall and up a faintly lighted staircase. Then down two more corridors, their turnings so shrewdly shaded as to seem secretive. With a grunt Goldstein hit his hand against a last portal of ebony leather. It fell open and still seeing the down-turned face of Paul, Delia followed into the room.

It was the room where she had first met

Goldstein. It had seemed crowded that day because of the continuous agitation of its servants and office boys and the swift steps of their leader, Bennie, noiselessly hurrying between his employer and the door. Now she walked across the immensity of its stretch which no dozens of servants could fill, realizing as usual that its decoration was what made it seem populous, oppressive.

It was a huge room walled with flat silk striped in what looked like epidermal colors. There was an occasional black satin slit for hot skins, some brown for island shades, Manchu yellows like strips from a Chinaman's back, slivers of blue as if it would seem (though it was not likely) that among theatrical literature either Goldstein or his Bennie had read of antique fighting Britons, painted and bright. Slashes of white varied this mixture, white like the arms of blonds with scarlet lines for their broad lips. The wall looked like a long background of carnal tints and here and there the priceless silk sagged as skin does when it drops away from maturing bones.

On the dark carpet was a ring of soft-bosomed chairs. They had protruding upholstered bustles like those forms of flesh left over from an earlier generation. Goldstein had hauled them out of a warehouse where he had hid the bones of his first and last adventure. This was their final asylum.

"I wish you'd change this room." She distrusted it tonight as she never had before. "I'd be blind if I lived here a week." She dropped on a chair. Her yellow head was couched on her furs: her eyes closed. What if Paul couldn't come Saturday, she thought. Her hands grew cold. She took off her long gloves and nursed her chill naked palms.

"What's the matter with this room?" Goldstein asked without interest. "I seen worse in my time." He circled among the chairs and on slow legs, finally let himself down in their dark satin. Delia listened to his interrogations with half-shut ears, wondering why he had sent for her, not what he was saying. She was used to his elaborate preambles and the surprise of his gutteral American speech. His Jewish accent he had lost years ago in the East River. It had been drowned out of him, summer after summer, by the persecution of Irish playmates, young, ardent, and belligerent who loved the Virgin and tormenting Russian Jews. And from the oily depths of that filthy stream Goldstein had finally come up an American.

She saw him now preparing his patriotic cigar. She had gone through such changes within the last twenty four hours that she looked at him with a moment's curiosity, wondering if he too had altered, if anything sweeping and reconstructive had gone through his body and mind, but he was just the same. He was the same slow man with legs clumsy from long standing, neck thick from shouting in cold air, face and wrists still red from the winds that had turned his flesh the color of the frost-bitten fruit he had once screamed on a street-corner to sell. He had still the body of a push-cart vendor with popping sumptuous blue eyes, pushed further into prominence by the weight of his bulging forehead.

"Yes," he said. He could talk now and crossed his legs to get his brain ready. The smoke that always started speech was rising from the end of his cigar. "I seen worse rooms than this. But never a prettier love-scene. You had ought to gone on the stage, Delia—you got talent for that sort of thing after all. And so sweet it looked, there on the curb, everybody in town looking on. Bright lights arranged by the city of N'York—and me. It was *my* lights you was standing in, too. Did you notice that?" Quite expressionlessly, his eyes bored at her through the wisps of smoke. She said nothing. He waited. "I heard he was handsome. He is. And a regular man. For once. You're getting better, I guess." Restlessly his fingers started twitching. The cigar, cradled between the fat digits,

rolled in a gentle lullaby. "I suppose you're
—you're in love again, ain't you, Delia? Yes,
she's in love." He dropped his lids. There was
no pattern on the carpet but he had found a
spot to which his eyes clung.

Ever since he met Delia he had fastened
onto her a persistent speculative interest in her
emotional affairs. He had persecuted her
with questions, and with his own answers.
Silent and uncomfortable, she had listened to
reproaches heaped on her head because of one
man, to new reproaches because of another,
and had, by saying nothing, managed to have
the discussions leave no impression once she
had walked out from them and lost herself on
the street. But even from her silence, Goldstein had always gleaned the news. He had
sensed the passing of one flame, the lighting
of another and had always managed to bring
them under his eye, casting his glance over
each handsome newcomer who satisfied first
his curiosity, then his contented contempt.
All of them, because they were nothing like

him, he had dismissed as weaklings. Except Paul. Him Goldstein had found worthy! Delia stirred uneasily. Praise for Paul was going to put her through just that much more pain.

But she aimed directly for the truth. "Yes, I'm in love. Not again, though. But for the first—and the last time. I—I—" The words clung to her throat and she looked at Goldstein with dumb appeal. The emotion she had been sure of twenty four hours ago but had not then tested, now deprived her of breath and means of communication. Ah, yes, she was in love. During the day with Paul she had felt free for occasional Platonisms and unusual loquacity. Now she wished she had not spoken a word, had never used her mouth except to embrace him. Embarrassed because she was not alone with such regrets, she looked toward Goldstein.

He was upright on his soft chair. His stiff face, bulging eyes, his swelling throat gave him the look of a man in a seizure, a man struck ill on the satin lap of some old bawd, supported by her coarse silk knees and kept from falling to the floor of a sensual-tinted room where whatever his gross desires had been, they had been shocked from him by some remembered sentimentality, some loss of hope, some affliction that deprived him of his force.

"Goldstein—." She felt as if she were witnessing a street-accident, one of those violent scenes where is visible the awkward disaster, come to some unknown body, of suffering and agonizing in public with all the helpless lack of dignity that should be hidden under the cool sheets of a bed. She wanted to leave her chair and go to him but his bloated blank face was a warning. She did not move.

He caught his breath. It jerked through his lungs. Then slowly he got back to his habits of the flesh. His arm lifted, his cigar approached his mouth and his lips, with mammal trained instinctiveness, opened and clung. "About this young man, then," he said with an effort. "The one you're so crazy about at last. Nancy said he was kind of a movie hero. Was going out into the jungle to make a fortune for his old folks and lift the mortgage."

Relieved she eased her body in her chair. She could always listen. Listening, Delia's sunken grey eyes took on that oracular expressive concentration that, like grisaille church windows letting in grey light over a preaching box, should have been accompanied by the sound of important speech. Yet with relief she heard some one else's voice moving on. Each word Goldstein said lifted from her the necessity of self-expression and brought the assurance of his recovery which, like the seizure that preceded it, still astonished her. She was grateful to the theater, too: its set phrases provided Goldstein, become so American as to suffer amidst all his and America's richness, from the national poverty of speech, with a means of clarifying thoughts for which he had never taken the trouble to find his own patent. Paul was a movie hero. The brick house in Philadephia was a homestead and mortgaged. Suddenly she began listening with acuteness.

"All the money you make here, contracts, work,—that ain't enough to satisfy, is it, now you've seen him? Now you're in love," he stammered. "You're going out to China with your sweetie, are you and watch him sweat in the sun. Bird of Paradise first act, palm trees, and blue backdrop. I know. You got freedom and money, things men would die for. But you got so much curiosity now you're in love, that you can't hear advice, you can't stick by your old friends. You got to give up everything and—and find out what you missed all these years. It ain't much. He's a man, Delia, like anybody else. Like —like me. And love's only—" He caught himself. "But you got to find out: you got to go and—and give yourself to this fellow to find out what it is to be a wife?"

At first she didn't understand. Then she

turned scarlet. She was rarely enraged. From
lack of practise apparently, her anger would
suddenly descend as now on some word, some
erratic act irrelevant to her emotions or her
life. Despite his persistent curiosity about her
habits, Goldstein had apparently never arrived
at supposing she had had love. She despised
women without courage. She probably despised celibacy and virginity, seeing in them
some plaintive timid evasion of energies everyone felt and should share. And, because it
hinted at these things, she felt anger at what
he had just said. How had he so miscon-
strued her life? Delia was quiet and non-
commital about her acts. No one talked about
her. Yet when her name was mentioned, eye-
brows had been lifted like windows in a side-
street when an interesting character strolled
by. These gestures Goldstein had missed.
He was like a member of her family, the last
one to be informed. And because of his own
disillusions, he clung to an idea of her virtue

as only a man without virtue would cling. The grossness of his own life had made him passionately romantic.

"You're wrong," she said. Her color heightened again with her words, made them red in the reflection of her cheeks. "I love Paul. But I'm not going away. And you're wrong if you think—" She stopped. She felt her lips with her tongue. There were no words there—but words would come.

"If I think you was in love," he shouted. "Say, I believed you at first." A half-breath of relief escaped from him. No whole breath. He was not yet recovered to the full extent of his lungs. "Oh don't talk to me. You're in love and yet you let the man you're crazy for walk off to the ends of the earth. That ain't love. I guess you're just a fake, Delia. Maybe you won't ever be in love as long as you live."

She looked at him.

"If you're in love, then do something about it." His arms lifted into the air. They looked pianistic as if, with some new talent and with his old knowledge of life, his criticism and wisdom was about to become aural, about to strike off, black and white, on an instrument he had suddenly become master of. "If you love him, you'd give up everything for him. Women always do."

Her experience had not taught her this. She listened prejudiced but with the open-minded attention she gave to statements she never believed.

"I've seen lots of men crazy about you, Delia Poole. Why didn't you like them?" Men he had despised he now seemed to be excitedly defending. Clumsily at orientating the shifts in other people's minds, Delia could only listen and fumble with consequences which though half-comprehended, were altering a friendship she had had for years. "It's this movie hero's going off to the great unknown, it's Nancy's saying he's the finest man she's ever met, that's what's got you with him where no other man had a chance. I guess you're romantic," he scoffed. Because women's romanticism had so generally evaded him, he located it now, using as an insult something he had wanted all his life. "You're spoiled, all of you girls. You get, you never give." His eyes tightened. "Where I come from, you bet, women are women. They give, though maybe they never get. That's right," he cried.

Her silence infuriated him as arbitrarily as his words had angered her a moment before. "Don't sit there saying nothing," he shouted. "Look at me. I'm ugly. Sure. Well, a prettier woman than you give me everything she had once. Or if she wasn't prettier—Some one who came from the old country to marry me. Oh, yes," he mimicked, "I been married, I done a lot you never knew. But when this woman—this girl—got off the boat we was only engaged. And I was poor. Apple-cart poor. But I had ideas of what I got now. Where did I get 'em? I don't know. But I told her. She loved me and I wanted to get away from Avenue A. If all the Jews ever get away from that street that plan to, they'll trample the rest of you to death," he said with satisfaction. He re-lit his cigar. For minutes he said nothing. "She ran away," he added. "She went to—Alaska. Goldfields. Miners lived in the hills. And were lonely. No women." He was silent. "When they come to town there's always women for 'em. These women sing and— dance and get paid."

The skin around her ears felt cold. Goldstein's wife had been a prostitute. The suddenness and vileness of his evasive disclosures, coming on top of his coarse faith in Delia, sickened her. All flesh was suddenly repulsive to her, including her own.

"She was gone five years. I thought she was dead. But she wasn't. Not yet. Nobody knew what had happened to her. And then one day she walked back onto Avenue A. Rich. She cried because she found I'd went with other women. I thought she was dead, I tell you. We was married," he added. "We had a swell wedding," he said with difficulty. "And—and that's the way I got my start. Why shouldn't I have taken the money? She'd earned it for me. She loved me. Anyway, I'd have got it soon, anyhow. She—she died."

"Oh."

"Well there's nothing healthy about miners, is there?" he cried with belligerence. "So don't ever come talking about love to me. I know about it." He tapped his fat chest. "See? Look how ugly I am, I was as ugly then or maybe uglier. But a woman did that for me. That's love. That's what a woman'll do if she cares. Not your sort of woman. You in love—say! You don't know the first thing about it."

She looked away. His contempt for her supposed inexperience no longer mattered. So this, she was thinking, was what had moved Goldstein from the tenements to Broadway. The mysterious hegira no one knew about had been made over the bridge of a woman's mouth, hastily kissed by miners. Some frail foreign creature with a satisfying Old Testament love that she carried even to Alaska which the ignorant Scriptures ignored, finally bringing it back from unbiblical snows to end in the new Jerusalem of Avenue A. A woman who had now been in her grave for years while the empty theatricality her money ran on showed its display of shirtfronts, white as tombstones gleaming nightly in the expensive first rows.

She looked back at Goldstein. His connection with woman's love still seemed incredible. But her concentration on his past dropped before the changed appearance of his face. He was struggling over some new problem. The room was not hot but his face looked damp. "So you're not going to leave us, eh?" he asked suddenly. He moved uneasily in his chair. "Now listen," he burst out in a staccato voice. "I guess maybe you ought to, after all. I don't want you to. But

I had ought to tell you the truth, give you some good advice. Maybe I was just—just testing you out when I insulted you a while ago. So long as I thought maybe you wanted to leave me, I could be mean to you. But now you say you ain't going to follow your Paul. If you love him, go with him." He clasped and unclasped his thick hands. "I must be crazy to talk to you this way but I'm right, I'm right. You been like all young women, flirting here, tasting there. I watched you at it for years now. But now you say you care. You're ripe then. Give what you got to give to the man you're crazy about or—or somebody else'll get it! Love ain't a lot of poetry after all, what you women think it is. It's flesh. Flesh do you hear. Say it's this and that and that!" His hands pattered over his heavy frame. "Give it to the man it's meant for. If you don't, you'll get into trouble, you might even—" She might what?

She didn't know. He broke off, what he

imagined frightening him beyond speech. "You're kind to advise me. But I'm going to stay here," she said.

"Then stay," he shouted, with anger and relief. "You think you know so much. Go to pot then. I wasted my breath, wasted my wind." He took out his handkerchief and dried his face, calming and cooling his flesh. "I tried to save you. What's going to happen to you, Delia? Oh, what do you know about life? Not that." He snapped his fingers in terrified disgust.

"I know enough," she said after a moment.

"What do you know?" he demanded. "Huh? Dance-music! God, you probably think babies come from saxophones. Even your pretty Paul knows more about life than you do. At least he's a man. Though he don't know much. If he knew beans when the bag's open he'd make you marry him before he left. Oh," he added with fresh fear, "are you—are you going to do that, Delia?"

"No," she said. She waited. "That won't

be necessary." She was tired. The room was hot now and tepid with smoke. Her bed was empty and mussed. She would go back to it.

"What do you mean?" Goldstein demanded. He could hardly speak. Slowly he began clambering out of his chair. "Where were you last night? Tell me. Delia," he cried.

She took one look at him and her instinct to tell the truth died. What difference does it make what I say, she thought, if it saves him from extra pain. Goldstein loved her. It had never occurred to her before. He had the defencelessness of the amorous man. "Last night? I was in my room. Alone." Her mouth looked plastic, heavy, overweighted, too loaded with paint to sustain anything more false than her breath, passing between the crevice of her lips and carrying off their scent of rouge. Once she had made up her mind to lie to him, she sat ready now to falsify every statement he would show interest in.

She owed him that much, she thought obstinately. All the years of their friendship came
to her mind. Amity was a serious emotion
to Delia. She set her jaw. Goldstein loved
her. Well, he would never know how she loved
anyone else. She tried to think of some new
lies. "We—we dined at the Crillon." She
had been able to think of nothing that wasn't
true but she spoke it with a false embarrassed
voice.

"Don't bother me," Goldstein muttered.
"I know that. Bennie told me."

"Oh, so Bennie—" She controlled her
surprise. So Bennie had been the informant,
Bennie bent double before his worship of lobsters in the Crillon from whose empty claws
he had risen to run to Goldstein's ear. "Did
Bennie also run and tell you I wasn't going
to take the early train this morning?" she en-
quired. She hated spying. She folded her
coat about her. It was late. On this impulse
of uneasiness she would depart. One moment's obstinate silence would get her home.

"No," said Goldstein in a daze, "I figured that out for myself. He said you hardly saw him. Hardly spoke. You was with a good-looking man. Well—" He shrugged his shoulders, spread out his hands. "I been watching you for years. You went dancing last night, didn't you? I guessed you went cabareting till dawn—your ideas of love," he scoffed. "And I guessed right, too, didn't I?" he cried in triumph. "Well?"

"Yes," she said after a moment, "you were —you were right." She stood up. She tightened the sagging of her gloves.

"Where you going? Oh you got time," he said in haste. He tried to push her back onto her chair. "I wanted to tell you—" His mouth hung open. He looked distracted. He turned away without finishing. "I wonder if you're worth it?" she heard him say. "Delia, I wonder if you're worth it after all. Look here." He walked back toward her and stopped close to her face. "You still got to go out to see your folks, eh? You ain't given up the idea entirely because you're in what you call love?"

He brushed by her nod, hurrying on with his words. "Well, then you leave on the midnight train. I—I got it arranged." Now he was afraid to look at her. "I sent you that wire telling you your vacation ended at midnight. Well, it—it does, you see."

Warning nerves began leaping in anxiety beneath her skin. "Paul is coming back Saturday. I'll see him for the last time. Then I'll go out home. When I return to New York he'll be gone." Her hands began getting cold.

"Oh he will, will he? And where'll I be by that time? In jail. Bankrupt! Yes, me!" He pointed to himself, sharing her astonishment. "I give you your chance. I begged you to go away with him. You wouldn't. Now take what comes. And listen." He caught her hand, shaking it in time with each of his words. "I did a little gambling this morning. I walked into Kolski's office and out again by ten o'clock. And when I walked out I left every nickel I had in the world on his desk. I bought the Columbus Theater. You heard me," he shouted. "Three months from tonight you and me will open that barn with the biggest show this town ever seen. The biggest, the best, the hottest money-maker or else the worst—oh God, what if it would fail?" The blood began pouring into his face. He looked stunned, as if he had just said something obscene and in front of a woman. Then he recovered. He talked against time. Afraid to look at Delia, he kept staring at and hiding his watch. He was going to stage an enormous spectacle. The biggest cast and payroll ever seen in New York. Money was going to flow like water, this city would be deluged by publicity and surprise and only his public exaggerations and private money-making instinct would survive. The plot for the piece would knock the town cold. It dealt with a medieval mir-acle that was supposed to have happened to some old French king whose legend the curious Bennie had unearthed in a starred book in the Public Library. "The moment he mentioned it to me, I got the idea all right." Goldstein's eyes fairly bulged with it. "Then here's where you come in," he hurried on, his voice smoother, more filled with fear and oil. "I'm going to turn the Columbus into a church." It occurred to Delia that Goldstein had gone crazy while she listened to him, hearing news of Romanesque arches that were to make a nave whose vaulting she was to contrive, whose capitals, carved with dragons and lambs— "papier maché; I got a moulder who'll make them sacred things cheap"—she was to design and whose decoration she was to arrive at, making it ready for the biggest cast in the world to march beneath in the biggest crusaders scene ever assembled in the largest spectacle ever attempted since New York theatrical history began. There were to be page boys blowing trumpets that were to be perfect copies, like the nave capitals, of medieval art, silk banners stenciled from museum rags, the chorus would be dressed like nuns and this vast body of mummers, rigged in twelfth century garments buttoned tight below twentieth century smiles were to march, sing, watch miracles, plots, pray for victory and finally get it in the last act of a combination musical comedy and church festival.

She saw his words of description rather than heard them. Too tired to hear facts, colors and pantomimes concerned with his projected enterprise jerked before her eyes in a kaleidoscope that she finally turned away from. Something else was more important.

"I'll talk to you about it tomorrow morning," she said. This was her answer to the whistle of the midnight train.

"Tomorrow morning! Hell, you'll be in Ohio tomorrow morning. Oh, yes you will. You been talking for a month about visiting your folks. This time you're going. I got figured out to the hour how long I'll be able to carry on the expense of this show before the old box office begins to relieve me. And if it don't relieve me the exact night I plan on, I go to the wall. Do you hear me? Oh, I mean it. Everything I got in the world is hanging on a time clock, Delia. It's a gamble but I had to—" He put his handkerchief across his mouth then wiped his face more calmly. "At my time of life, I ain't going to risk bankruptcy and lay out thousands of dollars for you to sit around five days in New York cabarets and hold your sweetie's hand. Time's money with me and you go to work as soon as—"

"I'll start to work tomorrow if you need me. But I'll start here. In New York. You talk as if Excelsior were the only——"

"It is," he cried. "It's the only place you can start because I—Listen, Delia." He tried to take her hand. "You said you was leaving on this morning's train. Well, I sent the plans of the Columbus out to your folks.

There ain't but that one plan. Well, is that my fault?" he cried as if injured by the penetrating suspicion of her grey eyes. "You can work out there nice and quiet," he began stammering with caution. "This show's the chance of your life. If we go big, Delia, I'll —I'll put you down for a share, honest I will. I know everything hangs on you. No one can make this church set, if you can't. Oh, God, that's true," he cried in a shrill voice as if the truth of his words had just struck him with fear. "Oh, it's your chance. There's a —there's a lot of books with art pictures waiting for you in the stateroom of your train tonight. All the churches of Europe's in them books. They're a present," he added as if that idea had just come to him. "I give Bennie two hundred dollars and told him to buy out the art books of the town. Do you think they'll be enough, Delia, or—" Suddenly he threw up his hands, looked at her a moment, meeting her eyes, then dropped his arms, dropped his glance and waited.

"Yes.   Considering what a reader I am, I should think two hundred dollars worth of books ought to keep me occupied for a few hours on the train," she said with irony. "If I go," she added.   She walked across the room. He thought she was going toward the door but she passed it and continued her march in a square.   She saw what he had done.   Afraid that she was planning to go away with Paul, he had tried to trap her (and himself) in a scheme that would hold her in Broadway even if it made him bankrupt.   Goldstein loved two things.   Most people only loved one or did the vast majority even arrive that far?   He loved his money.   And he loved her.   Yes he had two great passions.   In the midst of her speechless anger at being plotted against, her resentment was weakened.   His appetite and his capacity to suffer for the two violent elements in his heart forced her sympathy.   On principle she too would have committed violence for love.

Yet would she?   Despite all their years of

dissimilar amity, despite even her rise to luxury on Goldstein's helpful hand, wasn't she going to jeopardize his fortune for the sake of a Saturday with Paul? She should. Yet the helplessness of the fat man before her and above all his age, excited pity, excited contempt and excited consideration. She did not know how to distribute the novel sentiments she felt, walking on his carpets, resentment supplying the energy that moved her limbs and a conflicting pity paralyzing her tongue. If he had offered her intact the fortune he had risked to prevent her going, she would have thrown the bribe in his face. It was a feeling of superior strength, this exaggeration of her youth that kept her glancing at the miserable anxiety in his stale face and the bald sweating skull that doomed his apprehensions.

"Don't forget the first time you walked into this room," he begged as she passed him in her restless march. "I—I put you on your feet. I've done——"

"If it hadn't been you it would have been

someone else. I would have got on." This was true. He opened his mouth to protest again and sighed, saying nothing.

"But you've saved yourself, perhaps," she added, picking her words slowly. "By cooking up this trap you thought you could keep me from leaving——"

"Don't forget I got a contract over you too," he cried.

"Oh." She had forgotten the importance of scraps of paper. "I'd have torn that up," she said. He shivered. "You tried to trap me but before you sprang it, you advised me to leave. You told me to go away with Paul. It was good advice." After all, this was what saved Goldstein. He had enlarged her vision. With his coarse speech and—yes, even with his horrible recital about his wife, he had informed Delia of something about love and herself that she did not know. Unwillingly she deduced she had failed to give up everything for love. Probably she should have gone away with Paul. But it was too late now. It had been too late for years. Ever since Delia was a blond child. Yes, perhaps she should have gone away with Paul. And now she would not see him again. A lassitude settled over her frame. She felt cold. She tightened her coat. "I won't have time to pack," she said in a dull voice. "I'll go straight to the train."

He whipped out his watch. "There's a dresser been waiting for you downstairs for an hour. She'll pack your things. I—" They both waited a moment then with equal steps they started for the door. "Goodbye." She held out her hand.

Goldstein ground it between his thick palms. His hands had leaped for hers. "I guess I— I made you a lot of trouble. Now you won't see your Paul Saturday." The words gave him misery and they gave him relief.

"I won't see him perhaps for years. You'll never know what I've given up, Goldstein." He had started to bend to put his lips on her hand but he lifted his head. His blue eyes suddenly swelled with new confusion and fresh suspicious pain. But she pulled her hand away and passed through the door into the outer hall.

v

NEXT morning the marks of the East were gone.

As she twisted her yellow hair with final careless measures, Delia looked out the train window onto flat grey soil. The patched farms sewed together by gullies, the broken pines and threading hills of those scraps of land tucked in and wearing out between the beat of the Atlantic and the hard bones of the Alleghanies, had given way to the long morning fields of Ohio. There they were now—flat and useful, stretching in a long easy reach to the horizon. Virile fields, procreative and breastless, idling out the cold winter under a patient domestic sky. From where they had crept around her in the night they stretched on to the unseen confines of still distant Excelsior, ignored it, unrolled on and on, passing other slight civilizations in the spreading of their surface, until with a final effort, they rose and were broken to bits on the spine of the Rockies. half the length of the continent away. Fields sodden, drunk with rain, smooth and grey. Thus they would lie until with spring they sprouted a stubble of corn or later burst under an August sun with a beard of red clover that would wave like the beard of a wild man, blowing under harvest winds and hot skies.

Strolling out from the buxom suburbs of young Excelsior, Delia had run her childhood to an end over ugly fields like these. Now as she looked at them she felt grateful but alien. The shapeless farinous fields could appeal to the stomach but they offered nothing to the eye.

A gilt-buttoned official knocked at her door. At home on long immaculate legs balanced against the sway of the train, he was spending his morning quietly running about its interior, hunting tickets and telling time.

Omniscience had its oracle behind his gold
teeth.   On the tip of his tongue the moment
she asked lay knowledge of the hour, even the
minute, that would find them all rolling into
Excelsior together.   Her birthplace was a city
of homes and at the hour of her arrival, half
of them would fortunately be hidden by dusk.
The Protestant spires, gilded and filigreed by
the last glint of daylight, would look a little
romantic and papal, less chary of giving their
heaven an hour of picturesque praise.   Deep in
the gassy tomb of the covered station, her
father and mother would be waiting like impatient ghosts and just as vaguely they would
kiss her, not knowing their lips followed the
fleshier touch of Paul's.

It's just as well none of us has any violent
instinct toward confession any more, she
thought.   The scarlet letter!   Today it's no
redder than any other of the twenty six.

There had always been a void between every
generation and its offspring, of course, but
certainly it seemed uniquely broad now. Broad

enough, for the European war to have come between, killing a few of the younger American generation and setting all the rest free. Free for what? And as though it were an art peculiarly distinguishing their decade, sex had suddenly blossomed into a renaissance.

To her mother sex was malignant, whatever it was to the age in which she still lived. Delia, looking back to her hours with Paul, looking forward to her days with her family, felt their differences coming with a last fresh irreconcilability to her mind. Where Adam and Eve were concerned, her mother was still on the side of God and the angels. To her a Babylonian legend was as penetrating an explanation as any other of a force she did not understand, and for Mrs. Poole, too, after a certain moment, the Garden would have been defiled. After years of timid and reserved marriage, she failed to understand men. Nature outside of flowers was unnecessary to her. Yet beneath her iris roots, she knew moles were mating painfully underground. Her roses had pollenous relations with bees and the lawn buzzed with fertility summer and spring.

To her the only relief in the whole fleshy scheme was maternity.

Poor mother, Delia thought, compassionately. She has no appetite for flesh. She doesn't even like to eat it, let alone touch it. That must be why she likes the stage. No one ever really swallows a chop behind the footlights. A dumb show of pantomime appetite and papier maché meat. Kisses that are bits of business in the script. Four acts in the show maybe five but none of them intimate ones.

Yes, in the theater after all lay Mrs. Poole's relief from life. She had clung to the theater ever since she was a young girl and the local Opera House had been ill-lighted and a sin. Once she had even had the chance to become an actress but it was the winter she met James Poole. She was poor and she had married him in a spring of daze and trust, white satin and the odor of catalpa blossoms. A few months later from a front row she saw some healthy looking matron dying as Camille in the center of the stage. The white flowers and the red. For the first time the young Mrs. Poole, married and with child, comprehended with a shock.

Probably she ought to have gone on the stage when she had had her chance and twinkled as a virgin star. But she would have missed Delia and by irony Delia was able to shine for her, a sturdy substituting planet, capable of hiding even some of the coarser astronomical gleams from her mother's sensitive eyes.

But she couldn't hide all. Settings by Delia Poole and a background of affable beauties singing searching songs. A high-voltaged combustion of flesh and silk flaming the senses in dancing rows. Boy-headed girls with naked thighs creeping through connubial jazz in the disinterested arms of chorus men. Mrs. Poole ignored them when Goldstein's productions came to town and looked between the crevices of their knees at the scenery.

Grandmother is the only other one in our family who ever enjoyed flesh after all, Delia thought.   Wrapped in her Paisley shawl, twinkling behind her spectacles, the old lady had reveled in the Review.   Because of her religion, the theater had been a haunt of vice to her, first step on the road to hell, but since the law didn't stop it and Delia took part, she wanted to see what was going on.   If from any one, Delia stemmed from her.   The old lady had loved flesh.   And now hers was gone. It had fallen off in that quick process she always called "being at eternal rest."

Orpha Mills Poole, age 91, and The Lord Is My Shepherd.   That was all she had wanted on her tomb, Delia recalled.   A description of herself followed by one of God.   The old egotist had died, exalted with faith mixed with high hopes of immediately getting hold of her husband again in heaven and thus satisfying the ambition of a long widowhood.   Religious beliefs for Protestants had undergone extravagant changes during the last of her lifetime and while the infallibility of Genesis and geology was being fought out in her corner church, she had taken the opportunity to work out some private views on paradise. Thus by the time it was decided, early in the twentieth century, that the beginning of the world had possibly not taken place within the confines of a Gregorian week, old Mrs. Poole had figured out what was going to take place at the end of the world, so far as she was concerned, and was comforted. While angels played trumpets in open-mouthed admiration, she and her Jeremiah were to be reunited on the famous golden streets—both dressed fashionably for eternity in the pre-bellum broadcloth they had worn on their wedding day. He would be immortally handsome, manly and forward, a recrudescense of himself at eighteen. She would cling to him, looking her best, amorous, blushing with the double modesty of new angel and new bride, and eternal bliss would set in. St. Paul's relieved warning that there would be no marriage beyond the grave did not ruffle her.

She confined her scriptural readings to Solomon and the Psalms, went to church every Sabbath in silk, grew deafer when the minister tried to argue, and related her life word by word to her grandchild.

Here outside the train windows was the land she had ridden across as a child, high on a little red pillion, smelling the coarse easy odors of uncultivated spring, peering down at the infrequent country lads with her ready sensual blue eyes. This was the part of the world her family had homesteaded, these smug towns the scenes of her early triumphs, coming home from prayer-meeting. Young Ohio bucks had fought for the pleasure of spanning her waist with their clumsy fingers and thumbs. She had been a girl as slender as she was vain, laughing in the dark and sighing. Yes, she had liked flesh and men. Every man she met had apparently lived on in her memory, bearded and unforgettable. Silent amorous males, those Ohio pioneers, hunting sweethearts, kissing foreign women, chopping trees and building little towns. Everything they had done was told to Delia. Their pastoral passions grew into legends as Orpha Mills talked on and the originators quieted down in their graves.

The first news of men and women Delia had ever had, she remembered, still watching what had been once, perhaps, familiar family ground, had come from tales of her grandmother's youth. Numb with childish interest she had sat in a dusk flavored with the conflicting odor of pomade and sponge cake that had always hung over the old woman's house —listening, seeing people that words set moving through dark domestic space. Stories with dead friends and enemies caught in a mesh of recollections—held there, tied by an old woman's memory to their original posture and living shape. Hearty males and females, revived to plot and kiss again like immortals in local myths that could not die. Nothing they had done had been omitted in the retelling. All had passed on into little Delia's ears. The adulteries, for instance, animated always by bad women. There had been a crescendo in her grandmother's voice whenever it had mounted to say with satisfaction, "Well! Everyone *knew* she was a bad woman! Bad!" There had been quite a lot of Delilahs in young Ohio. Exciting attractive creatures and occasionally members of the Poole family, though always only by marriage, her grandmother had said. Brunette beauties who had lived in the little towns where Orpha Mills had matured, and had mixed themselves into the lives and occasionally the beds of Hector Beeson, Zimri Taylor and other vague connections. Farmers mostly their victims had been, who with their clumsy pioneering, their odd passions for zither playing, women and rhymed prayers had finally come down to live on in the ears of a yellow-haired child in whom their blood distantly flowed.

Well, doubtless they had been reported correctly. They had been men who grew to their strength when flesh seemed vivid and lovely whenever homespun was dropped—the only triumph beside crops. And they fitly lived like eponymous myths on the pomaded lips of a chattering Psalm-quoting old woman. Yes, flesh had been flesh to her. Her own she had kept fresh as a quince by massage each night before her prayers. And her husband's flesh, trifling dust for fifty years, she had spoken of with interest to the end of her life as though it still flowed with blood and charm before her eyes. He had been a steady adulterer, Jeremiah had, with a passion for Greek verse and new breasts in neighbors' gardens. But his relict had recalled his virility with no complaint. She had liked men. She would have understood the locked door that had shut in Delia and Paul.

VI

"How does it feel to be home?"

Ever since Delia had left Excelsior for New York, Mr. Poole always put the question to her on her return like a doctor, hopeful for good news.

Through the open window the air came in cold to Delia's face, acid to her mouth, with a taste of smoke which hung over the town as if as usual Excelsior had been busy all day working on a battle. The tension of the first few moments of their meeting was relaxing. They had hurried abreast through the dirty station, Delia big-boned and metropolitan by the side of her mother who stepped lightly and smiled as though to distant applause. On the other side walked her father, blind to spectacles and subtleties, harrowed only by the business of emotion and relief as he found cabs and trunks and piloted his family to the street. Now he pushed his hat back, smiling at last in the shifting shadows and motion that shook expressions like dice across his face. For a moment a street-light painted his skin yellow.

"How do you feel? That's much more important. I don't think you look well," she said bluntly. Her fingers patted his.

"We're getting a little old," her mother pro-tested. "To be the parents of our Delia we have to be nearly fifty, dear." She sighed. What little social animation Mrs. Poole had, during the excitement of meetings or small dramas, became always the reliable charm of the actress.

Now Delia heard that soft admirable voice in the darkness next her as though for a mo-ment it were part of a scene, helping carry on or hide a plot. The smell of lilac waved from her mother's tailored breast like spirited illu-sions struggling against smoke and gasoline. "There's your father's office, dear," she went on. "The old familiar tower."

Delia leaned in the window, looking past mounting black windows toward high roofs. "Yes, there's his nest." It was the highest coldest point on the first skyscraper the town had built. Years ago her father had at once rented it as though his conscience impelled him, a man who sold land, to patronize his neighboring adventurers who sold space in air. And there he had sat for a generation, working to spread Excelsior further and further over outlying ground while all around him girders kept springing up and stretching the town's progressive flatulency high and higher into the sky as though eventually builders and realtors together could turn the town into a perfect cube. Elevators to the sun and street cars to all outlying suburbs. Hooray, hooray for Excelsior.

"I suppose your fine partner Crapsey hasn't done any work since I last left or you'd have telegraphed me," Delia said, sinking back near her mother and her sweet odor again. "Or perhaps he's died of inertia and you haven't even noticed the loss." She moved in the small pause then felt the comforting pressure of her mother's hand in hers.

"No, dear, he's—he's not dead yet," she said with a hesitating laugh. "Oh, there's a package at home for you from Goldstein." Her voice sounded bright now, sweet and hasty. "And a telegram——"

"And a young man in Philadelphia has tried to telephone all day, I believe." Her father burst into the conversation with his air of rash energy and muscular good humor. "You're to put in a call for him tonight if possible. Mr. Harvey, Jarvey—"

"Jarvis." Mr. Paul Jarvis. Yes, her father and mother must be getting a little old, Delia thought. They must be old enough to have a daughter who had failed to say goodbye to her last lover. A daughter who had long since said goodbye even to the streets of her own youth. There they were in their familiarity— notches now in the rows of leafless trees of the boulevard where their cab was rocketing its way out the town's choicest thoroughfare. Each corner seemed to hold its resident memories. There was the shabby façade of one of the houses where she had lived as a child and a black haired boy, she suddenly remembered, had stood by her, with precious adolescence, kissing her as the sun set. Once the house had been isolated, like that first kiss, suburban. The city had crept around it and walled it in with her memory like a dead moth in a bee hive.

"We just passed our old place in Pratt Street," she said to her mother. "We Pooles have had as many different homes as gypsies. Or kings."

"Well, we're in our last now," her father said abruptly. "What was that old Greek's name who sowed dragon's teeth and soldiers sprouted up? Cadmus? Cadmus, yes." He jerked his hat off and rubbed the wrinkles in his forehead as if with the jolting of the cab they were pressing into his skull. "Cadmus. Well, I've sowed houses like Cadmus but I guess this time I've planted my last. I—I guess I've sowed my last." He sighed.

Father's getting old, she thought, shocked. His ambition is dwindling. The harvest of dwellings will be smaller now. Cadmus. Who was Cadmus? and where had her father ever heard of him? Probably in some story let fall by the dissolute Jeremiah, home from the Civil War and still preferring the classics to newer liberty and Lincoln. Then she saw her father's hand run over to her mother's knee, creep toward her wrist, feeling it, testing it.

"Oh, let's tell her tonight—now!" he suddenly begged. "She'll have to know sooner or later, Agatha. The thing sits on my chest. After all, what difference do the Crapseys make? Or any of it? We've got each other and you and Delia are strong and well. Nothing else counts, nothing else counts," he insisted positively. "Let me tell her while——"

It occurred to her that all her life she had been waiting for the Crapseys to do something vile. As a child and with a child's accurate suspiciousness she had disliked and feared them. The gust of protective sympathy she felt now for her parents intensified the recollective portraits that had harrowed her existence when young. For years she had refused to meet the originals. Now, not knowing what sleek crime they had committed, she wished she had called at their ugly house, or had lain in wait for them at the door of their mean-faced church and, using only her memory and her intuition, threatened violence if they ever brought harm to the Pooles on whom they battened and had always lived. What fatuous charitableness had made her father retain Crapsey as his partner all these years of Crapsey's idleness? She saw Crapsey's face as she had seen it during her childhood, his skin the color of the varnish on his empty desk, his long pale hairless head looking empty of anything except fetid piety. How much had he and his wife robbed her father of and meekly given to their church? There was their passion— their corrupt love for God, their pride in paying for the most expensive pew. Weekdays Mrs. Crapsey used the church like a holy pantry, organizing oyster suppers near the altar, supervising jelly sales of Christmas cake fairs and on the Sabbath, resting from her labors, she and her husband trod the aisle to the front row where they settled beneath the pulpit, controlling the minister's mind as they controlled his salary by the mere tightening of a thoughtful eye. Of later years, Mrs. Crapsey's energy had even led her among the poor. There in a settlement house she had collected unfortunate girls whom, as though they were rotting fruit, she preserved in spite of themselves, referring to them in her church reports as "fallen women." Fallen. The word would bounce from her chin to her silk knees and from there slip to the floor at her feet where it belonged. Fallen women. Fallen stars. Fallen Babylon.

"What have the Crapseys finally done?" Delia asked in a hard voice.

"The Crapseys weren't to blame. It was my fault, not theirs." Her father sounded impatient and tired but just. "Listen Delia, you remember my writing you about that War-fleigh property I was booming? I must have

written you or told you about it when you
were last here. I told everybody." He
laughed in a shamefaced tone but with eager-
ness. "The old Wallack place, it used to be.
A huge rambling old house with pillars and
a——"

"Oh." Delia stirred uneasily in the dark.
"Why, it was the Poor Farm."

"Well, yes. It used to be when you were a
child. I guess it was. It was—H'm." He
broke off. No one spoke for a moment. The
cab rattled, groaned.

A chill started parading down Delia's spine.
She had seen that rambling elderly mansion as
a child, driving by its unpainted pillars at her
father's side. Old men were slowly raking hay
from a mean and yellowed front yard. Little
hillocks were piled against the sagging front
porch and a white nanny goat with long legs
watched like a matron from the front door.
For years after whenever money seemed tight
in the erratic Poole household, the child had
lain awake at night, seeing the family march-

ing friendless between those haycocks, her mother's lovely brown eyes streaming tears as they passed the silent critical goat and disappeared into the unknown hall. This had been her nightmare.

"Curious," her father broke in in an empty voice. "I never thought about that place being the Poor Farm. I only remembered it as the Wallack property, as I say. That's what it was when I was a young man. Old Colonel Wallack——"

"It was a beautiful plot of ground no matter what it was called," his wife said quickly. "Was lovely and still is. Your father bought it and put in sunken gardens, dear, and terraces,— fountains with stairsteps and so on. Quite like an English estate. But it seemed a little far out from town, somehow. No one wanted to buy lots there even though everybody said ——"

"Oh, they said, they said." Mr. Poole's fingers drummed on the window-pane and he

peered into the darkness. "Speech is cheap
and taxes dear these days. Well, anyhow,
now you know it, daughter. That's the family news for this trip, unfortunately. I lost all
that ground. It's funny in a way. I've spent
my life here and made what money I had
selling this flat Ohio ground to people. But I
wasn't content. I had to make ravines and
transfer the dirt to make hills, plant limes and
locusts and a lot of fancy stuff."

She saw his stiff hand roll suddenly, lift for
a moment impotently, then drop into the shadows out of sight. "I had to do all that and
lose it. The Poor Farm. H'm."

The cab was rattling on gravel roads. The
wood-odor of suburban fields and hedges came
to Delia's nostrils. Her mother was sitting
silent in the corner, tense and handsome—in
an agony of sympathy and the chill of bottled
lilacs. Across from them leaned Mr. Poole,
staring through the opened window at the
night sky. His furrowed face looked blank

as though limes and locusts still burgeoned in his mind with memories of empty stairs where only rain walked and hope, not houses, sprang up from the ground.

"You know how much money I make, mother. And you never have taken any of it. Nothing but ridiculous gifts here and there. Now you'll take all of it. You must. You'll not dare refuse." The coarse healthiness she had always felt in her mother's presence seemed stiffened by pity until it was brutalizing her with its energy. She crushed her mother's thin arm, feeling the fine bones as if they were an unsurmountable reserve and defence. "You must come to New York and live with me. I'll take a house or you can find a flat. We'll live together if you want—anything you want." Even as she spoke her fingers slipped as she thought of her vanishing freedom. But what do I want it for anymore, she rendered subconsciously. Paul has gone. My past has gone. A future now with my family.

"Oh, we still have our own house, dear, and plenty besides," her mother exclaimed in soft surprise.

Delia's hands fell.

"You mustn't think your father's lost everything. Only those unhappy extra thousands. But we don't need them. Nor would we want to interfere with your life." Her mother's voice sounded clear, distinct. "We're home, dear."

The cab was turning through a narrow gate. Home. Slowly Delia looked into the dark. Behind a loop of the black driveway she saw bright lighted windows like squares of soft flesh held up behind the winter lawn. Against them were the coarse veins of catalpa branches and over the roof, sticking among the stars, the bony tips of the trees, skeletoned against the sky.

The cab stopped. After a moment she heard her mother open the house door. A dog barked.

"I'm glad you're home. I couldn't have

waited much longer." She and her father stood together on the narrow brick walk. He was blotting out the windows and even the sky by his closeness. She could smell the chill of dead gardens lying around their feet.

"I kept hoping you'd come yesterday, even after your telegram arrived. That's when I handed everything over to Crapsey. You see he—he wouldn't come in with me on the deal, at first, I mean. Then when I got tight for money he gave it to me—for mortgages. So when I couldn't pay up yesterday noon, he—he just took over the land. He had a right to. And he'll hang onto it until it finally begins to sell and tuck what I hoped to make in his pocket. He'll make a pile. He spoke impatiently, irritated by his accurate judgment. "Your mother didn't want me to tell you today but——"

He started rocking back and forth on his heels and pointed his big face at the sky. "Let's get at the truth of things before it's too late. A man my age hasn't time to evade and pretend with the few people he knows on earth, unless he's a coward. Let's have what few facts there are and accept them."

His voice sounded loud and impatient. She could see his teeth showing behind his words as though he had taken the wind in his mouth. He eyed the sky like a man who no longer is small and sees the glory of stars only as mere points of antique gaseous light twinkling on his unimportant defeat and his little human stoicism.

"But after all, the whole thing's of no importance. We won't talk of it any more. I've told you enough bad news for one night." He caught her arm and with his heavy loud-beating footsteps started swinging her toward the door.

"Do you mean there's more?" There was only the clatter of his haste, the racket of his nature and violent energy shaking in her ears. He pushed her, stumbling in tweeds across the doorstep and cried loudly. "Here we are, Agatha." He turned and slammed the door, he had always been a noisy man, and its cheerful explosion thundered through the lighted house.

A pale Sabbatical sun like a faint Christian halo hung low in the sky and from town the martyred sound of Protestant bells was reaching out to the suburb where Mr. Poole still circled the vitreous March lawn. For a fortnight a wash of unseasonable tepid air had been floating through the trees. Overhead in the opalescent space Delia watched their branches drift back and forth like seaweed. Beneath her soles the earth felt fevered. By the gate it had been observed that Mrs. Poole's anemones had come through the ground without warning and the peonies were cracking the mould a month too soon—both doomed to be another useless loss. Far on the other side of the city, on Crapsey's Warfleigh, young trees were probably swelling intemperately by empty steps whose flights on artificial hillsides led nowhere or were growing too green by dry fountains where Mr. Poole had hoped to see water sprout and Excelsior make its pleasanter home.

"I hope Crapsey isn't going to be a fool and trust those fine trees to God instead of to a reliable gardener," he said suddenly, with a shamefaced air.

Delia stopped in her tracks and looked at him, surprised. For two weeks he had been silent as to the money and faith he had lost. Now, standing on his lawn, a final afternoon of penetrating warmth sprouted speech from his tight lips and he started worrying about his shrubs.

"I was paying a man fifty a week to keep watch on the gardens out there but Crapsey has fired him by now, I guess. He begins to get a lot of faith in divine providence when he looks at two hundred a month. Everything'll be ruined by the time he finds out it's not faith but fertilizer plants need." His green eyes focused over the miles of roofs that lay between him and the distant plot of his affections. "However," he smiled grimly, "why should I worry? The thing's out of my hands now."

Yes, she thought, out of his hands and into Crapsey's pocket. Her father's vision of waving trees and hills had disappeared into his partner's sparse trousers and was keeping company in the darkness with coins and keys.

She turned and looked at the lawn about her. Her grey eyes narrowed in approximation under her blown yellow hair. Something like the sight before her was what had been lost—fertile sodded ground, companies of shrubs, files of tender young trees and her father's ambition running like a broad path between. That was the landscape she had helped sell over his head for sprays of fading freesias.

I oughtn't to have stayed that last night in New York, she thought for the hundredth time. Oh I wish—I wish——

He started moving again and she followed. Down toward the white gate, back to the quartette of cherry trees. Out to the wall again with its spreading of thin sweetbriars. Once more restlessly about the house, her father's heels pounding the sod as they silently walked the Sunday into dusk.

She looked at him, wondering if that tight mouth with its thick taut lips would speak and give her her chance again. In the last two weeks he had been abstracted. He seemed to have wrapped himself in a caul of speculation which he ripped through from time to time with loud jovialities as fundamental as his silence. And he had suddenly developed a sort of mundane transcendency in managing the women in his house—a kind of last virile organization. With awkward effectiveness he had kept his wife by his side ever since Delia had arrived. She and he had never been alone. Father, mother, child. A steady trilogy of Pooles, eating in union as if under his direction from their bird-decked plates. Talking afterwards in an unbroken triad beneath the lamps.

Now they were alone for the first time. A

few minutes before Mrs. Poole had drifted from the garden scene with a wash of blue draperies that had caught for a moment on the porch in a farewell wave. And her husband had not followed her.

No odor except of warmth came from the ground where Delia walked yet from every bush, each leafless tree patterning the lawn, each drift of unhealthy warm air, she kept smelling freesia. Their smell had clouded her room that last night and in those hours of perfume her father had lost hold of his hardy garden.

James Poole Loses Fortune as Daughter Takes Last Lover, she thought. That was how the story should have read on the financial page of the Excelsior Gazette instead of appearing, as it had, a mere stick—Important Transfer to Crapsey from Poole. Or perhaps if the true version of the story had reached the city editor, he might even have featured it on the front page, its quality being both social and sexual.

"Look here, father.   I've got to talk to you.
It's almost my last day.   I feel as if I deserted
you in not coming home sooner and above all,
I—I've been lying to you."   She saw him turn
to look at her with curiosity and concentration
on his face, in his pale green eyes, as if he were
hastily observing some new fundamental.

"I've been lying too."   A smile shivered
around the coarse bristles of his mustache.
"Maybe we both better tell the truth.   We
won't be interrupted here."   He caught her
arm as if he were guiding her to a conference.
They walked speechlessly into the small path
and its termination in a sundial, white as a
plate on the tabletop of surrounding hedges.

"This is where you always wanted to put up
a Greek statue," he said in their first silence.
All afternoon he had walked the garden in a
trail of slow glittering reminiscences that
spread behind him from bush to bush as he
talked, like the silica track of a snail.   Remembering something Delia had done as a
child, something Agatha had said as a bride,

something an author had written in last week's book which he read by the sweet-briars on the wall. Now he studied the space before him, collecting his recollections for this spot. "It was to be an Apollo of marble, I believe." He stood waiting, numb, she felt, to her words and yet eager to hang on them.

"No, not marble but faïence. A little—" She put her hand to her eyes. Yes, yes, he was right. She had once talked of a little luster god, white curls crawling over his shining scalp and below his forehead black empty sockets, like deserted grottoes. A small immortal, nude as a stonier Greek, his glazed feet, when she first saw him, resting on hyacinth chiffon in a brazen window in Vienna's voluptuous Ring. Nancy had kept pulling her elbow, fearful she would loiter and buy. Yes, she had later described that so-little male to her mother, having proposed that with vines the fertile god might decently ornament the Poole retreat. But all that was years ago. Years.

"Apollo's all right for Europe, I guess."

He stood near her, plucking and cracking dead leaves in his fingers. "Maybe he's all right for your New York. But we're still a long way from that, dear. Something that tells time is more Excelsior's style. Well," he burst out briskly, "What do you want to tell me? Yes, we might as well tell the truth." Get hold of facts, he seemed to be thinking. Now he was circling the sky with his eyes in a restless arc of reconnaissance. Lone star to trees at right. He took them in. Then back across the horizon and up to the star again. Beneath it, was the roof of his house.

"I didn't stay in New York for work—the other day. And you thought I did. I was so stunned that first night home when you told me about your loss, loss that—it didn't seem the time to talk. About such things. The first two or three delays in New York were—partly —Goldstein but that last time I stayed because I was in love. And you both kept excusing my delay, talking so proudly of my work." She stood uncomfortable, feeling humiliation and relief. Work, she thought to herself. The labor of hot responsive flesh. The honeyed sweat ground out from freesia. "I was only in love, I wasn't working. I ought to have told you." An intemperate impulse toward complete truthfulness rose up in her, like nausea almost, and stopped only just behind her teeth. For the first time since she had left home, years ago, she wanted to throw out the truth to her family and feel free from the bile of secrecy and complaint. After all, what she had done was only what he had done, and her mother had done, and every one else in the world. There for instance behind the hedge was that brutal row of marital catalpa trees she could point to, saying——

Her father was peering down into her face, taking it all in, looking it over with searching contentment. "Well, I'm glad you're in love," he said slowly. "It has its place in life though some women don't think so. I haven't had much of it myself, I suppose. But you're a beautiful girl. A handsome girl. Your mother was more beautiful, had more that classical face I admire, but I look at you and think you're lovely. Lots of men must have been in love with you and you've probably been in love with them. I—I hope you're happy."

He put his hand on her arm.

The garden seemed empty of everything except darkness and his presence there, and of his stifled knowledge appraising her without curiosity or embarrassment. All the secrecy of his parental life, the modest mystery of his generation of her, his maturity, his long browning years, were wiped out in the dusk and she felt only his loneliness, his wisdom and the final contact of his awkward hand. She was not only kin to him in this flashing impressionable moment but she was much more his admiring passionate contemporary. For an instant they seemed agreed on life and a final estimate of each other, father and daughter, standing speechless, hand in hand in the dusk.

"You don't believe in God either, do you?" His question came huskily.

The moment of illumination and closeness began fading. Soon he would be only himself again, collecting information about fundamentals like a man tardily playing the market. And she would be only herself—big-boned, devoted but silent, in his garden.

"That's right. I had to fight to lose him but it came easily to you, I suppose. Though it's lonely without him sometimes." He laughed, suddenly. "Your mother can't quite take his place."

"If I had come back that day when you expected me, could I have saved you in any way? I mean, if I'd had money——"

"Oh, but you never do." His voice sounded practical, commercial. "You earn it and spend it. You give us thousands in presents—dogs, cats, marble statues, automobiles. The place is full of your earnings. If you'd had bushels of money in your pocket that day Crapsey nailed me, or if I could have cashed the dogs and Persian cats——"

She could see the unusual glint of his

crooked white teeth gleaming below the bush of his mustache.

"But don't worry about it. It's gone. Let it go. You have your work. I had mine. I guess I better tell you about the lies I've been telling. Sit down a moment. Only a moment," he said with an effort. "Sit down."

He was forcing her onto the bench at her back. She sank on its cold carved corner and shivered. Guaranteed Italian Renaissance, the dealer had told her as she ordered it for her mother. One of the useless expensive gifts she thought, looking up toward the worried bulk hanging over her. Anyhow, she never need lie to him again. Quit lying and quit buying. For all her parents swore they didn't need money, she would sell that Hoboken Louis Quinze in her studio and——

"This is what I've been lying about," her father said. "To your mother, I mean. To everybody. This!" She saw his hand move in silhouette to his face. "That color you noticed the first night you were home. Not well! My God! I'm the color of a field pumpkin. It's humiliating. I can't get well and we'll let talking about it go. Not a word, do you hear? Not one. The thing I wanted to say," he hurried on in that concise strained voice, "is that, if anything happens to me, you must take Agatha to New York. I won't have her living alone," he complained in agony. "She worries about noises in the house at night. She's timid, delicate and you're not. Maybe this will interfere with your life, your freedom, I mean." He seemed to be dictating now. His voice rolled on and on, distinctly as if the garden were his office. "But I can't help that. Most men arrange their lives so that women never suspect anything. Now you'll have to ____"

Just behind the black hedge where they sat a door opened. A long shaft of light leaped at their bench. Neither spoke. Neither moved. They stayed motionless, huddled, discovered by brightness like a pair of animals caught by torches in an open field. The light played on her father's back but he faced out of it.   Eyes, mouth, all features were lost in shadow as though he had burrowed them into the ground.

"James, dear.   And Delia, dear too.   You'd best come in now.   You'll be chilled——"

The unexpected, the familiar pleasant voice floated toward them, passed over their heads, covered the lost sun dial like a little wind and drifted in echo over the garden road.   James dear.   Then Delia dear.   At last I am only an afterthought, she said to herself.   Mother has seen, then, despite his lies.   Her affection is brightened at last into constant attention.

"Father."   She wanted to move toward him but she could rouse no action except this clumsy flick of her heavy tongue.   "Father."

He was still looking toward the sod as though his feet had grown deep into the ground.

"You must finish what you started to say. If you're ill, something can be done to help you.   Oh, it can, it can."   She began crying heavily.   The sobs shook through her in irregular bursts, clambering against her ribs, striking her throat to strangle her, leaping through her opened mouth.

"There's only one thing can be done and—and I'll do it," he said. "You mustn't cry." He turned and looked down at her as though he were making some stupendous calculation. He was frowning. His face was blank and sallow, floating in a stream of light. Then an uncertain homeing smile pressed onto it in an old and unbreakable habit. "Your mother's calling me."

He struck through the hedge with a cracking of twigs and on heavy feet ran across the lawn.

VIII

Late that night she closed her door and walked into her room. Her ears caught a noise from two other closing doors in the hall outside. She stood listening a moment, then in a dulled routine dropped her clothes and started hunting naked around corners of her

room for her gown.   Clothes, papers, books,
paints were cluttering tables and chairs.   The
red heels of her mules clicked like hooves as
she nervelessly circled the room on her hunt.
Her spine drooped.. Her blonde breasts hung
apathetic, swaying like fruit over the trellis of
her ribs.   Naked as the day I was born, she
thought, but nervous now for them as they
must have been nervous for me.   Will she live?
was all father could keep saying that night, I
remember mother always said.   Will she live,
will she live?   Hanging like part of her nightmare against the foot of the bed, sobbing with
anxiety over a healthy baby.   Will she live?
Will he live?   It's my turn to wonder now.

    She walked to the casement, her eyes drop-
ping to the garden below.   There beneath her
was the sun dial where he had talked that evening.   A moon dial now and telling nothing.
The moon had come up late, secret and full
and was hanging heavy enough to burst with
white over the peaks of the trees.   He can't
be so ill as he thinks, she tried to tell herself.

Probably his nerves are gone, she decided, remembering the neurosis of his smile. America's ideal had settled on him, too young. Work. That was what he had always lived for. There had been plain poverty after Gettysburg with Jeremiah light-heartedly translating Homer into French to sing to the wolf when he came to the door and her father, a critical silent child, in bed in the parlor, getting Cadmus for a treat instead of candy as the candle burned on. Then almost before he was ripe to shave, his passion for land. His preoccupation with buying and selling it. Fresh soil with the Indians not so long ago cleared off like unnecessary rocks and trees that stood in the way of farms and towns. Then his life-time of labor in Excelsior, trying to beautify its mean suburbs and his final catastrophe of rotarian ideals and Warfleigh.

His nerves are gone, that's all, she insisted to herself. I'll see Dr. George in the morning and find out what can be done. Doctors can save him. They save everything nowadays like old women afraid to throw anything away. The world's full of people that oughtn't to have been saved. Why can't they save him? If George can't help him, there's New York, Chicago. There's always Vienna, still war-sick maybe but the home of healers. I'll take him there. Look at the china Apollo—something, something can be done.

Chilled with fears and nakedness, she swept at a silk robe hanging near her bed and wrapped it around her bare flesh. Thank God you can only have one set of parents, she thought. If you could have lots of them like brothers and sisters and for each one have to go through this pain, no one could stand it. She threw herself down on her bed. The tears rolled back about her ears, dropping into her hair like cold blood. She tried to stop her grief with her hands: to damn it. The outlet of her pain seemed to be flooding the room and leaking into the rest of the house.

When she finally sat up again she felt drained and dulled, as if she had already gone through the first violent shock of grief at losing her father from her world. And the noises of a suburb started coming back to her ears in a kind of mechanical consolation and respited routine. The wind was still blowing around the house, shifting and soughing, angling its substance through the bare trees. From the poplar outside her window twigs were scratching on closed glass. She turned sleeplessly and from her night table pulled at a line of books that toppled against her breast. A letter floated out and she plucked at it. Anything to keep from thinking.

Her pupils shifted back and forth across Mercy's expensive script. Mrs. Wellington was a woman who hated to be cramped. A word with her stretched full across a line like a hound on an inky leash, collared by commas. Her brief notes ran to pages. She threw paper away like money. Delia's eyes traced the familiar sentences. "Since you left, Compton Keith—you remember him—dear Compton has developed a devotion to me that I consider quite touching. He comes morning, noon and night with buds and bon-bons in his hand and asks me when you will return. I have never seen as much of him as I do now. He wakes me with roses, asking if I have had word from you and orders up Lucullan lunches, while waiting for the afternoon mail. His astonishment the first morning when I told him you had gone was quite primitive. He is a simple miner after all, charming fellow, and he seems to expect his treasures to remain on the same spot where he last saw them, in the manner of nuggets, I believe. Goldstein bumped into him here the other night. G. had also come up, I gathered, looking for news of you so you see you must write one oftener. Either write or come back, which ever seems cheapest. Personally I never find it much more bother buying railroad tickets than stamps, and then I can tell people face to face what I think, which ought to be and isn't a great economy. Goldstein heard Compton asking about you. Obviously he wished to be the only man alive with curiosity as to your whereabouts, I meditated. And Compton wished the same thing. It was instructive to watch the antagonism of opposite types. I observed them, thinking that East is East and West is best every time if you should ask your devoted—" Then a fresh line to give her name and its exalted capital breathing space. "Mercy."

Mr. Keith and his black hair and white flowers, Delia thought, letting the letter drop. Well, that's all over now. There's no man in the world I could care for now except Paul. Mr. Keith is too old, too tall and too late. All three.

Indifferently she opened one of the piled books, listening suddenly for sounds in the hall outside. Nothing. Her nerves. The world's wind. Something that creaked or seemed to creak near her father's door. With an effort at concentration she turned and looked at the pages. Whatever curiosity Goldstein had had as to what she had been doing, he had roused one in her in her last two week's work for him—a curiosity about the architecture of the faith that had persecuted his. What Christianity had housed itself in for a thousand years after Golgotha, lay before her in colored plates. Here was the richness, rareness, the expense of vaults curved like heaven and choirs built to tilt like his cross when, in poverty, the Nazarene died. The wealth of centuries spent in stone and all for poor Jesus' sake. Here was a picture of Vezelay with its red and white stripes erected as the Magdalen's boudoir for her worship in eastern France—the Nazarene a little forgotten in Gallic enthusiasm for a red-haired trollop with spikenard. Then Arles with its nugget of façade faces shouting for Saint Trophime. And pages farther on in the book, the hotter south. Yellow marbles for a yellower sun. The work of Latins confusing Christ with old painless memories of Apollo, showing him with beardless mosaic face smiling on twelve apostular sheep gamboling on grass at his pretty knee. A pagan blaze running through Italy

—a streak of solid chrome, starting near the vinelands of Tuscany, shining down to Sicily and the sea. *Giallo antico* in yellow columns holding up a church roof near Rome. An altar rail from Palermo with spindles as ochrous as the bawdy stamen of the Easter arum. Alabaster windows in San Vitale—thin flesh, they looked like, veiled with jaundiced blood and rattling lige slabs of color when wind roared through Ravenna. And from the wall behind the transenna, Theodora, the Bosphoros Magdalen, with a blush of topaz glinting still in her stiff glassy cheeks. Yellow. Yellow.

Delia moved uneasily in her bed. Yellow. That penetrating familiar color. The solace of churches and the salvation of spring. The color of the unnatural sun that had painted the March air all afternoon as the Pooles walked and none spoke of the insidious reflection shining in her father's face. Chrome. A pigment for old basillicas, for crocus and daffodil that would soon gild the local lawn but already blooming full-tinted in decay in flesh sleeping now beneath the same roof. Yellow. Fallow-shaded crusts by her father's plate when she had come in from the garden to dine. Conches of citrine-colored butter, rich in their insistent tone. And on her mother's fleshless plate, cadmium cracked from the privacy of eggs.

The books slid to Delia's knees. A smear of unhealthy color seemed to be drying like lacquer over her brain and below it in pain the drops of her tears came through.

Apparently she had gone to sleep in no dark relaxation but stiff in a full blaze of lights, her head hanging sidewise over a pillow. When she opened her eyes she saw the room at a distorted angle. The walls were awry. The door was falling off its hinges and in the black aperture her mother seemed leaning on space.

"Delia," she whispered.

Her face looked deserted, vacant, as if with all her sensibilities she had taken fright and hidden herself behind its nerveless flushed flesh. Her eyes were wavering. Slowly she seemed to be creeping up to a level with them to steady herself and finally peer out. Her hands began climbing across the surface of her breasts. The door yawned wider in the wind and a smell of drugs sifted into the room.

Delia jerked herself up in bed. "What is it?"

"Oh, my darling, my darling," her mother began whispering. A cluster of words practised silently on her lips. There was no sound from them. She stood struggling, working, her eyes running to the figure on the bed, then veering away. "Your father's killed himself," she said.

There was no other sound as she drifted back into the dark.

PART II

I

CLEAN autumnal smell smoked in the fireplace, a smell of the quick cremation of leaves and their salvation into ashes. On the mantel over the hearth a bouquet of wild asters bloomed, fragrant as if still in a fence corner. Outside the windows the October sun was as yellow as a harvest moon. Inert in a chair, rolled in a billiard green dressing gown Delia managed to maintain her note of spectacular disorder but the room where she sat, even after the confusion of last night, looked changed. It had lost its characteristic trimming of odds and ends, its scheme of hasty ease. It looked like an old orchard under new management by the policy of which shoots are pruned and fruit is forbidden to hang into the slow over-ripe comfort of mellow decay. Underfoot there was no longer any deciduous clutter of stale papers, journals, notes, addresses, filed after Delia's fashion on the carpet. No twigs of charcoal crackled when she walked. Even that difficult company, those dubious Pompadour, Bourbon and Napoleon chairs that had never been sure of correct precedent before, were now graded into a friendly settled scheme as if even fakes, under a knowing hand, could be put into their legitimate place.

On the old buhl table with its black pattern crawling in the bright sunshine, was a new picture of Paul, framed, like a sampler of a hundred years ago, in an old rim of flowered New England glass which had been Mrs. Poole's final organization of the room. Within the frame his figure had a curious effect. Instead of "Keep My Heart Pure, O God," or some such petition cross-stitched in small credulous letters, here was the more modern hope

given off by his strong limbs in white linen and
the moral suggested by his tanned unsmiling
face.   And where on a sampler neat pine trees
in pairs used to be found as part of the pattern, here behind him lay only the unsettling
plenitude of coconut trees, hanging myriad
and sullen under an oriental sky.

In the long sodden quiet that finally paralyzed the room, Delia managed to open her
eyes.   On the outer rim of her aching perspective she caught a glimpse of Nancy still sitting
with the same alertness she had settled down
with a half hour ago.   Small back still rigid
against the chair and with the same mutinous
instinct against comfort, her eyes, shaded but
visible beneath her hat, still were riveted to
the new portrait of Paul.   With a dizzy wave
of evasion, Delia closed her eyes and waited.

"He's about five thousand miles away, isn't
he?" Nancy finally commented.   She spoke in
the dry low voice used as a kindness only in
sickrooms.   "Though I suppose you're in no
condition to take a geography test this morn-

ing. It's a good thing for you today's Sunday and you can rest. After last night you certainly are a wreck." Then apparently she glanced back at the picture. "Five thousand miles. I looked it up in an atlas this morning."

My Lord, is she getting ready to go out there, Delia wondered. But she did not speak. Her lids felt like wood. She tried to open them and caught the blaze of Nancy's hair in the sunlight, making an aureole around her black hat. Then she saw her getting ready to speak. Delia wanted to close her ears, her eyes, her brain but she could only sit numb, head roaring, eyes dim. "You know your own business, Delia. Maybe. Still, sometimes I wonder. We've been together for so long perhaps I know the signs better than you do. And I saw them last night. Oh don't deny it." Without Delia's speaking Nancy had vividly imagined the accustomed protest. "Five thousand miles is just five thousand too many, for a woman like you. Too many for him, too many for yourself, too many to do either of you any good. At first when he left, I really believed you. I thought you were settled as you said for life. Well, you were. Until Compton came." Delia watched that golden rim of red hair, those harsh pretty features, seeing their colors, their anger, with helpless paralyzation. "I realized, after what I saw at the dinner last night, that Compton, six months absence and five thousand miles have —have been too much for your Paul. You see you can't stick to anyone any more. Oh Delia." Delia saw Nancy's lids go down as if the upper lashes were of gilded lead which tipped some delicately balanced machine made to be set in motion by the meager amount of water shed in small tears.

Delia turned her head to the fire. The motion made the blood surge in her skull. Her eyes felt like dirty windows she was trying to see through, her face pressed against a hot pane. For the first time since she had been awake she tried to think. But she had been keeping thoughts out of her reach all morning, putting them behind her, years back, years forward. Now when she tried to concentrate her brain only roared. She stared at the first fire of the season. Yes, Paul was five thousand miles away. He was so far away that the comfort of false heat such as was in her hearth, played no part in his life now while he sweated in the sun. The logs and flames came to her suddenly as a theatrical proof of their separation and a sodden moisture came to her eyes as it hadn't at Nancy's words. Only on her marble New York hearth was fire going to burn the difficult winter through, chaperoning her work by day, watching her perhaps with little flames on rare nights, or bursting with a higher more legitimate conflagration at Christmas, maybe, to please Mrs. Poole and honor that family festival toward which only she and young children felt delicately any more. Then holidays over, the coals would start their last semester and glow through short February till they came to their final effort in wet March—

the month when Paul had last sat in her rooms with her in his arms. "Please don't talk about last night. I don't care what you saw or think you saw." Her tongue was thick. "I wish the same thing this morning I've wished ever since he left. I wish—I wish he'd never gone."

"Is that all you've got to say for yourself! You wish he hadn't gone! Why don't you wish you'd gone with him while you're wishing and now that wishing anything's exactly six months too late."

Delia leaned her head in her hand. It ached from one side of the skull to the other. Ideas were beginning to move through the pain slowly now, advancing with the hesitation of weak stale drugs. I wish I had gone with him, she thought. Then I'd be out of all this. Everything that had happened in the last six months —and the last six hours—would have been altered by her legal spring flight as a bride. Everything, she thought. Mother. Nancy. Me. The fallacy of the illusion expanded until by an unexplained gyration of her brain it

exploded, for she thought of her father. His
death came over her with an intensity that had
not possessed her during all her months of
mute grief and a gush of slow alcoholic tears
started drenching her processes. Without any
other display she simply sat with moisture
dripping from her eyes, her voice making no
sound, her body no movement. No sobs, no
shaking breast. She sat there, dazedly alive
to the incongruous lack of co-operation her
tears always got from the rest of her body yet
weeping, weeping, going on and going on,
looking, with her silent face and phlegmatic
hands, as if she had suddenly been struck dumb
and paralyzed and these tears were the signs of
grief for her deprivations. Nothing she could
have done—bride or no bride—could have
saved her father. His fatalism was what was
breaking her heart now. She could have
started on her honeymoon to the moon. But
he would have gone on efficiently making his
way to his grave. With the same energy with
which he had gathered a little fortune for his

family's sake,—with that same force he had disposed of his sick mortality in a business-like rush, as if it were a bargain. After all why not? He'd only been offered knives and ether as temporary inducements against dying more at his leisure. Nothing could have stopped him. She saw her father, sure if he remained only of the indignity of one more human defeat, walking off and leaving his body and his carcinomous malady to fight things out in his eternal absence.

"Don't cry," said Nancy uncomfortably. Delia knew Nancy thought her tears were being offered to Paul but she couldn't explain. As they fell less regularly, she felt drained, spent, drowned. "Perhaps I'm hard on you," Nancy added after a few moments. "I'm—I'm proud of you and I guess it makes me hard. Anyhow," she slid quickly from confession to cynicism, "if you're crying because you didn't go out to the Philippines last spring, cheer up. You'd have been in trouble out there within six months, just as you are here.

There'd have been a neighboring planter. Somebody. There's always somebody where you're concerned." Silence fell on the room again. The logs cracked, fell. "Outside of being with Paul out there, the only other thing you would have gained would be not hearing Goldstein's wails about that confounded Columbus show. Well, that would be worth five thousand miles to avoid," she admitted with brittle malice.

"Yes." Poor Goldstein, Delia thought. Few pilgrims were making their way to the box-office shrine in his ill-fated medieval theatrical church. This morning Delia felt as far from it as if she had never spent months in its construction. She felt as far as if she were really on Paul's Pacific Island. Paul. Her heart jumped with shame. Paul in white linen. Yes, and Mrs. Poole, a widow in white. Everyone in fresh white linen but me, thought Delia, and I'd be mussed and probably barefoot, she thought in disgust. I'd be the first to deteriorate. A flower in my hair. But blue sky.

Peace. An island where one might be lonely but Nancy could not walk onto it with her angry questioning air. An island where monkies might scream but there would be no terrifying telephone bell with Compton Keith's insistent voice, rumbling over the wire. An island where there might be free orchids off the trees but no perpetual and expensive garden emerging from florist's boxes under her mother's acute eyes each time she apologetically entered the studio to put its furnishings straight. "There are always flies in the ointment," said Delia. She tried to sit up straight, settle the discussion with Nancy once for all. "I get in trouble here, you say. And out with Paul it might have been worse. I have mother to think of now. You probably find tarantulas in your shoes in the Philippines or the natives don't wear enough clothes. She's got shock enough here. But at any rate we're none of us naked."

"Make sure you're not," said Nancy. Her voice was sharp. "Don't forget last night's party showed her a thing or two. And if she got wind of all the rest you've done in the last five years, she'd be shocked more than at seeing the whole Philippine army without its trousers on."

What had her mother seen last night? Fear began clearing Delia's head. Despite Mrs. Poole's grey hair, an odd relict from her youth, and the little lines which had cut on her face faint narratives of her marriage, her more epic maternity and recent grief, it seemed that ever since she had come to live in New York Delia was sharing her existence with a young virgin. Life would have to be kept concealed from Mrs. Poole as it had been kept from Delia when she was a little girl and where babies came from was, according to Excelsior standards, simply one of God's mysteries. And even when brides began sharing this secret with the Creator, they were supposed to dislike it. "What happens in marriage can't be helped," mothers had whispered with embarrassment as they prepared their daughters for the approaching nuptial trial in the Pullman berth. And Mrs. Batey, Mrs. Crapsey's co-worker in the church, though seven enormous offspring had sprung from her womb onto Batey's hearth, still retained too much respect for herself, after twenty years of married life, to know what had caused them. She had merely had, so she said, occasional "periods of unconsciousness."

Why are we so different, the Bateys, mother and I? Delia asked herself helplessly. Probably Puritanism had finished for the women what men, thousands and thousands of years ago, had thoughtlessly begun. There was no record that men, during all that time, had stopped to ask women if they liked passion, and the response, finally deadened by Christian modesty, had apparently finally been bred out of most Anglo-Saxon females. It had fallen away from disuse as lizards, taking their time about it, had through evolution finally lost their wings. For only on Olympus, though the immortals had rarely said it, had the ladies been allowed to shout "No!" But every place else and ever since on the more cautious globe, this element of chance had been guarded against in the merely mortal rapes, abductions, polite purchases and politer marriages that, in progression, finally took to civilizing and satisfying most men and keeping the world populated at the same time. In all such arrangements the ladies had rarely been heard lisping negations, ladies having been, for the good of all, rarely asked to speak up. Medieval chivalry, of course, had encouraged the women to say no to their husbands, at least, but the fillip, the plumes and the tourneys seemed to have come a little late. Too soon Puritans, blue with colonial cold, made on a new cold shore, cold and blue new laws. Mysogynist St. Paul finally triumphed in Salem, 1650A.D. And the New World quickly settled down in prosperous confusion, determined for the next three hundred years to try to forgive woman for its original fall and look up to her at the same time for her purity, as with modest sexless instincts she ruled the American home, keeping it clear of the sensual candor she had never been properly invited to enjoy.

"Oh, well," broke in Nancy with impatience, "don't worry until something definite turns up. Maybe your mother will never find out. Love's ophthalmic. And you've housed her well away from the studio." Certainly Mrs. Poole seemed safely tethered in her small apartment in Washington Mews. It had only recently ceased being a stable and to Delia, nervous over her mother's arrival, seemed cleanly devoid of human associations. Bathtubs had been substituted for mangers and there was a hanging garden the size of a stagecoach in the back court. "And the coast is clear. All your old flames have long since left town. Except Grafton. And he might as well be in China for all you ever see of him. And Paul's gone." She took a quick breath. "Oh, he's gone, right enough. Don't worry about that. So the only person left on the horizon who might give your mother ideas is—Compton. And he doesn't seem to be hiding his talent under any bushel basket, does he?" Maliciously her eyes rose like bees to the field of asters on the mantel, took in the colossal chrysanthemum, potted and pungent as a white tree in the corner and then moved to the mass of dahlias piled on the distant desk. All the mathematical dimensions of complicated botany lay in their solid globes, in their mauves, purples, reds and cerise, odorless and expensive in the artificial heat of the room. "He may not be on the horizon. Yet. But after last night's dinner and flowers and then fresh flowers again this morning, she's liable to think so. She's not a fool," she cried as if Delia had said her mother was. "She knows men don't send women flowers because they're crazy about gardens, as she is. She knows they send them because they're crazy about a woman. And as for last night's dinner —I saw your mother's eyes. She didn't miss a trick. She knew what it cost. All those birds, those bottles, those—Oh well, what difference does it make?" She bit her lip and relapsed into sullen silence.

At the thought of the dinner, nausea began creeping through Delia again. Birds and bottles. Bottles illicitly brought from all corners of the earth it seemed, when she tried to think of them now, wishing they'd all been left unopened on their native heaths. Most of them she'd never even heard of before. White wines from France, Portugal and the Rhine, pale as the houses of Lisbon or the clay loam of Chartres; red gushing bubbles from Burgundy trod near Dijon by the feet of young boys: soft pink wine from Beaujolais, sweet-tasting like the leaf of a vulgar rose: Tarragon corked long ago by French monks working in Spanish caves and from Harlem a continual flow of manly American gin, made last week by jazzing blacks. And at intervals accompanying bottles on the table, there had appeared fish-eggs from Siberia, the brown bodies of friendly pheasants that had been flushed and shot in familiar country sunshines, and had died surprised. Sauces of negroid truffles which some foreign pig had rooted from Perigourdine ground, salads and finally an ice, its chill shock relieving her burning mouth,—ices arriving at the end of a long array of shifting plates, faces and foods that seemed melting to Delia, as the evening ran on, into a long masticated blur. "Let's not talk about last night."

"So you said. Still you were all right. Until after your mother left. Then—I've known you for years. I never saw you drink before. Why did you last night?" Her curiosity was sharp, well-aimed.

Delia shrugged her shoulders, knowing why and saying nothing. All right until her mother left. Thank God for that. But could she be sure? All evening her mother in black lace had been like a mast holding the room straight. One black thin figure erect in a sea of white linen, a wash of floating faces bobbing in the room. Then she had left. And the ceiling started to bulge, lift itself like a reefed sail to the farthest corners. Delia had felt herself sinking into a fog of noise and sensation in which Compton was the only steadying exciting form.

"Look here. Where did you go after the party broke up?" Nancy cried. "I've a right to know that. I stayed for a moment to put you to bed here. I knew you could never get down to the Mews. But you'd gone. All I found in your room was a lot of your topcoats piled on the floor. So I went home."

"I—I was hunting something warm. I don't get drunk very well, I guess. I need all out of doors to sober up in so Compton took me out to get some coffee and go driving. For hours." That helpless affection she always gave Nancy, in her sparse embarrassed way, loaded her voice now in a petition. Her candid face with its combing high plateaus had its customary look of primitive directness but it had been native so long that now it was only a picturesque habit. For her eyes, settled sumptuously away from those watching hers, looked guilty and had in them the dignity and silence of an animal. Behind her eyes though, her memory was revolving like a searchlight picking up night shapes. She and Compton had gone riding. Yes. Long deserted city streets. Lamps by the mile. His arms. Then the smell of country roads and earth, cold and unhuman. More trees. Rich ones, dutifully making a park. A long road winding among them and arriving at a blank door. Then fires, couches, wine—drunk and touched in the presence of books and large chairs and then windows as day started and showed, below the winter terrace and garden, the long walls of the Palisades, feudal as the wine-terraces of France but stretched here along the rich suburbs of New Jersey.

"So it was Compton you went off with. Riding. I suspected as much." Nancy sat as tense as if she were going through an accident. There was no sound, no talk. Then finally she said slowly, "I hope Paul never hears about that—drive."

"It—it was of no importance," Delia mumbled. Curious, but the feeling of Nancy's disgust was more than she could bear. Her own (she tried to feel it) and Paul's anger were not sitting in front of her. Nancy was. "I—I wouldn't worry if I were you. It won't happen again. I'm not going to see Compton again," she said in a sudden inspiration. She broke off, looking placating and foolish. She had had no idea of not seeing Keith again. She had even supposed, though she hadn't thought about it yet, that she would be driven to see him. And now she had said she wouldn't.

"Why doesn't he go back to his old mines?" cried Nancy unexpectedly. "What's he doing here, anyway? Or why don't you send him back across the hall to Mercy, where he belongs?"

"Mercy?" Delia asked. This was a shock.

Mrs. Wellington's relations with Keith had only seemed to Delia to be passionately social. Now Delia thought of Mercy as she had sometimes seen her in the early mornings, twentieth century corseting reviving in Mercy that superb straightwaisted free figure of pre-christian Venuses, as she curried herself for a new day in the long matinal parade that made up her fastidious toilette, Parisian in scent, Spartan in endurance, intimate ruffles of short silk gently flagellating her round thighs while she marched between wardrobe and bath, her curious habit of lonely shrill whistling accompanying her like a musical shadow in her mauve rooms. In Mercy's presence Delia had always felt devoted, loyal, honest and inferior. It seemed to her even now that she couldn't have robbed Mercy of anything. Mercy was too superior. She was a patron not a possessor. Sure of her taste, in her late thirties she had taken up men as other women take up art. "I haven't stolen anything from Mercy," she protested uncomfortably.

"Oh. You haven't stolen Compton. You just borrowed him, eh? To go riding with, drunk in the middle of the night. I hope nobody borrows Paul like that. How would you like that?"

Paul wasn't the kind that got borrowed, Delia felt. That was why she loved him. "Oh, let's let it all go. Believe me, Nancy, I'm not going to see Compton again." She meant it now. Obviously it was her only way out.

"Believe you?" Nancy considered its advisability. "I used to believe anything you said. When I first met you if you'd said black was white, I'd have believed you. Now you lie to me, lie to Goldstein—to everybody. Don't forget to lie to your mother while you're about it," she cried. "That's the only place left where it'll count."

Delia felt her skin getting red. "I don't make you lie. I let you alone."

"Let me alone? Why? Because you don't care what I do! What anybody does. You haven't any more moral sense than an oyster. You——"

There was a sound from the corridor. Then quite audibly came the neat tailored tap-tapping of Mrs. Poole's pumps. "Promise me you won't see Keith again. Promise it! I won't have Paul——"

"Yes. I won't. I won't." Her ears were strained for her mother's hand at the door.

"And as for last night," persisted Nancy. "You'd deny it, of course, but——"

"There was nothing," said Delia in desperation. And Mrs. Poole walked in the door. Mechanically, Delia's eyes hurried to her face. She looked at her mother's countenance as if it was the flat enameled face of one of those elegant old fashioned watches such as the old lady Poole's husband had carried and told other women the time by—one of those early mechanical experiments which, without a key to its silver nib, will not work—won't tell the hour, won't move its polite gilded hands, hung aloft between noon and dusk, all the springs ready, all the jeweled wheels oiled but inert without that puncturing insertion of the thick key. What had her mother made up her mind to after last night? And which one of her few but isolated maternal moods was she in? That was the key Delia had to have. Despite her years, she felt as if she were a child. Habit, in front of mother, was too much for her. As her mother came toward her in that inevitable blue suit such as she had, ever since Delia remembered her, always worn—a kind of eye-blue, lucid soft—and to which even in her mourning she clung now because her husband had admired it, Delia saw herself back in some of the early front doors she had walked through as a child. Doomed for reproof. Belated. Dirty. Guilty. And her mother waiting for her. From infancy she had known her mother's various facial expressions as if they were illustrations from a first picture book. Which one was this now? The one where, eyes

hard, face evasive, forgiveness would come
with few words and no embraces, affection being of so little importance that it could be dis-
pensed with, along with discussion of the
crime? Or would this be the mood where the
brown eyes swelled, looked molten, glistened
like expensive agate marbles, and a rare gar-
rulousness broke from the strained mouth below,—wordiness that was a kind of confiden-
tial despair which had sometimes broken over
the young Delia in a wave, strangling, swamp-
ing, then just before drowning floating her
off to repentance in a verbal tide against which
she had struggled, finally weeping out of sympathetic excitement. But there had been a
worse mood than either of these. Instead of
outbursts there had sometimes been glances
of absent-minded shock. Such as when that
black-haired boy had been caught kissing Delia
unrebuffed. And the time when Delia had
repeated a word seen on a fence. Then on her
mother's face had come a look of speechless
distant incomprehension. A look of fanatical

disgust.   Like an actress the muscles around the plastic nose tightened, the mouth took a new classical shape and her mother, a new woman, became remote, strange and unbearably handsome.   And on the child staring up at her, peering stunned at a profile hiding the mystery of judgment, at brown eyes glancing feverishly from beneath the oddity of premature white hair, a swooning but observant daze settled as if she were seeing a vision, a rarefied cloud of anger in which her mother stood aloft, suspended and from which she could not descend even to discipline, clothed too buoyantly in a momentary grandeur at which her child gazed, awestruck, frightened and fortunate.

But though Delia searched as her mother crossed the room, she could find no clue.   The presence of Nancy, watchful by the fire, was distracting Mrs. Poole.   As she moved toward the mantel with neat springing steps, her face, carried high, had only in it an expression of gifted but self-conscious shyness.   Her eyes radiated a kind of talented tenderness.   "So both of you children are up at last!" She smiled with nervousness. She eyed the hard face of her fox as she unlatched its skin from her throat. "I rather wondered, after I first went to bed, what had happened to you, dear, when you didn't come home after the gayeties of last night. But then I reflected it must have seemed like old times—Nancy and you here in your—your Bohemian studio. But I telephoned to be sure. About nine." She smiled again to apologize and show that she knew nine, in New York, was early. "But you must both have been sleeping too soundly to hear the bell."

There was only a fractional silence until Delia said, "I didn't hear the telephone. Nancy. Did—did you?" Her heart tripped on a beat.

"No, I didn't hear it," said Nancy in a commonplace tone. "And I'll wager you didn't." She looked at Delia's face. "I know you didn't." She laughed. Her voice was angry, suspicious but sure. There was another small pause. "Delia wouldn't hear the fall of Rome, Mrs. Poole—unless it took place under her bed. I wonder where we were at nine o'clock? Weren't you still drinking coffee?"

Compton. And coffee. Why did I tell her that, Delia thought. "I—I don't recall. We —we had coffee with Mercy in her rooms, Nancy and I. I expect no one was here to hear the bell when you 'phoned." She waited for the next moment. Would Nancy deny her? E'er the cock crow twice. Nancy would deny her. Would? Wouldn't? Delia was afraid to lift her eyes. Like two moist grey stones, half hidden by gold lids, her eyes turned in heavy speculative loneliness toward the floor.

"No, no one was here to answer the telephone," Nancy said. Simply that. It sounded without comment, almost without sense, it came out so dull, so heavy.

"Oh, well. You were both tired," said Mrs. Poole, picking up the conversation. "Everyone had a great deal to eat and—to drink."

She smiled, a faint stretching of her lips.   It was a motion that stretched them to an arch, like a little bridge over which her reproofs seemed to pass.

No one said anything.

"Well, we're only young once. And we'll only have prohibition once.   So we have to make the best of it."   Nancy said in a reckless tone.   "However, it won't happen again. Delia tells me Mr. Keith is leaving town. Isn't that so, Delia?" she demanded.

"Yes.   Yes."   Delia's shoulders sagged. An ebb of relief rolled through her body that made it feel weak. "He's leaving for the west." I'll never see him again.   Mother won't know if he's gone west or east or stayed in the same hotel, she thought.   A gratitude that was as keen as discomfort or pleasure was tingling in her nerves.   She opened her eyes.   Nancy was standing up.   "Don't go."   She caught at Nancy's hand.   She looked into her face. All Nancy's pride and trust in Delia seemed to have been knocked out of her: her affection

had been bruised, her belief completely dis-
heveled, yet without so much as marring the
minute slant of her smart hat or moving one
of her plastered immaculately arranged red
hairs. It was that that Delia noticed. She
looked the same, yet something upheaving
had happened. "Goodbye." Delia pressed
her fingers into Nancy's, gripped them. And
Nancy for a moment, clung. The feel of these
belated motions of affection coming after five
dry years in which, according to Delia's reactions, it was perfectly natural they had never
even exchanged what could be properly called
a kiss, upset her. The well of demonstrative-
ness in which Nancy's nature swam, was for a
moment troubled. It was as if someone had
thrown a stone in it. Then with tightening
muscles she moved away and speaking with an
effort to Mrs. Poole, made for the door. It
closed. And Delia, after a fashion, was saved.

Providing her mother said nothing. In the
first few moment's silence, Delia waited for
the maternal voice to begin. Your mother's

no fool. She could hear Nancy crying it. No.
No fool, unfortunately. But as she sat expecting the words, the click of her mother's
lorgnette came across the room. Mrs. Poole
had not yet come to a platonic acceptance of
glasses. There was the rattle of the thin silver
chain that moored her instrument to her ·neck,
the sound of her lifting arm. Then the turn
of pages. Mrs. Poole was silently reading.

The minutes passed by in heavy lethargic
relief. Able for the first time that morning to
relax, Delia felt herself almost drowsy. Slipping close to sleep. She stirred, forcing her
muscles to move an inch. No sleep. Think.
What was her mother reading? She tried to
feel curious. Why should her mother be reading now? Still, Delia mused, Mrs. Poole had
always fancied books. She had worshipped
them from the door of the library, without often going in. Had committed pages of
Shakespeare occasionally. Hamlet and the
more female rôles. Delia opened her eyes. A
serene sort of glamorous attention, a look of

recipience not implying too much faith, was moving across her mother's face—a look of polite cerebral sensitiveness such as always glimmered there on state occasions. She was reading verse.

Whose? Under whose printed mind was Mrs. Poole shading herself for the moment from reality, making of each page a parasol that shielded her from facts, and under whose half-circle she seemed to stroll considering, like those old beauties slowly twirling sun-shades over their big shoulders, while they mature and remember on the sands of fashionable sea-shores. Who was comforting Mrs. Poole after the violences of last night? François Villon? Without her lips moving, Delia's mind smiled. The pot-house poet seemed too pat after yesterday's wines. Yet her mother had always admired his lament as to where were yesterday's snows. Had more than admired. Had, perhaps because she had had nothing but snows, passionately appreciated the man. Printed, that is. He was dead but

she would hardly have read him had he been
still alive. His cry would then have been too
personal. And above all she would never
have wanted to meet him, face to face. She
liked the genius but disapproved of the man.
Even her favorite Will, were he still in his
Shakespearean flesh, could not have brought
it hot from dark dames and bright boys, into
Mrs. Poole's presence. For she felt the dis-
tinction between literature and life. She would
have shrunk from seeing the playwright's
frame, warm to bursting with genius and sensitive organs and veins. Better Romeo and
Juliet than their maker—sweet Capulets and
Montagus, aristocratic and aching, doomed to
die in immortal beauty and shed their exquisite
scandal only on the printed page. Marlowe
would have shocked her, too—wild Kit who
wrote of Hero to his precious age—Kit dead
and twenty of a violent Sunday played in the
bowels of the Golden Hind. No, he would
never have been invited into the little flat in the
Mews for he had been too young, male, per-

verse and wild, too life-loving and well-loined. Poe would have been uninvited, too, with his Raven bound on the library shelf. And even Wordsworth and his pretty primrose, for the poet had had a bastard babe in France. Bryant might have been accepted and Emerson, bringing a reasonable God like a new kind of autocrat to the breakfast table of his century. And the pure Jameses, above all Henry, who being less human than William, had been accredited with even conversing with the refined inky air of merely reading, or at least dictating aloud. Yes, they might have been received, though their genius would have upset her, timid, with the talent she had never used and always regretted, more than ever lost, at such an event, in the presence of great American men. But as for the more moderns, Moore or——

"Delia, my dear." The silver chain dropped to her knee. The silence that had been creeping around the room to the farthest walls where for long moments it had leaned, waiting, was now reeled up to the skylight like a curtain on strings. And in the lower spaces of the room Mrs. Poole's voice started its soft circulation. "I've been wondering," said Mrs. Poole as quietly as if she had been collecting her curiosity from her book, "I've been wondering about this man, dear. Who is this Compton Keith?"

"Well," said Delia, bracing herself. It had arrived then. "He comes from California," she announced rather unintelligently. It was only a general contribution, this statement. Yet his having come from the biggest state seemed to Delia at the moment quite indicative. Where else could he come from suitably? With his big robust body and thatch of black hair, he seemed to be a province in himself. He was as unique as a special region of earth, with gold or wealth underground and long valleys down which his speech flowed. "He's been a friend of Mercy's for years."

"Oh. It's very nice of him to keep you— from—from being lonely. While Paul is so

far away. Very—very nice of him." As she
hunted carefully for each of her words, Mrs.
Poole's head drooped a little on top of each
of her pauses as a swan's beak comes down on
each small floating crumb the bill incises. Each
crumb. Each smallest one. Caught. Held.
"It's very nice. Especially for—him." Again
she bent to catch at something in hesitation.
"Providing, of course that Paul doesn't mind."
She added this quickly. She seemed to be
sailing by.

"Oh I don't think Paul would mind. He
understands me by now, I think." Delia
propped her head against her chair, fastening
it so that her mother's face was her full sight.

"Of course, I'm old fashioned, dear." Her
mother spoke with a note of position as well
as apology. "Times change. Yet I fancy men
haven't. I know life a little, darling. After
all, I'm old enough to be your mother." Delia
heard the arrival of this little joke with a feeling of calamity. In twenty-five years, she never
recalled her mother to have attempted a sim-

ilar stroke. "Each generation thinks itself unique. But they're all alike, I believe." Her mother pulled herself erect. "Men always like pretty women: or like them best at any rate," she added. "And men are always encouraged if they can give women gifts—smart dinners, baskets of flowers. Each flower is a sign which men accept as leading them on. And on."

"I haven't encouraged Compton. Particularly," Delia mumbled. Like a lilac ray, the asters on the mantel entered and discolored the edge of her perspective. "He's rich," she said. "He's always giving something to somebody. A kind of habit. Flowers and dinners from him don't mean anything serious, I should say."

Mrs. Poole made a sudden move. Leaned forward. Her whole head looked suddenly minted by the lamplight. The grey hair was as hard as silver. The thin profile and bullioned skull were as implacable as dies used to outline old pieces of classical money. In her face were those incised fiducial eyes, the

stiff straight nose, the well-lipped, just-think-
ing mouth. "Serious! But who thought it
was?" The coin tilted. Then that classical
look, even that modern reserve, was wiped off
in a gesture and from beneath it she moved
out, individual, maternal and with a kind of
determined animal curiosity. "But why should
anyone think his attentions were serious? Least
of all your mother. How could anyone think
you were encouraging him, or that he had any
right to feel really encouraged, when you are
already engaged to another man. And you
are engaged to Paul, aren't you?"

She caught Delia's dull nod and dropped
back, a slight retreat, into her chair. "Well,
then, if you're still engaged to Paul, I don't
see what—" She broke off, uncertain. Her
spine was stiff. Her body looked tense, mechanical, fearless. Maternity was the only
trap Mrs. Poole had ever really fallen into
and it gave her her only ability to show herself
belligerent and unafraid. "If certain of your
New York friends are going to think, just

because a vulgar millionaire sends you a few flowers, that you must be interested in him and are leading him on, it's high time they found out the truth. It's high time they came to their senses and he came to his, too." The fear that her child was being attacked by this vague, voluptuous New York world, turned all her criticism into a passionate defense. Compton. It was all his fault, she was immediately sure. Men were always doing women harm. Men never thought. Delia had been idly victimized and her mother quivered with anger and pride. "Perhaps it's a good thing I've come here to live. With your mother here, people will change their ideas." A moment of egotism and some haughty secret instinct for matriarchy pulled the words from her mouth. Yet at their full unusual sound, she shrank a little. Her arrogance started to collapse. Her surety shriveled and she began shrinking back to normal. Her eyes wavered and after the few moments' dramatic expansion, she started settling again into a middle-aged hypersensitive individual who at fifty, a mother in a new loud city, in a new strained home, herself still draped with new griefs and old habits, wonders, in a minute's destructive intuitive illumination, if she isn't futile. Who, outside of her Delia, would ever know or care that she had come to the island of New York? No one probably.

"I think I'll not see Compton again," said Delia. "Whether he leaves town or not." She was unable to keep out of her voice an inflection which seemed to make this decision a special gift to her mother, a tribute of their position and Delia's love. She wanted to placate Mrs. Poole. But deeper than that was a realization she was too tongue-tied to make: the sight of her mother's distress and pain lit up like an interior illumination in Delia's emotions, the knowledge of how hopelessly but how indissolubly they were bound, one to the other. Mother and child. Mother and child, Delia thought. Nothing ever managed to cut that tie. And no one ever wanted to cut it. Everybody clung. She knew.

"Well, perhaps it's just as well, if Mr. Keith doesn't go away—though I thought Nancy was so sure he would?" Mrs. Poole ejaculated, starting to be pleased but breaking off to be a little confused. "Would go or had gone," she persisted. "I can't remember what she said."

"Already gone," said Delia with clumsy quickness. "I think he left town this morning."

The telephone rang. Compton. And not calling from out of town. From the Palisades. Waiting. Demanding. Asking for a special hour. Bending over her book again, Mrs. Poole said, as if she were reading aloud a quotation, "Answer it, dear." She waited. "If you are going to."

Delia felt her mother knew who was on the wire. Familiarity and a strict belief in theatrical principles had endowed Mrs. Poole, perhaps with rare moments of confidence in coincidence. But other stage-tricks might be flowing into her mind at the same time: Compton might have missed his train, as men do in melodramas. He might have changed his mind, for business reasons, as is so often done even in real life and wished to announce news of his temporarily altered plans. Drama was varied enough to infer all these possibilities. It wasn't necessary for her to know her daughter lied.

The bell had stopped. Now it started again. Its automatic burst, then silence, its repeat, then quiet again, went through the routine of what the company would have called perfect service. Delia made no move by the fire. Then it stopped. It may be the last, Delia thought in relief. He might have hung up at the other end. In the fireplace a log broke with a puff of explosion into the cataclysm of scarlet crumbs. And as if its slight sound had not been enough, the bell behind the buhl table started its solo again. It burst through the quiet room with an unbearable mechanical inquiry. The shrill undeviating whirr of standard clapper on a standard metal sharply burst into the silence, then disappeared, shot itself into it again, then withdrew on the same principle as a flash-light that snaps off and on in periods of investigation into a black hole. On. Off. Dark. Light. Quiet. Sound.

Delia lifted her eyes with an effort and fastenéd them on her mother, who sat durable under noise that she seemed to be ignoring in the rhythm of her book. There was no trace of actual suspicion in her face. It would be easier for me, thought Delia, if she didn't trust so much. The trial of the last hour, of the night before seemed worthless to her now, as her helpless emotion for the woman facing her rushed in a new relieved tide through Delia's brain. I'll never do anything that might hurt her again, she swore.

With a last automatic appeal, the bell stopped. Delia waited a long minute. But the electric inquiry for her had ceased. Unpunctuated silence settled over the room again with the tinkle of Mrs. Poole's silver chain writing small hieroglyphs of sound while, her mind trying to read her daughter perhaps, she still held her eyes on her book.

II

MIDNIGHT had settled over what was visible to her of Washington Square. In the last few moments the chill had lifted, the refrigeration of the rain had ceased. The cobbles in the Mews were draining more easily now and from the darkness of the stoop by her new door, she could discern behind the white arch sealing the end of the avenue, the tips of the square's jaded-looking trees. Tall sparse city sycamores, winter or summer they always appeared worn from having stayed up late at night and from being there early each morning, by day their bark rained on, snowed on as the civic season ran round, with smoke instead of wind for their top branches and at dawn horns and the clamor of early traffic as the only steady chirruping near their lower boughs. And just behind their frayed branches after night set in and visible to Delia as she stood watching now, was the cheap electric cross on the Judson Tower, a few of its bulbs missing, —symbol to nature and man of struggle, faith and insufficient voltage.

As she turned restlessly to go into her flat, a cab stopped at the end of the Mews with Goldstein climbing out from its door. She watched him struggle with the charity of the tip, the streetlight blazoning his apprehensions, then splashing through puddles with the thoughtless philosophy of a horse, he started for her house. Without seeing her he halted so close she could have touched him, and with that nicety which sentimentally coarse men have only for isolated pleasures, for those joys which alone can thrill them and which as a result get all the indulgence and finesse that their pleasures with others never obtain, he felt over his heart with delicately moving hands and drew forth a cigar, unrobing it of its tinfoil with the tender fingers of a girl idly destroying the petals of a rose.   She watched him at his task and saw each silver calyx fall until only the naked tobacco twig was left.

"You'll have to stay out here if you smoke that," she said, smiling.   He jumped. "Mother's in bed and cigars give her nightmares.   One puff is as bad as if you stayed all night."

"Have I ever asked to stay all night?" he demanded and let himself down, groaning, onto the narrow bench.

"No and you never asked if you could smoke either."

He held his match up to her face to be sure of her goodnature as if her smile were an added treacherous step in the dark.   Then assured, he started to puff, sucked in smoke through the flame, watched it burn low and tossed the match into the rain.   "Sit down." He reached up for her hand.   His fingers felt like wood, bent and carved about hers.   Their clasp was clinging, stiff, lifeless. "I got news for you, Delia," he said in a strained voice. "Grand news." He tried to laugh. His voice sounded muffled in the thin spray of rain that had begun to fall again—a bitter antiseptic dropping on the atmosphere after the wound of the storm. Across the cobbles the garden wall and the big mansion whose rear it bordered started sinking back into a bed of mist. Even the street-lights on the Avenue seemed turned down to give the neighborhood a moment of weak rest. "Delia, I'm in trouble. And I came down here to tell you I got to have fifty—thousand—dollars. Quick." The hand that had lain in hers for the first time in all their years of friendship, withdrew. She saw him use it to prop his head, cover his eyes and in that little privacy, tremble with a long unmerciful breath.

She was too stunned to speak. She couldn't grasp what he had said. Goldstein whose protecting oriental munificence seemed to her as bright and sure as one of the lights on Broadway, Goldstein into whose silk-striped sanctum she had wandered one rainy hungry morning and come out to go through the next several years as opulent as if his silk still hung on her shoulders and made a carpet under her feet. Goldstein crying for money. That's what we live by, she thought in a moment's chemical penetration. That's the difference between him now and what he was at my age—money. It's what he eats by, drinks by, what he cries by now. All the dollars he's had in those intervening years are shedding their tears through his eyes. She sighed, took his hand again. Now that she was beginning to appreciate his words, they had knocked out of her any words she might have said, like two objects colliding for their own destruction in mid air. As if an accident had just occurred, her eyes felt that photographic intensity that comes immediately after a shock. She observed with flawless precision the unimportant new slant of the rain.

"I guess I'm about to go to the wall, Delia.

After all these years. I been fighting and trying to keep mum. But I gotta have help now. Or never. Honest to God," he cried, "I don't know what New York wants to look at if it lets the Columbus close up. Why ain't it good enough? But this town's getting so tough it wants to watch Christians in a lion's den and I'd give it to 'em too, you bet, if I could find any Christians. Delia," he broke off excitedly, "Where'm I going to get fifty thousand dollars? Tell me. Help me. Where?" From the darkness of the stoop he bent forward as if in muscular agony and stretched his heavy head into the light. His face was shiny with sweat and rain. The fat of his cheeks that normally cushioned the weight of his eyes, seemed to have melted below its normal level, leaving his eyes swollen, insular, high. "I suppose bankruptcy's always got its aggravating side but the worst of my case is that if I could only get enough money to run another couple weeks, I needn't fail at all. I could be packing 'em in, turning 'em away from the box office. Because the show's picking up. Better every night. If I could just hang on, we'd be safe, I could pay what I owe, turn the corner, be rich again," he cried, "if I just didn't have to go broke first."

"The Columbus," she said, as if to herself. "Goldstein—" But she didn't speak her mind. To her the Columbus had always been damned. She thought of it and its spiteful inception and what it had cost her last spring. Now apparently all that synchronized sinning, all the rehearsed babble off stage, the marching breasts, painted priests, the hundred hired virgins (sopranos), the stars, sub-stars, the blondes, bells, lights, regiment of scene shifters, —all that vast corps working for a rising and falling curtain and a plot which had its adulterous crisis at 10:47 and its virtuous ending at 11:36 sharp,—all this was going to collapse. Maidenhood would no longer go on triumphing in Delia's wonderful theatrical church of canvas Romanesque, composite of San Zeno, Vezelay and Arles, where as if to show what the cost had been to her, nave seats sold at fourteen dollars apiece and a clerestory perch, so high, so near heaven that virtue on the stage could only be seen and not heard, cost more than a good book.

"I'm sorry, my dear." She kept patting his hand, tapping it with her fingers, her warm palm. "No one ever knows what New York will like. You gambled on something and apparently you've lost but that doesn't prove what you did was no good. I believed in it as much as you," she lied. His animosity against Paul had made Goldstein triumphantly proud of this show. But not knowing his secret passions, New York had found itself slightly indifferent to his paynims and victorious crusades, had found itself diffident about going to see what his billboards prophetically assured them was the Greatest Spectacle of the Century, where stars, heroes, choruses even, wore chasubles, albs, amices, greaves, Historically and Artistically Correct,—probably more artistic and correct than anything used in the real crusades a thousand years ago when French warriors, occupied only with faith, dashed off to fight and die in Asia wearing, stabbing with, bleeding on anything they might have picked up around the house.

"Well, I did it once—turned out one thing that made me proud, that show. That's more than most men do. Make money and make beauty," he said with bitterness, "trust us Jews once in a while for that." True. As cheap as Broadway was, still in this one production, the imagination of the Slav, the lust for beauty-loving of the Hebrew had soared out of Goldstein's chaotic mind. And color, lamps, bodies moving in costumed struggle had approximated something that was nebulous, fiery, fine and which hung over Broadway as over a new Jewish wilderness, like a glorious pillar of fire by night. "Yes, it's been good, what I did. But who's going to save it? Who's going to put up the long green? Haven't you got some high-life friend who'll pull us out of the hole? They gamble twice fifty thousand a year on cock-eyed ponies and cards. Why in hell won't they gamble on me? They'd get their money's worth of fun if it's excitement they want: I'm liable to come in first as last. 'Three on no trumps. Oh, partner, I played that heart trick wrong'," he mimicked. "Christ, these rich!" He caught his head in his hands and in a collapse of resentment stared at the palatial outlines of the mansion whose refined American brick buttocks swung back to the Mews, aggravating with elegance left over from former society days the tawdry artistic surroundings into which it had now sunk. "I thought Bennie was going to be able to swing a loan," he went on. "But you should have seen Kolski's face when he began smelling the loan was maybe for me. Bennie had to pretend he wanted cash to buy a movie in Harlem, Jersey—Oh, Jerusalem, maybe. I don't know. He just sneaked out. Movies! I bet he'll have to take it too, and me pay for it, just to keep that tiger of a Kolski from suspecting the truth. If he had an idea how things really

stood with me—" His face broke out with
sweat. He hunted for his handkerchief.
"That's just how I'm caught," he gasped. "If
I tell anyone, I'm lost. If I don't tell anyone,
I'm lost. Oh, I can't believe it, Delia. After
all them years I took getting over here, here
close to Fifth, close to nice houses, nice air
where everybody has a swell bathtub and nobody sleeps six in a room, close to all this,"
he waved his hand at the trees, roofs, the comfortable sights in view, "to go back to where
I started from and begin all over, I can't do
it. Can't. Can't. To go back to those tenements, just for a handful of cash to keep things
going with the Columbus till it starts paying
like a goldmine, it's—." He stopped short.
"Like a goldmine," he repeated and turned to
her. He pinched her hands. Except for his
quick breathing he made no sound. "You
heard what I said." His voice was changed.
It sounded now thin, hopeful and new. "Ain't
it goldmines that that Keith guy owns, Delia?
I just happened to think. If it's——"

"So did I just happen to think. But it's coal. Not gold."

"What's the difference?" he cried. "My God, if you had to buy coal to heat a theater, you'd know there wasn't much difference. Delia!" His hands leaped up her arm. "Do you want to bet me he ain't rich? Listen!"

"I don't want to bet you anything." She tried to move away. His hand fell off: found its heavy mate. She could hear them moving, straining, scraping against each other at her side. "I don't know how much money Keith has or how little. But he's no theatrical angel. And anyhow, I can't speak to him for you. Really I can't. I'm not seeing him any more. I haven't for ten days."

"Oh." The salvation he had been about to cling to rolled away. His voice had been lost with his hope. He said nothing, folding and unfolding his handkerchief in a patient mechanical exercise of the flesh. "I suppose the reason you ain't been seeing him is because you've had a lover's quarrel. That it?" The bitterness of a disappointment that had been purely material, transferred, leaped across to the field of his emotion. Worn with monotonous days of worry, jealousy broke out with an element of novel relief. "Say, look here. If on top of all my other troubles, I got to——"

"You've got to do nothing. Nothing," she said quietly. "Except keep quiet if you can and let me scheme. Let me think." With the restlessness of a man on whom jealousy acts like a fever and whom hope affects like a chill, he furnished for her ears the continual sounds of his conflicting distress while, before she was even ready for them, thoughts, ideas, images began leaping into her mind.

At the mention of seeing Compton again, inhibitions, sensations, instincts passed and repassed through her brain each acting like a sponge, each dislocating with its slight pressure what preceded it, and in that same small thrust wiping out any trace which the prior perception might have left. Her head seemed alternatingly empty as water, gurgling, blowing in a tide, then filled like a backwash where minute forms of life floated, turned dead bellies up, swam frantic for their life or clung. She wanted to see him. She knew that and had been waiting alone with a vague appetite all evening. And she wanted to help Goldstein. Indifferent to analyzing herself, the almost muscular gust of energy she felt when she thought of his helplessness, nearly clarified her mind, nearly threw Compton and thoughts of her mother out. Goldstein. What could she do for him? Delia had passed most of her life giving silver to beggars, monkeys, men without legs, finding publishers for poets, poets for rich friends, bread for artists and so on, she always having opened her hand with that ready argumentative generosity rarely found only in women of strict virtue. Now generosity was a violent almost self-indulgent habit. Yet thoughts of her mother, what she had promised her, what she had promised Nancy about never seeing Keith again, numbed her a little. Besides, how about Keith himself? He wasn't a Broadway lamb. Delia, having worked for her money, had a level-headed practical sensitiveness toward the money of others, where risks were incurred.

"Admitting I might possibly see Compton, couldn't you get along with less than fifty?" she asked. Vaguely she was conscious of trying to throw her moral struggle onto the number of dollars involved, as if, had Goldstein asked her for only a dozen or a few, the meeting with Compton would have been facilely arranged. "Fifty thousand is a whale of a lot of money."

"Since when?" he demanded. "Say, I've paid you more than that in my time and then plus some. And I never heard no screaming about whales when you cashed your checks. Do you think you could? Do you think he'd give it? But why shouldn't you see him? Tell me that," he demanded, edging closer. "Say, if there's something between him and you, I'll——"

She was still thinking of Compton's money.

How did it feel to lose large sums as her father had, for instance, on his fantastic Poor Farm Heights? What if she asked Compton for this money and it was lost? Somehow his cash seemed peculiarly solid and terrestrial, pulled as it was from beneath the crust of the earth. Not the kind of money to be scattered, Danaë-like among the thighs of Broadway where dissimulation was the basis of art— where an actor's life-work depended upon his repeatedly pretending he was someone he was not, and Goldstein's blonde star drew her thousands a week for her superb imitation of a virgin.

"Tell that Keith it's for some kind of new highbrow art," suggested Goldstein, moving into her thoughts again. He nudged her. "All them rich guys are nuts on art stuff. Tell him it's something like the Moscow——"

"Nonsense. If I ask him for it, I'll ask him if he wants to throw fifty thousand dollars up in the air and trust to luck to be underneath it when it starts coming back toward the

ground.   No hocus-pocus about it.   Putting
money on Broadway is like putting money on
the shell game at a county fair.   Only Compton won't have as much fun as at the fair.   I'll
tell him——"

"Say, why don't you hit him on the head
and take the cash away from him if that's the
way you feel about the theatrical business?"
Goldstein demanded.   "This is a hell of a
moment to start being ashamed of our job.
You've lived by Broadway up till now and
believe me, you're going to start living without
it, so far as I'm concerned unless you help get
me out of this hole.   We're all going to go
smash together, can't you get that in your
brain—not me alone, but you, Nancy, your
mother too, for all I know.   All of us, all of
us."   He swung his arms in a violent family
circle around his head.   "We won't have two
coppers left among us if we can't get out of
this jam."

"Oh, I wouldn't mind that so much.   I'd
find something else.   You would.   We all

would." She was sure really only for herself.
Delia was too used to luxury, too used to hard
work not to feel that she had only to step out,
hungry perhaps, in some elegant tawdry finery
to replenish it and her meager stomach in this
city where opulence and slavery were the com-
monplaces. "I'm not worrying about that."
But almost involuntarily she took his hand,
that inexpressive, sightless member of his
eager jaded body, his hand, any hand suddenly
arousing in her a peculiar tenderness for such
servant pieces of flesh as a class—digits and
palms that slaved for the body entire without
any of the retributive pleasure of seeing, like
the eyes as they worked or the nostrils as they
sniffed and dilated, but offering patiently the
mouth its food which the palate loved, button-
ing the garments which the flesh accepted
with excitement and hanging always loose on
the end of dangling arms, as Goldstein's did
now, empty, pathetic, dissatisfied, touching,
fingering the air. For the moment they seemed
to have taken on a new employment and as she

touched them under her warm clasp they seemed discovered as the final organ of friendship.

Animated by thoughts, of perhaps seeing Compton, a rare and ubiquitous affection for all human beings, a kind of heady friendliness, seemed running all through her body, prompting her tongue to any genial promise. And the satisfaction that Goldstein's agony which he still ground out at her side, was going to be wiped out, relieved her conscience of any sensation of guilt in the plan she was conceiving, rousing by its slight friction only a curious glow in her blood and eyes that, turned on the cobbles, the brick wall, the night air she watched, gave all these dull objects a new and lively character that made them glossy and stimulating under the temptation of the slender rain.

"I'll ask Keith for it. For your money. And I think he'll give it. I'll bring it to your office at noon."

Goldstein got up, moved away from her,

walked a few steps and then suddenly lifted his arm. "Now look here. Listen to me." He struck his chest. "You'll ask him, will you? For fifty thousand dollars. And he'll give it, is that the idea? Just like that—oof. A man who's in love with you will give you all that cold cash, just because you cry for it. ·My God," he cried in agony, "Men ain't governments paying out pension money to ugly widows they don't love. They're men, see? And they buy what they want. Otherwise they never give up the cash. Delia, listen to me." He clamped her wrists between his hands. "You ain't going to ask him for nothing. Nothing. Do you hear me?" he shouted. "I ain't going to have you buying me up with some rich swine's bloody money. I'd rather die first, I'd rather, I'd—. I can't, I tell you, I'd nearly rather—" Tantalized by ideals of suicide, poverty, giving up success and power when saving them was so near, he threw his arms over his head and swayed and motioned in his anger and humiliation. "I'm going to ask your mother," he cried. He stumbled toward the Poole door. "I'm going to ask her advice. She's no fool. She knows a thing or two. And if she thinks you ought to ask—"

Space seemed to be nothing but a black color through which she threw herself to come between Goldstein and the entry to her house. "Are you crazy?" He was about to answer and she wound her scarf against his mouth. She could feel the wet heat of his breath, the muffled guttural of voice soaking through. "Mother doesn't understand these things. I don't think she likes Compton and I'm sure she doesn't like threats of bankruptcy thrown at her in the middle of the night. Don't you ever try that again," she warned pushing him back into the cobbled path. "What you want to say about me, say to me. What you think I should or shouldn't do, curse me for. But not her. Do you hear?" she inquired in a little panic. She shook his arm. "Don't you ever try to rag her or I'll—" She don't know what. Call off the loan from Compton, for instance. That would be a punishment. To everyone but Keith. "If you've waked mother up, I'll be furious. She sleeps so lightly that —" Delia heard a sound behind her. Turned. Because she most dreaded it for a moment she thought she saw, opening in the door, the blue of her mother's bathrobe and a segment of her white listening face, stiff as a somnabulist's pulled deep from dreams and set to drifting in fright above bare feet. But there was nothing. Only a certain cracking of green woodwork, the tapping of water from the eaves and its gurgle underground. She drew a deep breath.

Once again Delia would be safe and Mrs. Poole spared knowing what was in her daughter's life or mind. No shock at least at present would fall on that pale maternal skull, its white hair, its padding of white pillows, white sheets balancing the cranial oval like cotton around an egg, prize in some rare series, some bird-

collector's showcase and settled at night for
safety amidst wadding in a red mahogany,
carved, Excelsior-made fourposter box.

"All right. See him then. Go see him.
Tell him you love him and—and that I'm
broke," cried Goldstcin. "Yeh, sell me out
for—for money I've got to have to save me and
then laugh and kiss behind my back. Oh my
God," he groaned. She could see him close his
eyes. "I guess you were sitting out there in
the dark thinking about him when I came
along. Would you tell me the truth—for once
—just for once? Are you in love with that
Keith, Delia? Huh?" He fumbled for her
arm and in his uncertainty she began pulling
him toward the street.

"No." Not in love. Yet. Or probably
ever. Yet whatever it was, she wished now
that she had been conscious at its high point, at
its drunken consummation that dawn on the
Palisades. Unable now to recall either her
body or Compton's, she had only an unsatisfied
recollection of the witnesses they had couched

among—high chairs with gold on their Spanish leather faces and rows of books, their embalmed spines turned toward the agitation of
the room. And windows. Companies of
them. Windows unnumbered, opaque, confusing like mirrors with the faint light of dawn
finally reflecting in. The windows and the
rain of that dawn were all she really remembered. They were the only relics of that night.
The sound of a storm on the lawn and pallid
glass squares, faintly grouped in a large room
but sure, shedding now on her unshaped recollections that same useless penetration, that
same needless light they had aimed at the room,
doubtless, where love was being made.

She heard Goldstein sigh and with an effort
turned to him. His hat was off and he was
wiping his face. If he had been weeping, the
moisture now passed as part of the rain and if
what struck his eyes was only rain, he had the
benefit of her suspecting he had had tears.
"You were waiting for somebody when I come
down tonight," he said. "Oh, I know that!

Know it like my name. I'll go now." He put on his hat but waited a moment, defiantly. Footsteps were sounding on the pavement in the next block. In the night quiet and humidity their sound beat so clearly, seemed so close that the man, invisible in the mist, seemed walking in their wake.

Then pinked by the rain as if it were a shower-bath that left him ruddy, healthy, gymnastic and male, Grafton emerged under the light. As his hat came off, his smile went on and a youthful spark of pleasure and surprise settled in his small blue eyes. "Grafton!" Delia smiled.

"So I was right, huh? Not Keith, no, but this one," Goldstein whispered. He pinched her arm. "What's he doing down here if you wasn't sitting out waiting in the dark for him to come? Answer."

"Oh I haven't seen Grafton in months. Years," she said with impatience. She shook off Goldstein's hand. She didn't speak to Grafton but turned her eyes over him, feeling as she hadn't felt for a long period, a sense of pleasant relaxation in his presence that seemed almost undisturbed from her last sentiments, left over from years ago.

"Well," said Goldstein with heavy uncertainty. She heard him move away, stop under the light to watch them both. With his problem settled, she had dismissed him from her mind. And when, after a moment, he jerked at his hat and mumbled goodnight, she only nodded her head, loosened her thick scarf and stood waiting.

Between her and Grafton was stretching a long penetrating explorative glance such as sometimes, between old lovers, rises up between them like a monument to their former days, when everything was known, no question lay unsatisfied, no moment lay unexplained in their mutual life. For the first time since she had left him years ago she felt interest in him, wondered what he had been doing, whom seeing, whom caressing with that sanguine loyalty that was part of his temperament rather than his heart. Unable to reach into those recesses of his secrecy and faith where part of herself had once been locked, her memory kept pausing before them like fingers fumbling around secret panels in a cabinet that is now empty but whose laquer and mechanism, like the pink gleam and smile on Grafton's face, suggest and survive, long after they have anything to hide. "Where have you been? Walking?" His smile broadened. "Whom do you know in this neighborhood?" she insisted.

"No one. Not even you any more." He tilted his head and laughed. Grafton looked as if he enjoyed his freedom. He used it up to the last grain and then said, "I walk down here occasionally to look at your house. It's quite nice. Some day I'm going to ask you to present me to your mother."

She relaxed a little. He was still childish after all. But the old trait of sentimentality in him made her feel more at ease. Visible by day only in clubs and offices where he strutted about, hearty and empty-hearted, by night his domesticity and memory moved him through the streets "for his health's sake," he said, promenading with admiration before other people's connubial doors and pausing, like a watchman, near Washington Square. Grafton was odd.

"Since you come down this way so often, why haven't you ever knocked and come in? I've often spoken of you to mother."

As she said it, she probably believed it. She had evaded all mention not only of Grafton but of any other men in her speech and recollections before her mother, yet at this moment, watching him with close pleasure, Grafton seemed so much a slow part of her growth, he seemed so mellow with her past that he was like a well-used old belonging which one may safely bring to light any time without the embarrassment of saying definitely when it was acquired. The ease she felt in his presence aroused a certain tenderness and charm. Old memories of his smiling patience clouded around her and seemed wetting her with mist.

The years in which she had not seen Grafton were like the half hour she had just lived through with Goldstein—incidents which in new lights lost their original value. Not only the Avenue and its trees but the more recent field of Delia's memory, through which Grafton had not strolled, were all being washed by the rain whose fine spray, loading her garments and bare head, removed all recollections except those heavy ones concerning Grafton and they, like flowers or branches that had long since been cut and wilted, were freshened, revived, had almost a false air of living on roots again, reanimated by moisture and pressing around her with perfume in the damp air.

"At this moment, you look exactly like that portrait you did of yourself. Oh, Delia, you've hardly changed at all. Years—and yet you look the same."

In his weak blue eyes he seemed for a moment to be enjoying double vision. Not having expected to see Delia at all that night, he was now confronted with what seemed to be two

of her—the old and new, like two camera portraits taken years apart and by accident on the
same plate. Not side by side like bride and
groom but overlaying each other, posed in du-
plicate line for line, shape for shape, one face
looking through the other, the last resting on
the first like, not another person, but a new
expression, a new skin in which was placed the
composite of her eyes, those two blending sets
of them, varied and original, with (around
them) shadows like events adding their blurr
as the paint on her more recent mouth added
its confusing bias. For the carmine, serving
as a standard to measure the elapse of time in
which the nude shoulders furnished a historical setting beneath the later tweeds, had even
a period of precedence that divided the false
from the true at least to eyes like Grafton's
which, once having been perfectly contented,
could never again be cheated.

"Yes, you look like the portrait. My portrait. Don't forget that if I never get it back,
like a lot of other things, you're keeping it as

my gift," he announced with his glazed stiff smile.

"Come by and see me." She laid her hand on his arm. "We'll hunt it up. It's somewhere in the studio."

"Well, when shall I come?" The brightness in his eyes sharpened to a glitter. He spoke promptly. Once having loved Delia with all his strength, Grafton would love her again if she gave him the chance and lying with her in his arms, think, if not speak, of how he had once perfectly loved another woman—the earlier Delia Poole—performing in this appreciation a loyalty and an adultery that would have given him no pain or even pleasure. "When shall I come? Tomorrow? Lunch? Dine?"

"Yes. Tomorrow. Come at—" She broke off suddenly. Tomorrow. I must be losing my mind. I've got to see Keith she thought. And Goldstein. What was the matter with her? After all these years, she wasn't going to let the Moses of Broadway slip back into his

original tenement and finish his life among
fetid air, frying onions and sidewalks peopled
by old women still in their bridal wigs and the
fine bosoms and haunches of hatless Jewish
virgins, their frontside or backside voluptuous
and mondaine under the cheap broadcloth, the
remarkable tailoring that puts style and glory
on the asphalts of the East Side. No, he must
be saved. And Compton. She shivered,
glanced at Grafton, more quickly glanced
away. What transference of her emotions had
affected her that for the last half hour she had
slipped over Grafton, like a lasso, the emotions
she had been planning for another man? "I
can't see you tomorrow. I'm sorry."

"Oh." He laughed. "Well—" He tapped
the curb with his stick, shrugged his shoulders
and waited. Then he turned away. "When
you want to see me—if you ever do again,
Delia—you know where I am."

She did not answer. She had to see Keith
tomorrow. Today. It was already early
morning, though the night still seemed going

on.   How could she have forgotten?   The
street was dead and quiet.   Sound seemed to
have been done away with.   Noise from the
arena of Manhattan seemed to have ceased because of the futility of ever mounting to those
black tiers of space where hidden stars sat as
an audience in the sky.

"I'll telephone sometime.   No, I'll drop by."
He laughed.   "You'll see, Delia.   Goodnight."

She stood for a moment, then turned and
walked through the damp Mews to her door.

III

SECRET on its balcony the orchestra hid behind the management's palms and at regular
intervals played with the servile softness which
distinguishes hotels so smart that good music
is used only as another phase of its superb gas-
tronomic valeting.   Cadenzas fit for a concert
hall vaulted out in an odor of lambchops and
with the same meek sycophant arch, the identi-
cal attentive droop assumed, further below the
chandeliers, by the waiters' spines.   For work-

ing in that warm area lying between soft carpets and crusted ceiling, both melodies and
men seemed to have undergone a similar emas-
culating process before being hired—some
kind of operation that left them segregated
and unique, useful only to a clientele which
(of course) adored music and (naturally) admired democracy but in circumstances in
which the hotel staff unfortunately, never had
a normal chance to take part. Indeed so completely altered were the orchestra's powers
that the nasal reediness, the natural manly
noisiness of the 'cello floated over the tables in
a dominion no more virile than the occasional
voice of the maître-d'hôtel, as if, heads of their
bands, he and it had suffered the most cruel re-
finement of all and one that left them isolated,
attuned and paired in lonely command of their
forces in the room.

"Well, Delia." Keith leaned back in his
chair and with a hospitable air offered his
rumbling laugh in place of the silence that had
finally come on with the coffee. The appear-

ance of the silver-looking tray marked the last
dwindling vocal effort of the dinner. The pot
might have been filled with some bean-brown
anæsthetic that was to be sugared and inhaled
while coma marked the meal's end. "A man
never knows—" He deposited his ashes carefully, watching the cigarette end with the habitual inspection of a frank but shrewd man
for whom even details got a watchful courtesy.
"A man never knows when to believe a woman
—except when it's too late." He laughed. "I
couldn't believe it when you said Philadelphia
wasn't a good place for us to come. Now I'm
beginning to believe it's true. Probably because it's too late." He looked up to be sure
of missing nothing she might agree to.

"I'd have preferred another town. Paris.
Petrograd."

"Or Paradise."

"Or Paradise." She finally smiled. But
the motion across her mouth, charming, candid
but forced, was like a belated dish, something
savory and tasty coming to the table after

neither of them wished anything more to eat.

His fingers started tapping among the spoons and flowers, mixing silver and pollen, petals and small silver bowls. "Delia, I may be wrong but I've got the idea—And it's not a brilliant one! Just about what a man in my position and of my experience might think. I've got the idea that—" He broke off and watched her as he made ready his words, prepared them for her mouth, her eyes as if those were the points where sounds were to sink rather than into her hidden aural organs. "To put it bluntly, is there any man in this town, Delia, whom you love?" He laughed, suspicious but still uncertain of what he wanted to say, "Ever since I said on the train that it was this particular town we were coming to, you've acted—I suppose the word is gun-shy." He drew back from the table. "Did you ever see a good hunting dog that had gone wrong?"

She ought to have glanced at him. But she couldn't think of anything to say. Words might have steadied her eyes. Some races or

families, even some of the allied professions
have a glib talent for words. Lawyers, sales-
men, priests, chattering of writ, right and exquisitely attractive prices. Latins, excited by
the passion and beauty of their Mediterranean
and still talking of it after years of immigration on our cold Atlantic shores. These keep
their vocabulary like a piece of lollypop sweet
under their tongue. But the Pooles were not
Latin. For solid generations they had all had
mute tongues except the old lady, quiet only
because she was dead or had no audience in her
grave. Anyhow, Delia was capable of doing
anything and explaining none of it. "I don't
know anyone here," she said with evasion. He
took hold of her lie and like that miracle of
Joseph's rod in early Catholic mariolatry, hurried it, with a middle-aged man's enforced
credulity, into a burst of good-natured blossoms on its scented end. "I dare say I only
imagined it then. Likely you've never known
anyone here. Or you might have been here
with your family, your mother. Now there's

a charming woman, Delia. She has a charm that—" Ready to go on with this admiration of her mother, Delia saw him lean back in his chair with that obstinate patience, the vivacity, even the interest that can be shown by men waiting for the appearance of big game— for the hooked fish that has not yet risen with a comet of angry scales, for the wild deer the gun-shy dogs may have found but so far away that endless even precious anecdotes dealing with possessions, women, fortunes—all kinds of fragile articles and civilized bits of bric-a-brac, remembered or lost—can mingle foreignly with the constant slap of faint waves, the squeak of pinching boughs in wild areas of earth which know nothing, if left to themselves, but the taciturnity of their own violent interests and the competition of seasons, breeding and death.

Yet she caught nothing of his words but the sound they made, rolling on the heated air. Ordinarily when she had been aroused, the banal phrases men had said had flowed with a pleasing delirium to her ears. Waves of exciting sensation had waved in which the words eddied, floated, rolling in to her ears finally with costly meaning and freight. But Compton's voice meant nothing tonight. It had come in the wrong place and twenty-four hours too late. She felt as removed from him as from that pair which, neat and silent against the room's farthest wall, sat like sample citizens of the town, lingering over their coffee with the ancestral air of gentlemen in whose family small coffee has been a polite tradition for generations and for whom the black beverage, by a juggling of law and environment, had finally taken the place of their forefathers' port that still seemed to be served, or its color anyhow, in their ruddy American cheeks. Though native sons in a native hotel, yet in their pride and shyness, their large civilized skulls and loose tweeds, they seemed in defiance of William Penn, in defiance most of that rebel George Washington, actually to be slipping back to England where they sat,

growing slowly but perceptibly more Angli-
can, more British, with Saxon blue eyes like
insular islands turned in displeasure on whatever Yankee bustle managed to enter the room,
as from their Ritz chairs they gave the cultural
impression that 1776 was only a brief mistake.

They were unknown to her. They were
Pennsylvania strangers in Bond Street
clothes. But she felt no more strange to them
than to Keith. There he sat. He was smiling,
talking, waiting. He was flushed. But something was missing in her. The fever and
laquer her sensations had always supplied was
lost. Once stuffy alcoves had had to Delia,
eager and not overly particular, an overpower-
ing charm. The odor of cheap food, coarse
service had been as stimulating as a banquet
of bleeding birds. Rain at a rendezvous had
not been a disappointment, clouds and water
having seemed like inconsequential curtains
added for secrecy's sake. Even the sun in
spring had been only a lucky flick of color on
what was already a festival. Because of

healthy eroticism, Delia's early years of New
York poverty and freedom had been fine and
glamorous, their events pinked and yellowed
to a charm, even a glory, in much the same way
that a commonplace country scene, some
shabby mill and brook, arrive at a sort of
ideality at sunset when the last helpful rays
seem to glorify, poeticize them, gilding bushes,
shadowing scum in stagnant waters, ennobling
the flat face of the miller and his singular interest in the price of wheat,—putting over the
whole site a pastel gaiety, beauty, charm that
can finally make an ideal of a colored postal
card or any other native sentimental picture
saved for the private mental album.

But at this moment all capacity for glamor
had gone. Drinking coffee in Paul's town, a
city in which she had never looked on his face,
still she could only keep remembering, as her
last glamorous sight, his struggles with her to
his first great terror and delight. "I think I
must be getting old," she said suddenly. Her
voice was loud. "I feel differently than I've

ever felt before. Something—" she pulled
herself together, stopped speaking, shrugged
her hands. Why explain, she thought, I'm
like one of many other women to Compton.
She watched him, critically. But she looked
away when after a moment's staring it occurred to her he was, to her, like a few other
men. She hadn't thought of that before.

Compton leaned forward. "Are you sorry
you came, Delia?"

She looked at him. "Not yet." She smiled.
She was glad she hadn't had to lie outright.
For where women of fifty years ago had delicately blushed at falsification, a selfconscious-
ness still pumped a quick rush of blood to
Delia's face whenever she told an untruth.
Discomfort heightened color, seemed to add
contrast. It played up that yellow thick scroll
of her hair frankly blousing over her skull in
an unsagacious primitive roll, deepened the
candid grey of her eyes, seemed to call attention to the color not the paint of her mouth,
—all the tints, the details of her head receiv-

ing a momentary psychological focus, as if the
act of lying put her in a peculiar condition for
sitting unprotected for her portrait.   And
probably because of her clothes, her pelts, collars or chains, smart in cut but corrupted by a
slight look of permanent beauty that could
make them unfortunately lovely next year as
well as this, particularly when added color
flooded Delia's face she suggested those creatures to which her profession should have made
her devoted—women done in her similar
chromes and yellows where the tints not only
decorated and permeated but even marked as
a special class those female figures of Venetian art whom she ignorantly resembled but
whose luxury and license (had she heard fully
about it) she could have affected as suitably as
their ripe velours above whose folds her
modern face, like new provincial wines in an
old Doge's flagons, would have fermented the
unique anachronism.

"Let's take a turn about in the air.   It's
not cold.   It'll give us fresh ideas.   Clear

our heads," Compton said without warning. And before she had put down her coffee cup, his fingers, hands, muscular arms seemed to be directing her motions, getting her through the foyer and out through the big door. Then once in the cab, before she even knew why she was there, she felt him watching, considering, planning how to please her. With the wind blowing through the lowered window she looked out on the street.

The pile of masonry dominating City Hall Place loomed up in the empty Quaker night with a thick European, a ponderous baroque profile, as if it had come unaccompanied from the Continent many centuries ago and the frame in which it stood had been made in America long afterward. Then its bulbous pediments were lost to sight as the driver, proud of his town and used to tourists, rushed for Pine Street to show it off. And the endless red brick of Philadelphia's early domesticity set in. Up one street, down another, back to the first and around again the driver led until miles of houses seemed to have been erected in a competition whose rules made them all nearly alike,—each a charming pattern and doubtless claiming to be the original for the little type of Noah's ark still visible as a form of faith in happy Christian nurseries. And as the streets unwound each house seemed to retain, though built flush to its neighbor, that aloof unique air of the Ark itself during the forty days when it sheltered the only triumphant first family left in the neighborhood and snobbery was, for once, complete. Occasional patches of trees appeared before the biblical manses, completing the Old Testament illusion by seeming to stand ready to furnish, as often anyhow as God sent a remarkable freshet, leaves of a sort fit to be borne back as bundles of good cheer.

And because Paul had once described such a narrow brick house as his, all of them looked to Delia like the Jarvis home. Compton had set out to clear her head of his rival. Already thinking of Paul when she left the hotel now she had nothing before her eyes except windows, any one of which might have belonged to him. Only Philadelphia could have produced this resistless illusion. There couldn't have been any tracing of an individual in the architectural mixture of Venetian palazzi and handsome corn-fed hotels lake-fronting the wind in Chicago. And how could Paul have felt any trace of her or any house she might have occupied had he been rushing by night through the boulevards of Excelsior where neo-Queen Anne, Elizabeth, even among the really old homes, neo-Victorian confused the local scent originally laid down in democratic styleless dwellings built in her father's early days by Republican carpenters ignorant not only of women rulers but of architecture as well.

As the cab made another turn and she looked idly toward the corner light, without any shock, with only surprise to find co-incidence operating like any other feebly enforced law, she saw the name of Paul's street. They had probably followed and crossed it a dozen times, seeing it merely as one of the town's several arboreally-called old highways, those Cherries, Pines, Spruces that still suggested the laying out of a quiet Quaker grove. "You asked me if I knew anyone here. I don't. But I once did. Do you mind," she spoke over her shoulder to Keith, "if I tell the driver to pass by the house?" She called to the chauffeur and leaned forward watching. Any house would satisfy now—Paul's or a stranger's. She wouldn't know the difference. And it wasn't sentiment that moved her anyhow. Only an inexplicable insistent emotional curiosity. Then with a soft slurr of the wheels and depositing her as if she had been expected, the cab stopped before a lighted door. Soft beams, patient and pale, shone from a lunette transom whose old crescent glass, like the moon getting light from the sun, weakly caught brightness from some globe within and shed it meekly on the black world outside. It even imparted some dim life to the white door which without warning, swung open, emitting a man.

The hall globe blazed on him, on his shapeless nautical clothes and his trader's profile. It was a nasally-pointed peaked profile, edging a skull through which the light seemed to shine dimly like an old fashioned oil ship's lamp. Delia looked at him as she would have at some old relative of her own family, some remote male finally appearing in flesh she had seen described only in the faint likeness of a daguerreotype.

"Well," laughed Compton in discomfort. "Do you see what you want?"

She motioned for the chauffeur to drive on.

"I wasn't looking for anyone." Sometimes Delia had a way of speaking softly, in which volume partook of nothing vocal but seemed to have more that easy heaviness and finish associating with the parabola of thick shapely limbs as male dancers jumped slowly in the air, their vault finishing, as her voice finished, by giving an impression that such a flow of ease could never happen again.

She felt that in the Jarvis home she had seen the finish of a council of war. What had the old man been saying? Something about Paul? An uncomfortable feeling of responsibility settled in her mind. Had Paul written them the dissatisfied letters he had written her? Had he any idea, because of his anger, of leaving his work and ruining the family hopes?

"I want to talk to you a moment," Compton said. She had forgotten he was with her. Without noticing, she had come back to the hotel and was now in its foyer. "We can talk down here in the lounge, have coffee— whatever you want. But I must talk to you," he insisted.

"We'll go up to my room." Whatever he had to say would be more quietly delivered there. She hoped he wouldn't talk forever. Now as to Paul—Her mind came back to him as they stepped into the lift. How patient would that old Jarvis pirate be?

"So this is your room." He stood at the door. "And hardly the way I expected to enter it tonight." He laughed. He walked in with his coat on his arm, carrying his hat and stick. He sat down on the edge of a weak chair, looking at her as she leaned, transitory and awkward, on the side of her small bed. Her hat too was prominent. Over escaping loops of her hair it crouched, suave and set, like a permanent convention for hired bedrooms.

"I guess we came over here for nothing," he said finally. She did not answer. "It wasn't to have been like this. But this will end it— unless you change your mind. Well, any other town than this would have been better," he added as she remained silent. "You're right. And I'm right too. You *have* known somebody here, just as I thought. But that's your affair." He sat hard, reminiscent. Then he jumped to his feet and turned toward her. "And I've had mine. But never anyone like you. I'm terribly in love with you, Delia. I

thought I would be the first time I ever heard
of you. But I was terribly in love with someone else at the time. Then there was somebody else, and somebody else. Not really
many of them but they always lasted so long.
Commonplace, charming women," he said with
enthusiasm. "The kind you'd sit next to and
never notice. But they always seemed at the
moment the most desirable women under the
sun. Sometimes I wonder what I've done with
my life,—on whom I've spent it. On unimportant women. I've been unfaithful to them,
forgiven by them and I've adored them.
Usually it doesn't matter to a man what a
woman is. A sweet dull blonde or a sweet
dull brunette." He spoke with unemotional
candor talking to Delia as if her experience
allowed him the accuracy he would have used
to a man. "But you're different. That's why
I'm so mad about you. I'm past thirty-five,
Delia, and I've known just two extraordinary
women in my life—you and guess who—
Mercy, of course." He remembered to laugh.

His laughs seemed an outlet of physical energy such as Latins wave off in their constant gestures. He moved his vocal chords as they moved their hands when talking to women, their heads on one side, showing white teeth. "So you see, you and Mercy are a problem. A problem." He started up and down the room. "Especially you. I'd do anything in the world for you, Delia. Anything."

"You did a great deal in your office this morning," she said with discomfort. "I'm grateful." He stopped walking, looked at her sharply on hearing her words but when she made no move, did not lift her head, open her arms, he only smiled and said, "I wouldn't have mentioned it. Since you do, why—it's all right, all right." Fifty thousand dollars. Oh certainly Compton had known women who must have cost much less. Still— "I just said I'd do anything for you," he repeated.

She nodded her head. Men would do anything for a woman. Goldstein rebuilt a theater and Compton had given a large check.

Men would do anything for women they wanted to get for themselves.

"I would do anything for you," said Compton. He tried to finger her hair. "And now that we're here alone in this town, you won't do anything for me. Try to feel what you did this morning in my office. It was written all over your face with stenographers and secretaries looking on. You were marvelous, marvelous. Pretend it's last night when you sat before your door, thinking of me. Or so you said. Oh, Delia." He stumbled against her, caught her hands. "I can't let you go. Whatever you demand, I'll say yes to. Only say you won't leave me. Ever. Other women have been—just for that moment. But you're something I want always. All my life. Oh, I mean it. Say yes, say yes. I've never asked this of a woman before. Look, Delia, on my knees. Say you'll never quit me and I can be with you as long as we live, that we'll never be separated, that you care as I care for you."

He slipped against her shoulder, his bulk

weighting her breast until she felt bursting under the added pressure of her own flesh. "For as long as we live, Delia. Oh, say yes, say yes."

"I can't now," she whispered. "I'm fond of you but I—I don't want to marry, Compton." Her hands that had refused to touch him before tendered him gestures, spontaneous, embarrassed, blind.

But his muscles stiffened. The blood had tilted to his face and as he suddenly lifted it, it looked sanguinary, guilty, as he presented it to her eyes. The chaos that had blurred his features had been distributed. "I didn't mean marriage, Delia, I—" He got to his feet. All the civilizing tendencies that have nearly paralyzed the free callousness of the male were struggling in his face, muscles of politeness a few centuries old straining beneath those mounds of masculine flesh, old as the hills and settled in pads around the jowls and shrewd eyes like seats of self-preservation. "I should wish to marry you. I should feel honored but—" He kissed the palm of her hand. "I'm sorry."

For a moment she had been stunned. Then that commonplace rather masculine instinct in Delia which smiled at funny stories, that recalled them, retold them while she worked with her female face as solemn as a nun telling her beads—that risible instinct loosened her mouth, wet her eyes, discovered even her voice and in one of the few times of her life, Delia laughed out loud. The solemnity of the moment before, Compton's passion, her pity, even the ghostly figure of Paul were all pushed aside. She could only see herself and how ridiculous she had looked and Compton's fear, hearing outside the scale of her own laughing the added chromatics of his voice, uncertainly come to swell hers.

"By God, I ought to want to marry you," she heard him insisting. "I have sense enough to say it anyhow. Even if a little late. You're superb. Oh I ought to be glad to marry you, if you'd have me, and yet there's something in me that won't let me change my ideas. Men aren't like women, I guess, Delia. And I'm a man. I—I would never marry a woman if I had been her lover."

She thought a minute. "And I'd never marry a man if he hadn't been."

"Well—" He lifted his hands almost in forgiveness. "We're different. It's a pity I'd heard so much about you." He walked around the room. "I'd heard about you for years before I met you. I'd heard—everything. And all it got me was that one night and even though you ignore it now, you can't deny it!"

"I don't deny it." She felt her face getting red. She waited a moment and then said with curiosity, "What do you mean you'd heard about me?"

"Well, Delia, that's difficult." He laughed with embarrassment. "Still, I'll say what I heard about you was what any woman would expect to—hear about any man. Let's put it that way. Except that men, along with not being Gallahads, aren't famous as you are, and so their reputation is of no importance in the long run. I mean—" He stopped clumsily.

"Oh. Oh. My fame lies in not being a Galahad either, does it? And my reputation goes all the way to California where you lived, across states that have heard of me without ever having heard of Galahad." The red that had been in her face flooded back. No one had ever spoken to Delia as Compton had spoken. The vulgarity of public appraisal had never occurred to her. Her skin burned anew. Outside in the hall she heard the hum of the mounting lift. Someone rang for a maid. A whang of bells. Once, twice. The lamp dropped brazen light into her eyes. In an age of electricity, thousands of years after the parable of who should throw the first stone—in an age with lifts in hotels and the modern miracle of wireless in the air the peculiar preoccupation with women's virtue went on like something persistent and eternal that even in the New World did not change. Light women. Lost. Or fallen. Once a so-called "bad woman" had been to Delia like the sideshow at the circus she never got to see. Bad women. Bearded ladies. And now, almost like a companion for the dog-faced boy came young Galahad, dragged forth from the past like a freak of nature—a youth who spent youth in a swoon, his sex safe in the holy grail. Many young women in America led their own lives—yet virginity as a theory was apparently still well mixed with the republican civilization of the twentieth century—that fantastic decade in which no one had any new ideals and every one patented a new invention, that upsidedown renaissance in which forgetting what little classical culture the country ever knew proved as stimulating as remembering all of it had been to the Florentine moyenage. Yes, a woman's reputation still counted, according to what Compton had just said.

Still scarlet, she got up and walked the square of the room. She couldn't meet his eyes but peered at some French prints, peaceful upon the wall. Countesses with a lifted limb simpering on their beds. Humbler scenes where loving swains hid their heads under straw and husbands, frightened and fat, were hunting infidelity with a lantern and a broom. "I never thought what people might say about me. I thought my—private life was private."

"No woman's is." He laughed. He knew he had been clumsy. Now all his passion went into trying to make amends. "Only conventional women ever remain hidden. Mercy, for instance. Not, of course, that Mercy has anything to hide," he said with haste. "Oh, what difference does it make! You're wonderful, Delia but—You're like a palace. It—it isn't something which can be hidden from the rest of the city."

"No." Mercy. She looked at Keith. Well, he was right. Mercy was admirable.

She was discreet. Marvelous mondaine
Mercy, she thought, dazzling not only Compton but everyone with her fine mélange of little
laws and witty hats—hats that were her perfect characteristic, tactful to the mode yet in
their buckle or brim displaying some shrewd
individualism, some brilliant contempt that
was like a penetrating criticism she might have
voiced on life but which she forbearingly let
take shape, for men, in the silence of silk and
velour. Ah, there was a woman civilized
enough to have arrived in New York in her
thirties but without prejudices, lies or tales,
ready to mellow from her undiscussed past all
the elements that had made her wise—the passions that might have come in with the big
Leghorns of her western youth, the loves that
accompanied the tilted toques of her increas-
ing twenties, or the Parisian confections that,
sitting flowered and high, started dating her
ripening seasons—fashionable memoranda of
the emotions of her life that had entered with

the cockades of one spring or were hidden under the feathers of the next, Compton finally arriving in a season of cloche shapes and black to view, dazzled, the result and hear her voice like a seasoned melodious clapper, tinkling beneath the half-concealing dark bell.

"Yes, Mercy's is the better way." For the first time Delia envied her. Who could have said to Mercy that she was public like a palace, a florid splendid building but whose every cornice was known to the country's eye? "She's —she's miraculous."

"But so are you in your way." He spoke hopelessly now, helplessly. He saw that in the last five minutes he had lost her more completely than he had during the entire evening's length. The clumsy prejudices with which he had defended himself had placed them miles apart. The room still held them both but Delia was out of his reach forever. "Would you mind telling me something? You did know a man here once. You have loved some one here. Do now perhaps. That's what's ruined our night. Who was he, Delia?"

She picked up her coat. "A Galahad. With brown hair." She smiled a little. "I'll just have time to catch the midnight train."

"Yes. You'll just have time."

She could think of nothing to say. Many ideas came to her mind, even words. But she represented them all merely by standing before him, the curious handsome alignment of her odd clothes over her flesh, the ornament and style of her lovely colored face offered to Keith as her entire vocabulary.

After a moment he followed her to the door, through the hall. Then she heard his footsteps branch off, carrying him down the corridor to his empty room.

She paid her bill and walked out into the night air. She felt as if she had lost something. Her youth and her belief in herself. I'll never feel the same again, she thought and turned toward the station through the lighted streets.

IV

FROM a victrola in the corner of the room rose that familiar modern sound of rubber in contact with steel, the friction of two leading quotations on the world's stock market, giving off from this amalgamation (as if even Wall Street had, as esoterics claim for all entities its super-vibration) a type of competitive struggling music, native to a century of newly-rich men with inside information and patented ideas. From this wonderbox, rigid and mysterious as a clairvoyante in a séance, came the sound of its inner voices visiting the room in the form of the Deep Second Street Blues, intimidating not only the ear but seeming to raise almost before the eyes a vocal picture, a struggle of exciting racial insanity in which bugling black bass and pale oval treble clutched, retreated, swung dark and light sounds together, screams and blows—combatants on the floor of the disk while around them stretched the stringy square twang of zithers sagging, holding, sagging on the edge

of the fight like ropes around a boxing ring.
Jazz. Yet, viewed impartially it was the same
as the music of the Morris men of England
when villages danced squares, life was simple,
love fecund and Robin Hood served as a god.
In its suitability it was not different from the
tinkle of spinnets to painted ladies, stiff with
silk and smiles, when a Bourbon and Watteau
were temporary kings of France. Though
jazz and blue, it was the same as Italian Opera
for Italian males who, had no opera ever been
written, would still have sung something on
Neapolitan streets where their high voices,
sweet as scent, disturbed the night stench of
the town. It was a new version of what Wag-
ner had been to his Germany with his then new
bellow of brasses, fight of sentimental gods,
solos long, glittering as Prussian campaigns,
and melodies amorous, repetitive and tiresome
as the constant passion of convenient domestic
love. Jazz, like these others, was native to an
epoch. It was America's national accompani-
ment to twentieth century Woolworth Gothic,

the reign of ten cent stores, pious presidents, short working hours, shorter hair (even for men) and the personality of Fifth Avenue, neé Main Street, stretching more opulent, rich, headstrong, more matronly every year.

It was normal music to Delia and Nancy at work in their common room. Both of them in the new zodiac in which Rome's rams and twins were replaced by more telling modern inventions, had been born under the sign of the saxaphone. But for Mrs. Poole, absent-mindedly straightening the studio this old November afternoon, jazz was a torture. She had had a childhood when "Shoo Fly" was considered coarse for little girls and now grey hair, misgivings and maturity left her like a shipwreck on a new and savage musical shore. But hatted, veiled, she kept up her polite strained smile. Beneath the hat in her head she kept coming back with elderly confusion to the point at which children start—"Why?" "Why?" "Why is this and that?" Why was Delia, why was youth, why was this screaming, sensual, twitching procreative music? And again, why was Delia? In perfect deportment she walked lightly about the room struggling to understand growths and decays in nature that called for a philosophic heart.

Ignorant of her mother's unhappiness, secure a little while longer on the rim' of a generation to which mental telepathy is fortunately not quite common to all, Delia sat leaning over the splendor of the buhl table, writing with pencil on cheap paper to Paul. She wrote slowly. Guilt paralyzes more frequently than germs which, setting up a secret and slow mutiny, finally surprise and overpower certain centers discoverable in the brain. Delia felt guilty. Though she had committed no infidelity to Paul that night in Philadelphia, she had had her hot intentions. She was honest, with herself at least, and admitted her wrong. Had she gone through with the affair she would have felt no guilt, probably. For it was only in discovering how tied she was to Paul that she appreciated her fault.

Curious. In some way the sight of Paul's city, the smell of its streets, above all the bleak whiteness of his little house where heads seemed clustering in a life and death consultation had changed her as much as if the white door had been that of an operating room and Philadelphia's common mist rare altering ether from which she emerged emasculated to find that her youth with its peculiar responses was a special organ that was now gone. She would never be the same, she had kept saying to herself and for days she had felt dead, used, emptied. Her life had changed.

Now the shock was passing. She had come out of it as big handsome patients come out of sickbeds, feeling somewhat refined. As the accident of her victory grew dimmer and she grew more sensible of the narrow escape she had had of treachery to her mother and Nancy, Delia began to pluck up courage. She even thought these two might be proud of her if they knew (which she took care they didn't) and regard her at last as someone who had come through fire. Delia was primitive. In her state of ruddy health, glands and ethics were the same things. But she hungered for sympathy, peace, her own desires and praise.

"I think I can leave the room now," her mother said. "It's a little tidier. But I wanted first to ask you—Oh, Delia, how do such things get in print?" she demanded heartbroken. Then, as if this last phrase had already been silently rehearsed a dozen times, she spoke it with that unnatural nervousness of a first public trial: "I thought, my dear, that Mr. Keith had left town. Or anyhow that you had promised not to see him again."

In the silence Delia heard Nancy's thread, like a new form of flagellation, whipping uninterruptedly through flesh-colored cloth. The stitches did not stop. Delia felt the tension of curiosity but it only seemed to force Nancy the more passionately to her work. A moment ago everything had been peaceful, safe. Why did you see Compton Keith? Why did you say he had left? I'm losing my luck, thought

Delia helplessly. All her life she had been lucky until lately. In danger she had always had the victory, in love and gambling she had too often won the prize. "What do you mean, mother?" she said. "What did you see printed? There?"

She held out her hand. The magazine her mother clutched Delia had seen on Broadway kiosks and knew by name. She had even once been offered what was called "stock" in it—a fifty dollar hush money fee similar to those indulgences issued by the medieval church to frantic sinners who, if they paid cash on earth, were promised relief from hell hereafter. It seemed to her now that hell was where she had told the editor to go as he made his proposition. I wish I'd taken it, she thought. I could have taken it and told him to go to the devil at the same time. Why didn't I? She opened to the marked page. A Night out in Philadelphia, it was headed. Millionaire Mine Magnet Courts Broadway Beauty—Out of Town, was the second line. Then with oriental malice, Anglo-

Saxon innuendo and the Gallic talent for bedroom farce, her night in Philadelphia was de-
tailed.   She was referred to as D. . .a P. . .e,
the Only Woman Stagecrafter in Town.
Fickle breaker of a dozen hearts, the millionaire had taken a shrewd course, kidnapped her
for a night where no other rivals would be in
his way to attract her impressionable eye.   The
Quaker love-nest got its line.   Even the room
numbers.   Irrefutable and accurate, the figures spun before her eye; Nos. 48 and 64.   Yes,
that was right, she recalled.   But who had furnished these details?   The mention of Mercy
was easier to accept.   Fascinating Widow, oh,
of course.   Problem: had she lost her well-
known hold on the millionaire's heart?   However a fortune like his, couldn't it easily bring
balm to at least two, if not even more, feminine
hearts?   Ladies, it concluded, must live.

"Where did you get this?" she asked.   Her
heart was beating so rapidly that her lungs
seemed fluttering.   Her breath caught.   Her
lungs seemed full of blood not air.

"I found it here.   On your table.   Hadn't you seen it?"

"I never read magazines.   And I never know what's in the room."   She let it drop on the floor.   "I went to Philadelphia to see Keith. On business.   He gave me fifty thousand dollars for Goldstein to keep him from going to the wall."

"Oh, well of course then—" her mother started, uncertainly.   Mrs. Poole was incorruptible but she belonged to the older generation of middle-westerners to whom, though they had had no evidence in years to prove their faith, a dollar was still a dollar.   It was an initial minted digit of sober wealth and patriotic faith, a whitish emblem serious in its way as the thirteen original stars which, as if trying to keep up with the cheapened currency, had risen to 48 to a flag.   To Mrs. Poole dollars in quantities were serious.   "Still," she protested with sharpness, "no matter for what purpose you met Mr. Keith, even if it was to help a friend, he should have protected you

against any such attack as this. It's a man's
duty to protect a woman, not expose her."
Confused as she had been all her life by life, in
a moment like this, tapping with gloved hands,
peering out at facts through the screen of her
veil, she clung frantically to the polarity of
the sexes and its one justification—that the
brutality of men fitted them to be women's
protectors. "I have always disapproved of
your Mr. Keith," she started again then
halted. Thousands. Fifty thousands. That
meant "business."

Money couldn't have tempted Mrs. Poole
much less calmed her where a principle was at
stake. But if cash were veiled by talk of
"business", if even candid bribes were figleafed
by talk of "funds," "loans" and the like, she relapsed into polite ignorant silence such as she
would have held at a lecture on astronomy or
physics. For after a lifetime spent in America she comprehended only the simple notions
of profit and loss. The rest, everything that
made the country rattle, roar, die rich and die

young, was only a confusing theory which she
had never penetrated. Like one accepting a
miracle she saw it as a force strong enough to
have jerked the phenomena of skyscrapers out
of the ground, that it was a national instinct
which could pull lazy men out of their beds and
onto the streets every morning and that its
sound was that of juggling clicking figures,
standing for mysteries called "upkeep," "overhead" etc., before standing for the final secrets
of profit and loss,—items these last almost like
scandals, appropriately discussed only in the
hush of conferences that had the theatrical isolation of lodge meetings or at long luncheons
where the brains of the country shrewdly mixed
fountainpens with forks or, hurried at drug-
store counters, bolted callories by the clock.
This, to Mrs. Poole, was "business" in the cities
while over the countryside she vaguely noted
the vast parade of things someone had made to
sell to someone who wanted to buy f.o.b.—cases
of commodities, boxes, bags, vats, all being
rushed by the millions of tons over land that

was likely changing hands even while the cinders fell from the freight train, or was trying to revive its faint crop of weeds around suburban factories, put up yesterday, but already belching smoke in a feverish symptom of healthy prosperity. And as the evening sun came to fields, capitals, towns, according to their little turn in the big service of the sun, the prosperous profit-getting parade that had started on hegira that morning, turned home again as all wives knew. Doors opened, a family was fed, crawled to sleep and the night was either starred or rainy, cold or deadly hot as the American seasons ground out their reliable routine like members of the fiscal year. And women married, there were babies and thousands of girls left home to go out into the world.

That was all Mrs. Poole had ever gotten out of it. And of late a sense of disaster. After God and the Crapseys had divided their claims on James Poole, his widow had nothing but the embittered memory of his life to re-

member and to keep, a minute income a year.
What used to confuse now frightened her. It
could be remorseless.   Spell terror, poverty.
Her eyes clung brightly to Delia's. "Nothing
is worth the risk you took.   Especially if you
took it not only for Goldstein but—but for
my sake.   I have my little income and it's
enough.   Oh it is.   We could make it do for
us both, dear.   Live with less.   I can if you
can.   Oh I can't have you doing things like
this if you've done them for—for me."   She
stood in the center of the luxurious tawdry
room, offering as she had once offered in child-
birth, all her material strength to her luxurious
weedy haired Delia who sat with eyes hidden,
mouth ruddy, blown, listening to her mother's
cry.

Delia said nothing.   Not having been allowed the dignity of silence ever since her
mother and Nancy joined forces over her life,
her silence now took on a new undignified
form.   She should be speaking, she knew that.
Thanking her mother with tears, calming

Nancy's suspicions, padding this moment with words, gestures, calm smiles, gilded protests that would keep the bright happiness in all their lives. But she could not. She sat there like a figure in a cube of glass, visible but untouchable, observant but incapable of sound.

Her mother waited for a sign, a syllable until the tension was unbearable. "I've simply distressed you for nothing," she said with penitence. She took Delia's silence for numb grief. Or at any rate for something so unwieldy that it could not be broken without passionate aid. "I should realize that a woman in your position isn't—responsible—," she selected the word tenderly, "for what malice prints. And after all," she added but in a different voice, one rather sharp and shrewd, "you've been home in your own bed every night during the last week." She blushed.

"Yes," said Delia, "I have." Why hadn't she thought of that?

"So Numbers 48 and 64 in the expensive hotel went untenanted for the night," commented Nancy. "Ah, Delia, that's the way you waste your money." Almost indolently she rose and crossed the room to where the magazine lay open faced on the floor. Without a word she read it through. "I suppose at any rate the story of the loan for Goldstein's the truth?" she asked afterwards. She took hold of Delia's nod. "That much I can believe then. These magazines are always notoriously unreliable," she added to Mrs. Poole with muffed irony. "Well—" She stood for a moment looking at Delia, looking around the room, craning her neck in a triumphant slow procession of small muscles. "If you're going now, Mrs. Poole, perhaps you'll let me go with you to your cab? I have to go out on an errand."

"What for?" Delia asked. Why should Nancy leave now? Why evade the agony of one of those long explanatory scenes in which Delia could point out the truth in a few words?

Nancy looked at her with hard uniforming eyes and did not reply.

Still feeling the tension Mrs. Poole stood by her daughter's side. "I'll mail your letter, dear." The letter to Paul. Too late, thought Delia. Or probably. Still— She relaxed a little. Her mother's eyes were of a tenderness to calm any fright. Then with that rare display of affection which, like candles on a Christmas tree, she allowed herself only as a festival and which, because rare, made the touch of her lips, the festoon of her arms as special as the poinsetta or sweep of the cedar's boughs, Mrs. Poole bent and kissed Delia goodbye. "Don't come home tonight," she suggested. "Dine with some of your friends, dear." This was what hung on the end of the branch, wrapped in paper, tied with silver cord—a little gift of pathetic freedom that glittered like baubles or tears or the top tinsel star.

Moved, Delia shook her head, bending to kiss her mother's cheek and then helplessly watched the two depart. "You'll be back?" she called with new energy after Nancy but there

was no answer. She heard me, Delia thought.
And wouldn't answer. She walked toward the
window and pulling the shade stared down toward the street. What was Nancy going to
do? What had she believed? The worst probably. For several minutes she stood there,
watching traffic yet seeing nothing of it until
Nancy came into her view. With Mrs. Poole.
Then Mrs. Poole disappeared into a cab and
Nancy without the slightest hesitation turned
into the office of the Western Union. In-
credulous, fatalistic, Delia watched her. That's
the "errand," she thought. A cable to Paul.
Wires to All Parts of the World. Little boys
in little blue uniforms running around the
earth with gilt buttons and messages which are
not true. What happens here today can be
told in Hongkong tomorrow. Or the Philippines. Or in hell. Service. Electricity has
made the world small.

It's over, Delia thought. Not between her
and Paul. There might be a struggle or
trouble but she never thought of losing him.

She was thinking of Nancy. This was the end of a friendship—this exact minute, during this ticking of the clock, this passing of that particular motor bus with a woman on top with a red rose in her hat. While the bus was swinging down the street, Delia was losing a friend. She walked back to the fire and sat down. With a rare choice in comfort, as if she couldn't put up with any more physical pain, she chose a large breast-like chair and sank on it. It was over. The minutes passed. Delia was thinking, or maybe only remembering in confused kaleidoscopic patches, what she felt and what she, during their long years together, now saw. Nancy. Their amity had been diminishing ever since Paul had arrived to make it a triad and yet the confusing of its dissolution swaddled Delia's head in a haze. How many years? Seven. Once, she thought, Nancy loved me better than any thing in the world. She reddened a little. But it was true. Love was the only accurate word. Love had given a peculiar intensity to what otherwise would have been Nancy's mere affection and friendliness. Outside Delia's window in the gathering electrical effulgence that was New York's protest against the demoded restrictions of night, were certain lamps, probably not too brightly glimmering, by the bedsides of certain chorus girls. They too, when Delia first came to New York, first came to Goldstein, had offered affection that could have been intense. Flowers, sent as tentatives to Delia's door and bought in gallantry out of small salaries. Sweets, as brown as amorous brown eyes, fondants as white as unrefined teeth.

Delia was glamorous, physical. But she was primitive. So unerring was her naturalness that there never had been any scenes. The Russian singer with the pearl earrings, boy's jackets and short hair had been abruptly left sitting in her cab. As Delia had said in irritation to Goldstein, "Why should I talk to her? You know I don't speak any French." She had never arrived at stating the truth any

more exactly than that nor had the theme ever
been mentioned between Nancy and her. As a
matter of fact, perhaps it was only the domesticity she never felt for her husband Harry
which Nancy let blossom on Delia, arriving on
the fleeing Harry's heels. Perhaps, had
Harry stayed, this tenderness would have gone
to him. Maybe he missed being happy only by
a narrow margin. Missed the home-made coffee, the buttons and sewing bag, which, the
routine once started, his wife poured over
Delia, a coffee-loving, buttonless substitute.
For with the peculiar adaptability of an unoc-
cupied violent woman, Nancy picked from the
three graded female emotions (wife, mother,
friend) all the essences, all the follies and
threw them on Delia without any of their
proper rewards. For Nancy was filled like
that swan's egg holding Castor and Pollux,
with a mixture so rich that she could, as the
egg did, make of brothers more than twins, of
lovers more than friends, of companions more
than comrades before life and in death—

strange partners of white and yolk. But Castor and Pollux, if ever, were historical long, long ago. And since then Jove, not having Nancy's needs in mind, had never begotten twinned girls. Though ignoring Nancy (as indeed life did) he might easily have had a hand in begetting Delia. Thicker-hipped and adorned with her own rugged hair, she could have confused early citizens with an idea of a parent god. For Delia had, set even in the midst of a mechanical civilization, some of that primitive archaic allure marked in ancient females who in small select numbers had received in absentia grain, prayers, milk, worship or hyacinth buds placed on credulous rural shrines. And what Nancy had brought and would now bring no more was what had always been, is always being placed before graven, silent, lovely faces—the gifts of honey and wine.

And now the gifts were finished. With her unerring instinct to select and stick to the wrong thing, Nancy who had passed from

Harry to Delia, was now passing from Delia to Paul. Probably she thought she had never been appreciated. But if in all these years Delia's affection had been satisfied but mute, now while Nancy was not there to hear a sound, in the region of her heart Delia felt a wrenching as if something that had been lifted out had left its roots that could lament and wave in the inner cardiac air like mandrakes crying on a field at night because they have been cut.

She sat by the fire, thinking she might hear a knock. But no one came back to tap on the glass of the door.

v

As the days passed Delia learned to do without food, hunger having deserted her as her money once had when she first came to New York. And like a last economy, she slowly gave up sleep like some luxury of the nerves which, fighting for it as she might, gradually went further and further from her

reach. For the first time in her life she had
nearly all of the twenty-four hours that make
a day on her hands. Days became enormous.
There was no night. There was simply a portion of the day that had to be gone through
without light from the sun and in whose darkness she methodically stumbled from bed to
lamp, from easel to the street, in a routine that
never changed. Nancy had temporarily disappeared, sending professional messages only
from the whirlpool of new energy revived in
Goldstein's office. Mrs. Poole, tender and
tactful, spoke merely of the weather or of
Delia's loss of appetite, proffering egg-nogs
with little comments that reflected only her
love. But she had suffered suspicion. It had
affected her like having been in an accident
which, while it had shed no blood, had been a
great shock. Where the trust of Nancy and
her mother had made walls and roofs around
Delia's life nothing now remained except the
space they had once enclosed, like the inky flat
plans of huge medieval buildings that can still

be found on archived parchments to prove the cubic glory of edifices of which no stone above ground endures and for which no one grieves.

Only Compton and Mercy were natural and optimistic, she with modistes, smiles, and fittings and he with impatient faith. Paul had made no sign. Only Goldstein seemed really active. For the Columbus was reviving, just as he had prophesied, and he with it. Already he was planning a new spectacle like a man, who barely out of the woods where he has nearly died, starts figuring on a new jaunt into another wilderness. And Delia worked, glad as she bent over her boards that the chorus girls of Manhattan still wore clothes or at any rate did not sing completely nude as did the Parisian coryphées who demand nothing public from the management except backdrops and a tune. Long hours with charcoal kept her mind drugged. But her nerves were too free. They kept listening for sounds at the door. News. Word from Nancy about Paul. The janitor, the bootlegger, insurance agents, the newsboy,—the hand of each one raised against her door all started to be news from Paul until the owners walked in and she looked at them in blank defeat.

A week after she had seen Nancy the last time, her bell rang and she shouted, "Come in." Years of clinging to her easel had finally turned Delia's voice into a servant. It was what she sent to the door, training it from its low native stature to something high enough, official enough to usher callers in through the door. But after her call, the silence and wait were so long that she turned on her stool, wondering. The entrant, whoever he was, under the clamor of her shouts, had finally decided to start his way in which he took a little uncertainly, accustomed perhaps to more formal routine. As she looked up, he walked in. Under the emmigré French portières of her inner door she saw a doublebreasted blue coat, a singlebreasted wax face, not a fold of flesh gross enough to lap over another, skin being as scantily used as if it cost cash and rip-ping open to emit an underlining of voice that was as strong, as pliant, as smooth as silk of superior and lasting quality.

"I rang." He spoke like a man who never lied. His statement had the impatience of a middle-aged financier who never deals in inaccuracies and never makes mistakes. "I rang," he repeated. Then he looked at a card in his hand. "I am looking," he read off, "for a Miss Poole."

Her heart began its irregular motion. "I am a Miss Poole." Nervously she pulled her hair back from her face, her hands moving not like an artist's at a curtain which he lifts to show off a portrait in which he takes pride. They were more like the hired hands of a nurse trying to relieve a patient's distress.

He ignored her. Having located his audience, he said, "I am Mr. Jarvis," and sat down.

"Yes, I knew you were. I've seen you once before."

He looked at her for the first time. He

went over her face carefully to criticise his memory if such a fantasy were possible, or to mark her features like a dead letter, Unknown, and leave it lying for the proper channels to take from this notice. "You are probably mistaken. It is difficult to imagine by what chance you and I would have met. I never forget people I have seen," he persisted, "and I never saw you before."

"You never saw me. I saw you," she corrected. Her voice was respectful. Delia was in one way anyhow old-fashioned. She thought people after fifty were entitled to a special polite tone. It was their righteous solace for age.

He had listened attentively to her two sentences as if they presented all the trickeries of a verbal contract. Then he made up his mind. "Possibly you have seen me. It is of no consequence. It has nothing to do with the matter in hand." He gave her an impression of not being so much rude as of being too rich and too accurate. Poor men lack the privilege of candor and the neatness of petty conclusions. But this old man had an exactitude for every dollar he owned in the bank. Neither patience nor sensuality had ever befogged nor illuminated his vision. "As I am very little accomplished in visits of this sort," he started with satisfaction, "I shall make no attempt to lead up to what I have to say. I shall talk bluntly. I have very little time to give to it. In forty years I haven't left my office to go on without me as I have today. I am," he added, "a very busy man."

"And I'm a busy woman," she murmured. "Do you mind if I go on with my work?" With a certain generosity that seemed to be trying to include him with her profile, she turned away from him and bent over her easel with her methodical inspired lines.

She had surprised him. "I disapprove of women in business."

She watched her crayon a moment. "You disapprove of women in general, I expect."

He did not reply. Those people who had

dared dispute with him in his youth, he had long since forgotten. All he remembered now was the routine day by day of vocal chords saying hastily, "Yes, sir," and the sight of letters ending with "Esteeming your favors we are, Mr. Jarvis, Very truly yours, etc." He had probably lost interest in anything else. At sixty he had selected, had tested, had made up his inflexible mind as to what he wanted to ignore, like an invalid following a strict diet.

"You've come to see me about Paul," she said. Her voice showed no excitement but her heart was jerking. "Or I hope you have, at any rate."

"You astonish me. I should not have deduced, judging by the ill-will you have showed his career for the last half year, that you had any interest in my nephew at all."

"I don't know if you would call it interest," she said slowly. "I'm in love with him."

"That of course, is merely your statement."

"Well, mine's likely to be more authoritative than yours. I'm the one concerned and be-

sides I daresay you don't know what love is,
Mr. Jarvis. And it seems to me at this moment
that I—I know a great deal about it."

"None of this concerns me."　He pushed it
all aside by a sparse flick of his hand.　"I want
to know why he should have been sent a cable a
few days ago which has upset all of his plans.
Also," he added undistractedly, "mine.　You
are the person who can answer me because you
are the one who sent it."

She clung to her crayon.　What it was tracing was of no consequence now.　Scratches on
wasted paper.　"No.　I did not send it."

Paul's uncle was not in the habit of being
wrong.　Incapable of apology, he sat with his
head carefully balanced, his eyes rolling a little
as if he were dizzy but had only to wait a minute for things to settle into their normal triumphant relations which as yet they had never
failed to do.　"I doubt if I believe you did not
have something to do with sending it."　If
he were in the wrong, it was going to affect
him like a phenomenon.　She wished she could

deny him entirely. She had never seen anyone look more righteous, intelligent and sure.

"I'm not the only woman who's in love with your nephew," she evaded. "I am I trust, the only woman he loves. But I had nothing to do with sending that message. I wish it hadn't been sent. Though I must admit," she added with an effort, "that it was sent perhaps because of me. Would you mind," she turned toward him, leaned, "would you mind telling me what that message said?"

"I naturally would not tell you, if you did not send it. Things of that sort are matters of common principle," he replied.

He doesn't know what was in it, she thought.

"If you didn't send it, why do you care what it contained?" His face was not one that lightened or darkened. It simply opened or shut, according to his moods and to let his ideas out and keep anyone else's from entering in. But his eyes suffered temperature. Their brown turned to bullion when he thought he had scored a point as now. Then in a moment the brightness ran down and was visible only in a patch of gold faceting one of his front teeth and which served for the nucleus of his expressions like the mercury bead resting at the bottom of a thermometer, ready to shoot up in a registering flash the instant heat is applied. "I will, however, tell you the result of the cable. For of course you had, on or without your own admission, some unforgivable hand in bringing it about. You're entitled to the severity of the results." His voice hardened. "My nephew is on his way to San Francisco now. I trust," he articulated with choice bitterness, "that you—and the other women—will be gratified. He has ruined himself."

"I'm sorry if his voyage means that. Personally of course I'm glad he's coming."

"Women are never able to take any but a personal view of everything. I am not one of those weak-kneed feminists."

"No, I shouldn't have fancied you were." She sounded abstracted. "Are you going to give Paul the sack because of this?" She turned toward him and put her question directly.

His face became as hard as ice. "I am not in the habit of discussing my private affairs with anybody. Anybody!" He threw out his arm in one of the few gestures of a lifetime. "You've ruined his career. That ought to satisfy you. There isn't anything else you need to know."

"H'm." She and Jarvis both turned, surprised. On worn rubber heels Goldstein had walked quietly into the room and stood looking at them, curious and displeased. "I gotta write something," he mumbled to Delia. "I just came in to—" He shambled over to the buhl desk and with his back to them, sat down.

Jarvis turned scarlet. "I had no idea we weren't alone," he said to Delia in a strained voice. Lack of privacy affected him like the final unendurable breach of all those to be expected in a female artist's rooms. "I came here to tell you what I thought of you for your heartless interference. But we have too little in common, I find, for you to understand what I might say. I shall go."

Before he could rise Goldstein swiveled on his fat haunches and over one ponderous shoulder eyed him with oriental fury. "Say, how do you get that way?" he demanded. "Who do you think you're talking to, anyhow? Delia, who is this guy?"

She waited a moment. "No one you know," she said shortly. "Don't bother, Goldstein. Please."

"Whose life have you ruined, that he keeps talking about. That's what I want to know. Say, what does he think this is? A ten-twenty-thirt? What's all this last act stuff for?" He pulled his limbs from beneath the narrow desk, got himself on his feet and started coming across the room. The slip of paper on which he had been writing was still clutched in his fat hand. "Tell us all about it," he commanded.

Delia held her lip in her teeth a moment. "This is Mr. Jarvis," she said. "Paul's uncle,"

she added with more animation. "Now don't
say you don't know who Paul is, either."

"I'll tell the world I won't. That brown-
eyed cinema hero, that monkeying mollycod-
dle who damn near broke up my business last
spring? Forget him? And he's your nephew,
is he? Well, tell him for me that the next time
he sets foot on Broadway and tries to ruin *my*
career, I'm going to run him back to Holly-
wood where he belongs, him and his six-reel
kisses on the sidewalk and his plot to save the
family fortune, if any. And if he saved theirs
the way I nearly lost mine because of the way
he acted, he's a hell of a fortune-saver. Is he
back again?" he demanded of Delia.

"Coming."

"Oh, good news." His thick eyes narrowed.
He walked closer to Jarvis, still stunned in his
chair, his hat in his hand and his knees locked
together in a private vise. Goldstein stretched
himself, shot his hands into his pockets and
towering above the seated figure, stood pulling tweeds against flesh and tailoring against

the protuberance of his stomach.   "What would you do," he interrogated, "if some whippersnapper came around and tried to steal the best business asset you got—an asset you made thousands out of, somebody you paid thousands to—and the whippersnapper, without a penny in his pocket, tried to steal what was yours?   Well, Mr. Whatsyourname, that elegant young meddler who tried those tricks is your swell nephew.   Last spring he wanted this lady here to throw up her contracts, break 'em, 'eat 'em, wrap sausage in 'em—oh contracts for a fortune a year meant nothing to him for he loved her, sure—say, if what he did wasn't attempted robbery, what is? A rich man might have had the nerve for he'd have been offering something for what he stole and could give the lady something for the very bread he took out of her mouth, but your nephew—! Did he ever have a cent in his life?   Tell him I'm waiting for him," he bent down to shout, "and if he tries them dodges again he can pay me for her contracts, do you hear?   I guess that'll put a crimp in his passion. And in your remarks to Miss Poole here, too."

"I was not aware that my nephew had interfered with your business in any way. Whatever it may be," said the old man with cold disgust. "I only know this woman has helped lure him back from the Philippines where I had placed him to start his career. That's ruined. What about my contracts?" he inquired with bitterness. "Why shouldn't she pay for them if he is to pay for hers? Though it's probably asking too much of a man like you to demand legality. You wouldn't know what the word meant."

"I know a lot of words," Goldstein warned him. "Don't start counting on what I don't know or you'll be surprised. Well what are his contracts worth? If you pay him, I'll bet they don't add up to much. How much? Have you *got* a contract?" he jibed. "I bet you're one of them hand to mouth payers that puts nothing on paper without a struggle. Have you got a contract? Well, I have. And

we'll just write down in it what you pay your
little boy and what I pay my Miss Poole and
subtract and by J. C. you can hand me the
difference! And it'll be some difference.
You'll be paying me fifteen or twenty thousands!" His face swelled with anger and
success. All the agony he had suffered as a
youth was nothing to this middle-aged triumph. "To think of the times I was sweating
blood at how much I paid her, me not knowing you'd come along and I could get back at
what last spring cost me." He pulled out a
hand hot from his trouser's pocket and wagged
it under Jarvis' nose. "It scares you to have
your bluff called. Used to being a big bug,
ain't you? You can't big bug me. How
much do you pay that miserable half-crazy
nephew? Huh?" He waited a fraction of a
second. "Well, not much, I bet. Say, I've
heard all about love one another and turn the
other cheek since the first time I got mud
throwed on me by guys on the East Side. Oh
you're kind and charitable. Free with your

cash, aren't you—you are not! Say, when it comes to good wages, helping a friend out, lying for 'em a little if necessary," without expression his eyes hunted Delia's for a moment, "gimme a plain old Jew. That's me." He nodded his head, put on his hat, rammed it down over his bald scalp and stood covered, patriarchal and oriental in a woman's presence. "We gotta go," he said to her. "We gotta get to the church on time."

"Yes." She glanced at Jarvis again. Her hair was falling down. Beneath its yellow comet-tails her grey eyes were as phenomenal as an evening sky. "I must know if you're going to fire Paul. It's my fault he's lost his job—if he has. I've involved him. What are his family going to live on until he gets an opening again? I'm responsible, don't you see?"

"I don't believe I do." He looked at Delia for a moment as if she were infectious or violent, ignorant anyhow of his immunity and his old supple strength.

"I won't have them living without money. They've had enough of that. I'll send it to them until Paul gets on his feet. That's what I mean. And that won't take long. I know dozens of men here. Rich ones, poor ones. We'll get Paul a job within a few days. You mustn't think, Mr. Jarvis," and her voice became respectful again, "that just because you fire him, he can't get another job. New York's full of influential people. And if his parents need money for the first few weeks, they're going to get it. I'm sorry to disappoint you," she said more slowly, "but everything's going to turn out all right."

"You may be right," he said with moderate mildness. "At any rate, it is absurd for you to consider members of my family as objects of your impetuous but—but impressive," he had hunted for the word carefully, "your impressive charity." She had slipped off her smock. He looked at the dress she wore beneath, forced now to notice its expensive handsomeness, to be ignorant of its style and be driven back to computing only the luxury of its velvet and brown fur. It was the second time he had looked at her and this time he seemed to be sizing her up, as if her strong flesh and its rich textile covering were a prospectus he could rely on at last. "I am beginning to understand why most artists end their days in the poor house," he murmured. He glanced about the room. "Why only a minority of them ever eat unless they are finally fed by the generosity of the state." His head did not stir but his eyes moved cautiously around the room, the pupils caught by the gleam of gilt, the shudder of sham ormolu, the twinkle of satin and state. His retina was caught, informed and held by the gaudy signs of a dashing Empire. "I suppose this is the sort of thing they buy instead of bonds," he said to himself aloud. He stood up. "You seem to have a certain amount of money. I suppose most of it goes into oil-wells. Goldbricks." He seemed to take his correct diagnosis for granted.

She shook her head. "I buy Liberty Bonds."

He was annoyed. Her sagacity upset him a little. "Safe," he said. "But not sound." He couldn't resist that. "One can hardly afford to accept less than five percent," he said dogmatically.

"Yeh," said Goldstein. "It's all I can do to hold myself down to fifty sometimes. And speaking of money,—" He lifted his hand. The check in it fluttered for a moment before Jarvis' quick eye. " 'Pay to the Order of C. J. Keith $50,000,' " read Goldstein with glibness. "Now I suppose you'd bank that in five percents too. Wouldn't you? But us artists don't do things that way. That," and he struck it with his flushed fingers, "that's a little wedding present Miss Poole and me is giving to a happy pair we know when they step into the church this noon. When you can lay your fingers on fifty grands as easy as we did on that, Mr. Wisecrack, come around and tell us what to do with the rest of what we earn. And bring your nephew with you. You'd make a grand pair." His eyes caught Delia's and in their gross coppery flesh, she saw them light for a moment with a bewildering, animal humor.

What a man, she thought. She laughed. "Goodbye." She turned to Jarvis. She stepped toward him, fording carpets, brushing by the hedges of chairs. She extended her hand. He looked down at it, touched it, without looking at any of her but that one member. "Give Paul my love," she said. "Give Paul my best——"

"Yes," he interrupted. "Of course, of course. Certainly." He stared at his empty hat a moment, lifted it to his thin skull and walked out of the room.

VI

UTILIZING the prescribed silence of the church, she at once settled motionlessly into its quiet and chill, wrapping herself in her coat and her new thoughts from which her grey eyes looked out on windows and stones, forms of which she saw nothing. "She's got a bad house," she heard Goldstein whisper after turning himself about in his survey. Squeezed within the narrow limits of the pew he was leaning heavily across Mrs. Poole's chest in an effort to approach Delia's ear, too far removed. "Weddings are terrible unless you invite the whole neighborhood and Mercy ain't got twenty people here. It's a shame. She ought to have a big crowd. Invite the neighbors," his whispers persisted. "Get in all the relatives that don't usually speak to each other. Have lots of young folks. Then pull down the blinds, have supper, fiddling, champagne, honey-cakes and jigs. Be gay, you know. Dance. Carouse." Before his whispered list had stopped, his head, resting just below Mrs. Poole's chin had begun jerking slightly and around her ankles his foot started tapping a rabbinical rhythm that clacked on the cold Christian floor. "Say, you ought to see the way we used to do it on Avenue A!" And without any more musical memory than lay in the muscles of his neck, he began openly to beat time, beating off matrimonial yiddish melodies he had once whirled to, each motion he made waving the flounce of Mrs. Poole's veil until, with the light of Gothic windows falling on it, it seemed nevertheless to be the fichu of some foreign silent bridesmaid on whose breast an excited guest, worn out as he danced, was for a moment laying his head. With a sigh he finally drew away. "Did you ever see a good yiddish wedding?" he whispered to her.

Already nervous, she caught at her lips to keep them from twitching and whispered, "No."

"Y'oughta see one," he advised her. "I'll take you down some time."

She nodded to thank him, kept on smiling politely and flushed. It was only with her conventional flesh, not with her mind, that she reacted when Goldstein drew attention, and in a church of all places, to the difference in their race and faith. Being no longer anti-semitic, she felt nothing mentally. But her

face though so little distant from her brain,
underwent a slight self-conscious change when
he spoke as if the just emanations of her mind,
by the time they were visible around her lips
and eyes, had been falsified, precisely as the
noon light which entered the church only by
the guardianship of glass, was perverted to
red, blue and green—was constrained by re-
fraction into forming even the bodies of saints
and the hills upon which they stood celebrat-
ing, as indeed they might, phenomena in which
the loss of the simple yellow of the sun was certainly not the least miracle.

As far back as her thirties Mrs. Poole had
torn herself loose from Christianity without,
however, depriving herself of Jesus and God.
But the habits of the strict salvation of her
youth had left their mark if it was only the
embarrassment she felt in the presence of those
whom her Protestantism had once so safely
regarded as lost—that wretched race, who
knowing they were the murderers of the Savior
of Mankind, obstinately added hypocrisy to

crime by pretending to have not only a good religion but even tender legitimate ceremonies —marriage, feasts, New Year's—of their own. As a child this had seemed fantastic to her. Even shortly before she married, she could remember having heard her young voice, high with the excitement of rare bravado, saying that a Jewish wedding (one was going on in the neighborhood) was probably just as good as a Christian one. She had only meant "as good for them," "since they didn't know any better" or something of the sort. For she knew no Jews, none of their able morals, and their sufferings for their theology. She had spoken only because she was young, poetic and pragmatic. But now, in her middle age she had come to a feeling of real justice too late to have it bring her any good. Everyone was broad minded nowadays. No one had any prejudice except against the law. Free from all the old comforts of Protestant smugness, Mrs. Poole sat in the pew realizing she had nothing left out of her long religious struggle except a belief in a vast impersonal God who wasn't even conscious of her shameful flush in his holy temple. She sighed and turned her head.

There was a sound from the back of the church. Devoted to pageantry, Goldstein had the candor of a connoisseur. He turned and craned his neck. "Here they come," he whispered with excitement. "Oh, say, she looks elegant."

But outside of Mercy's extraordinarily smart hat and gown and the fact that she was conversing on the rector's arm, there was nothing unusual to see. It was characteristic of her that having decided to be married in a church, she gave its chilly carved nave the air of a fashionable restaurant toward one of whose reserved tables she might have been advancing with those smart hungry footsteps that were in reality leading her to the altar. She seemed at her ease. Only the rector looked dazed but holy. In all his experience in legalizing love there had never been a moment like this nor had he ever seen a bride who seemed to him so tender, so womanly, so intuitive, so spirited and wise, so special in those general gifts God meant man to require of his helpmeet, as Mrs. Wellington, leaning with perfume and a French model gown on his arm. In his embarrassment as they first left the vestry, he had tried to shake her off but she had chatted and clung. Now halfway to the choir, conscious that in their parade up the aisle all liturgy was being broken, listening to her words and sensing her personality gave him an expansion that was like a vision racing around in his delicate head, and a newer, broader, freer, less formal Church, bits of harmless fundamentalism, some geology, the notion of the Zeitgeist, his Bishop's drawn face and Mrs. Wellington in black all soared through his brain in a confusing revelation that left his little mouth strained but made his soul feel chosen and proud.

Excluded from this hagiography and buttoned into a laical cutaway, Compton followed on the dreamy rector's heels like a dark male swan, swimming evenly up the aisle.

From near the rooftree as if a host shouted the organ let fall its improvisations. The rector with difficulty disengaged his arm from Mercy's and turned. The vision was fading now. With the shock of falling back into real life, a stern frown puckered over his scholarly feminine forehead. With a long stride he placed his back to the fragile altar as a fighting man uses the wall, opened his book, lowered his tone and read.

Unfamiliar with the panoply of episcopal prose except where shreds from that same early century had hung like brilliant British markers from her American books at school, Delia listened in a daze to this magnificent orchestra of sound. This Church in which she did not believe and its service had taken from the past (as it did in every language) that beautiful verbal attention which solemnity offers to those moments of christianizing birth, mating and death. For hundreds of years the incoherence of the individual on each of these big occasions had been cared for by the ready

sonorous paragraphs of the chapel which, spe-
cializing in human trials, crises and the weak
changes of the flesh, clarified the mortal's momentary confusion by noble thoughts that had
been worked out by immortal celibates to
whom none of these catastrophes save birth and
death of course, had occurred. Believing or
not believing, these rituals to any ears had their
terrifying, their moving sounds. For between
the hand of the doctor at one end of life to the
hands of another at its end, ecstasy occurred
but infrequently to mankind and then only
through the optimism of the flesh roused to
bridals, birth, then on to paler reunions. But
the Church had been on hand for the high
points.

Trying to ignore the mature figures of
Mercy and Compton, listening with silent
heads, Delia kept hunting in her unconscious
eye for their proper substitutes. Mature.
Mature. They were too wise, too sensible.
Only reckless youth surely was concentrated
enough to withstand this service and stony set-

ting in which the beauty of centuries almost
crowded out the littler beauty of individual
love. Despite Compton's triumphant face and
Mercy's loyal civilized eyes, this pair, because
of their settled years, seemed to be borrowing
from the church polite permission only. And
if permission had been denied, their emotion
wouldn't have burned the book, snapped the
arches and torn their troth asunder. But
what youth felt for youth, what Delia, for instance felt for Paul—Ah! She tried to imagine she and Paul were standing by the altar,
blind to its white trappings with their vacant
embroidery of blue, deaf to the sound of the
rector's voice, unintimidated even by its terrible words. Blind they would stand there,
blind and deaf to all colors, all scent, all sound,
recipient only to the tint of each other's hair
and eyes and the faint human noise of their
quiet breathing as they stood sceptically waiting for the end.

"Till death do you part," the rector said.
Delia felt her mother tremble. She turned to

the veil.   Beneath it her mother was crying.
She pulled her against her arms.

The organist put foot and hand to his keys.
A roar burst from the complicated pipes stolen
from Pan.   The fugue was sufficient in noise
and inaccuracy to drown the felicitations of
thousands and under the rain of its notes, the
scattered few witnesses rallied to Mercy's side.
Two choirboys whom she had excluded from
the simple ceremony appeared from the vestry
and added their medieval color to a modern
season wearing only black.

"The rest of the women wear it because it's
smart but I wear it because I'm in mourning,"
Mercy cried in Goldstein's large ear.   "In
marrying Compton I feel exactly as if I'd lost
him.   Howdoyoudo, howdoyoudo, Oh howdoyoudo."   She broke from him to speak to the
smiles and gloves gathering about her.   Mercy
spoke to everyone.   Everyone spoke to Mercy
but spoke to no one else.   Individuals unknown
to each other, eyeing each other with polite but
curious eyes, had at this definite act in Mercy's

career, rallied around her like short torn threads of different colors and qualities which had at different times all been wound on the same spool.

As Delia approached her, her eyes twinkled, brightened. "Don't forget I married as much on your account, darling, as mine. Or very near it." There was a fractional pause after her words then she drew Delia awkward in the embrace but honest, repentant, admiring in the burst of affection and farewell that met in their rouged lips. "Let it be an object lesson," she murmured against Delia's cheek. "Go do likewise. You'll have to sooner or later. One can't go on leading one's life forever. You'll see what I mean." As if illustrating what she had just whispered in Delia's ears, she nodded toward the nearing presence of Mrs. Poole, refined, nervous, treading delicately among people she did not know and thought everyone else did, coming only to touch Mercy's fingers, be introduced again to that public sparkle that had once gleamed in Mrs. Wellington's and

now shone in Mrs. Keith's eyes. In the brightness of this sparkle Mrs. Poole stood for a moment, congratulatory, widowed, spiritual, mur-
muring conventional phrases from her own
wedding and youth.

"I was just complaining to Delia of her bad
taste, Mrs. Poole. Two of the nicest people
she knows are married,—you and I. I consider her celibacy a criticism. It's as if she—
howdoyoudo, howdoyoudo!" Mrs. Poole had,
in her surprise, been about to speak but Mercy
turned with animation to another face, greet-
ing it with friendly remembering mechanics.
But her mind, if Mrs. Poole had known it, was
still with Delia intact. What would happen to
her for instance? Would she—"Howdoyoudo!" Mercy didn't know. She had been more
drawn to Delia, drawn as if with a bond of
intimacy and lusty tenderness that united
them, than toward anyone she had met in years.
Had indeed loved her. But loving women, to
Mercy, was not practicable. Friendship for
her social nature didn't have enough shape.

Male and female, created he them. That was what had stamped its complicated design on the world.

About to leave on the edge of the small crowd, Delia found herself facing Compton. Hearing everything, saying nothing, he stood smiling with pride, ignored above everyone's shoulders. "You're just the informer I wanted to see. Should I marry?" she asked. Her lips parted broadly. He looked the perfect, the waiting bridegroom. Their celibate dawn together on the Palisades seemed dim, forgotten, unimportant. He looked only marital, successful at last in what he had feared to be drawn into that night in the Philadelphia hotel. "If I, of all people, ought to marry, you of all men, Compton, ought to know!"

"Delia," he flushed, "I'm not a man. I'm a bridegroom and am in no position to know anything." His self-conscious laugh rumbled out into the organ's last bloated chords. "I don't know anything except that it's all over at last and that with my wife's permission,

I'm going to kiss you goodbye." Without waiting for Delia's, he caught at her and she felt the hot flash of his scraped lips. "Now that's all I can do or say. If it's any encouragement——"

She stood without answering, remembering his other words. Men loved women, were unfaithful to them and forgiven by them. That was his hearty creed. She looked at the flower in his buttonhole. Drawn from a long line of obscure unimportant adulteries, Compton's position was public and distinguished at last. And to Mercy, for all his creed and middle-aged ardor, he would probably never succeed in being unfaithful, let alone forgiven, for what he did with his flesh and with others she would not count. He would have to find her full equal probably before she would ever flatter him that he had been at fault.

Once out of the church and onto the street, they adjusted their steps, fell into a speechless walking rhythm, Goldstein and the two Pooles. They settled into union like an old family group, giving the appearance as they strolled along of a relict of a misalliance between Russia and Ohio which, having started years ago, still kept its outward shape in New York, held together by the blonde, inter-racial creature who walked between the parent sides. In the cold sunny November air, the city seemed nordic and lively, with tall white buildings like ice floes from which the inhabitants descended to race after dollars as a means of keeping warm. Mrs. Poole was silent, sad. Whatever marriage failed to offer women (her mind was still in the church), at any rate matrimony stood for one of the big hopes in human life and in their disappointment women's lives were filled by items that substituted for happiness and kept loneliness for old age. Goldstein strolled scowling, defiant. His temperament left him exasperated with erotic optimism. Unable even with chorus girls to get away from domesticity as an ideal, he saw the world about him walking to (and from) the marriage altar with the longing with which his ancestors used to eye the Philistine's rich vines. Grapes, grapes everywhere and for him not even water to drink.

"Well," he grunted. They had come to the corner of the Avenue. "It was their wedding but I'm the one who's got the champagne." He still clung to his conventional ideas. "A wedding ain't a wedding unless you pull a cork. They're bad enough to make you blue even when they're good. And when they happen in the middle of the day and are dry, they're terrible. Mrs. Poole, Delia, how 'bout a little glass?"

They both nodded in dull negation. The stimulation all of them had borrowed from the church was rapidly disintegrating. Having witnessed the big moment in two people's lives, all three of them were now left with diminishing thoughts and their own 365 days a year to fill. Mrs. Poole was watching the buses as if, from the vast selection which New York offers its visitors, she would soon make a wise choice. Delia stood sagging in her high boots, phlegmatic, her mind new with hope for Paul.

"Don't want no champagne nor no wedding neither, eh?" she heard Goldstein say to her. "I was listening to what Mercy said. And she's right. Shouldn't Delia marry, Mrs. Poole?" He had raised his voice to throw it over the traffic.

Mrs. Poole looked ill at ease, surprised. She could never get used to talking publicly and suddenly about slow private things. "I'd— I'd like to see her marry," she tried to shout easily. She was so rarely called into counsel. "I want her to marry but she must be sure," her voice mounted to a panic. "Sure! It must be the right man!" At committing herself, she looked almost frightened. Sure. When Mrs. Poole was young, if a girl married at all it had been automatically considered that she married not only the right man but the only one in the world for her. But those days of the absolute in love had vanished. It had gone out with other forms of credulity in Mrs. Poole's lifetime and she showed the strain in the emptiness of small lines, small sagging pockets in her face which beliefs had once filled and made plump. "I want Delia to marry but—" The traffic that had been longitudinal now took up its median and rushed by their corner on its free line. The roar of liberation drowned Mrs. Poole's soft voice. At her command she had after all only the small percussion of words,—mere syllables struck from vocal chords by the private enterprise of maternal anxiety and the antique habit of human speech. It was not enough. It was only a voice, one voice raised in competition against the inventions of horns and wheels, the sentiments of the century. And with mouth empty but still ajar, she stood and accepted her defeat.

Alone at last with the Avenue's thousands, Delia turned uptown, free. She had known for two hours that her separation from Paul was finally coming to an end. This was the first moment of privacy she had had to let the news out of her brain and offer it its excursion through her blood. From her head the nervous sensation of ecstatic lightness that had been making it feel empty (which in such moments it is), at once started descending through her torso, crept down her thighs, moved to her feet as methodically as if the course of the unweighable emotions followed that law of gravity discovered thousands of years after passion had settled into its practices. The heavy sensual languor she had felt on meeting with Paul the last time had worn away in the months that had intervened. Delia was in a way purified. She only knew she felt hollow with elation. Those so many pounds of bone, flesh, yards of viscera and a lump of a heart to be dragged about, each of which ordinarily added its avoirdupois to passion, seemed to be functionless, drained of weight. Her body felt like a feather. She would see him soon. And as if her speed would bring him sooner to sight, she kept swinging up the Avenue.

Even the fact that they would quarrel before
the exhaustion of tenderness set in, did not
clog her stride. It was her nature to think that
everything would be all right. With that peculiar trusting egotism by which one of two
lovers in a crisis optimistically credits the
other with desires and views which if they were
only mutual would indeed reduce all quarrels
to a long kiss, Delia blindly endowed Paul
with the full hopes of her mind like a form of
goods more appropriate to a worldly union, it
never occurring to her they might be refused.
She wanted him to forgive her and she supposed he would. Their future hung on that,
meaning as much to her as to him, she argued.
And nothing else could count.

Her first premonition met her as she pushed
into her room a few minutes later. There sat
Nancy. Delia and Paul weren't the only two
people moving with desires over the earth.
There sat the third by the fire and looking so
changed that she had, in that familiar room, the
unfamiliarity of a new person. Delia walked

forward and surveyed Nancy, unbelieving.
No one in a few days can become unrecogniz-
able but a shift in the emotions can transfigure
a face. Animosity and secrecy had distributed their expressions until Nancy's ability
to look like herself had in some way been lost.
She had paled and flattened as if, no longer
equipped with her usual affection for Delia,
the surface of her face had fallen a little as
consequence, leaving the nose and cheeks in
hard critical relief. During the late years only
new clothes had given her enough novelty to
catch Delia's familiarized eye. But now the
novelty lay in her face. The features were
the same, the old green eyes, the little tight
mouth. But they were curiously like the old
ones done over and resembling the originals
no more than those occasional handsome hats
which, during their initial poverty together,
the women had seen return season after season from some cheap milliner who had re-
vamped them out of all their original charm.

"Well," said Delia. She moved on into the

center of her room and seated herself. "So you've turned up at last. You ought to have come earlier." She watched the effect of her words with close satisfaction. "An old gentleman from Philadelphia was here at noon. Highly upset and hard to manage. He was looking for the unpopular person who sent a certain recent cablegram to Paul."

Nancy caught her breath. "I sent it." Her secrecy wasn't shaken. Only her red lips moved.

"Yes, I know you did," said Delia dryly. She pulled off her hat and stood for a moment, ornamenting her head with her hand. "Since you seem to be managing his tour, would you mind telling me when Paul arrives?"

"New Year's Day. Or so he says."

"Why not believe him? He can't stay on the boat forever. Why shouldn't he be here by then?" With her big hands she unloosed her fur coat but stood still inside it, overprotected, overwarm, watching the face, the rigid body of Nancy. Then she relaxed. "New Year's. He'll arrive just after the first Christmas in five years we won't have spent together. Do you realize that?"

"I appreciate that it's one way of dating his arrival. But Christmas is like any other day to me, Delia." She shrugged her shoulders. "I never had your childish enthusiasm for festivals. Parades, Christmas trees, turkeys and all that." She spoke with bitterness as if this had been a deep seated grievance she had wanted to discuss for a long time.

"No, I daresay you never had. We're fairly different, I'm beginning to realize."

"We always have been," Nancy cried. "Be accurate if you must be anything. It's nothing new that we're unlike. After individuals are no longer friends they merely notice the difference more. That's all." She waited a moment, testing. "I'm sorry the old man is furious. You'll never believe it, but I didn't mean to make Paul pack up and start home."

"Oh. You just had an unexpected bit of

luck, eh? Well, some people are fortunate. And inaccurate," she added.

Nancy's white face hardened like china in the process of baking. What softness had moistened it a moment ago, was flattened out, stiffened by the hotness of her resentment. "You don't know what I said in the cablegram. But I'll tell you this much about it,—that I wager I was accurate. I'm not your mother," she said with contempt. "Don't think I believed that lie you told her about Compton and you in Philadelphia. I used to believe you but I know better now. Even one month ago I believed for an hour what you'd said about him and that ride in the dawn. Sixty minutes later you yourself gave it away you'd lied. Why shouldn't I have taken it for granted you were lying the second time?"

"Probably because it wasn't necessary." Delia slipped into a chair. Limbs sprawling, fur spread wide as if the animal had just been struck down, she settled to defend herself and to watch.

Nancy looked uncertain, confused. "What difference does it make? Maybe the second time was chaste—by accident. The first time was enough. I should have cabled him then. You can't play with Paul as you have everyone else, you'll find out. He'll never love anyone else as he did you and you sold him out for a man you didn't give a rap of your finger for. You spoiled Paul for anyone else. That's what I can't forgive you. I could love him. Yes, I admit it. And he'd never give me anything except left-overs from you. And you! What are you?" She stiffened herself in her chair as if her contempt were organic, something which could only rise to her lips from a straight free passage of bile. "All these years I've been standing in the backyard of your glory, do you think I haven't finally got a notion what you are? I loved you at first. I adored you. You were worth it then. And I sat to one side watching you give yourself so often for nothing—for a whim, for a moon-

light night, for feelings that didn't count—
that I saw you finally become worth just what
all free things are worth—nothing!" She
snapped her fingers. "Just nothing."

"Well, I'm glad you've arrived at what you
think is the truth. I wonder if I am as bad as
you say?" She wondered aloud. "I'm hearty,
I like love. Have loved often and never tried
to hide any talent under any bushel basket until you began frowning, hinting. So I began
lying. I guess everyone lies except animals,
Nancy." She dropped her head back and
passed her eyes over her familiar ceiling.
"Animals are about the only lovers that are
left in peace. It's about time we envied them
instead of pitying them and offering them
bones." She sprawled without words for a
moment. "You think I'm rotten. Not good
enough for your friend, not good enough for
Paul, not good enough for anyone, apparently, except perhaps a few confidence men
in Sing-Sing. Now I'll tell you what I think."

She jerked herself erect. "You've a damned cheek to have set yourself up as my guide. If you're good, as you call it, it's because you haven't wanted to be anything else. You oughtn't to take any more pride to yourself for being chaste than a bedridden grandfather. You haven't got an ounce of passion in your whole make-up. You're as chaste as a tea-cup. If I've deceived Paul, I'm sorry. Terribly. I drank too much—and I'm sorry. But while you're criticising me, just recall that while you may have disapproved of the way I led my life, you were never perfectly sure that I was no good until you fell in love with the man who loves me. And whom I love." Nancy's lips tightened to hold their color and blood. "You've always been better than I am. Paul has always been. There's no question of that. But don't forget that you never felt yourself to be a paragon until you saw your chance to stick a knife in my back. The moment when you walked into the telegraph office to get Paul for yourself,—ah! that was the moment when you were most exquisitely moral of all. Oh, you make me ill."

"I—I sent that cable partly for you too. If I had no influence on you, I thought he might. I give you my word. Delia!"

Delia could hardly hear her voice. "Oil and water," she said. "Keep them separate, Nancy. They don't mix. You and I were friends until you fell in love with Paul. And when you fell in love with him, you began hating me as you would have seen had you looked at things straightly. Which you never do." The poverty they had once shared, the work, the pleasant platonic ease they had known with Delia set in the core of it, as guiltless and grateful as the seed in a peach, surrounded with affectionate flesh so honeysweet that it rots before it gets ripe,—all that was over. Done. "I don't know why you felt so maternally for me," she added. She tried to speak kindly. "Until you began feeling connubially toward Paul you felt maternally for me in a way. A mistake. You should never have dreamed of trying to act like my mother. You lacked nine months preparation for it twenty-five years ago. Anyhow, I don't like supervision, interference. I didn't leave home to have lovers. But I left home to be free. And I won't give that up—until I have to." Free. What did it mean? She wasn't sure. All she could discern was that morality was ethics that should apply only to the head. People shouldn't gossip, tell lies, should pay their debts, give money to beggars and be polite. Moral. "But flesh," she said aloud, "doesn't come under 'good' or 'bad.' Passion is natural. People are born in bed and die there and unless they're liars, like to spend a certain portion of the intermediate time in the same place. I'm right about this and you're wrong," she said and she got up from her chair. "The world has always had lovers. And yet as near as I can observe, for thousands of years the concentrated aim of society has been to cut down kissing. With that same amount of energy, plus a little of yours, society could have stopped war, established liberty, given everybody a free education, free bathtubs, free music, free pianos and changed the human mind to boot. And they haven't done it. And you won't do it." Methodically she fumbled her hands over her hat and hair, succeeding only in substituting picturesque untidiness for what had been easy dishevelment. With her own coarse system she applied that extra-coating of rouge that she always ministered to her lips before taking them to the street and with bright mouth, and unpowdered face in which each plane of her high cheeks, each contributing arch that made the flare of her nose, displayed its handsome native line in the shine of her flesh, she turned from Nancy toward the door. "I've talked. And you've talked. And there's nothing more to say. And there never will be. Goodbye."

"Goodbye," she called again from the door. She stood a moment, listening, then closed it quietly and went down the hall.

VII

"I JUDGED by the way you opened the door that you were expecting someone." Grafton waited to be sure that her mother had left the room. "And then *I* walked in." He laughed.

"Yes. I thought it might be—" She changed her mind and without finishing, folded her limbs beneath her on the sofa again.

"It's still the same man, Delia?" He watched her, the flames in the fire, the shivering of the candles on the stale tree and their reflections on the spiral furnishings he had never seen before, sending his pale blue eyes around the unfamiliar walls in his first moment's domesticity and appreciation. The minutes passed. Neither spoke. She could hear the ticking of the small cherrywood clock her mother had brought from Excelsior. "Well, Happy New Year. It's supposed to be bad luck to wish it before midnight but you'll be with somebody else by then." He picked up his glass of synagogue port. "Here's to you Delia—and to Paul."

She wondered how he knew Paul's name or even if he had heard it, remembered it. But Grafton was like that. He grew older, his blond hair ebbed from his forehead. But out of the years, the months or whichever immediate yesterday lay behind him, he could always draw out the required name, whatever it might be and even if it had never concerned him, like the individual who from his neat wallet always produces postage stamps of the right denomination for other people's letters that are never written about him, for him, or bring him any luck.

She heard her mother's soft steps turning in the kitchen. "She'd love to have you stay, Grafton. We let the maid go tonight of course and there's probably nothing to eat, but —" Happy New Year. Happy New Year to everybody. The maid was going to start hers in Newark with friends. The goose which would represent to those in the front of the house in the Mews, the big moment of the festival as he came steaming onto the table tomorrow noon, had already been her kitchen companion all day. She had received him naked and raw, at the back door and tended him from sink to pan.

"There's not much to offer a guest," said Mrs. Poole, returning with a silver dish in her hand. "But we have the guest. And we have his flowers and our holiday feelings." She warmed to the spreading of the meager supper with pathetic pleasure. The social instincts she had always stifled like grass under the darkness of an Excelsior bush, for some reason burgeoned now, December 31st in cold and unfamiliar New York, in the late forties of Mrs. Poole's existence. While dwelling in the town where all knew her, she had known few and had often eaten alone. And to show how little was her appreciation for food which after all social intercourse lives by, she now crowded among the cold plates on the little table the overwhelming mass of Grafton's roses as if they were a dish in themselves. Her eyes kept dropping on them, a gift from Grafton whom she had never seen, had barely heard of a moment before—a stray floral emblem of his fidelity and hers to Delia who was about to leave them sitting alone by the fire.

Methodically Delia ate, tasting nothing but when the correct moment came, rhythmically lifting her glass. She preferred water and her mother could hardly swallow anything else. But twice a year ever since her marriage, Mrs. Poole had always served her family an inappropriate wine, malaga or some other dessert-syrup which Ohio druggists in the old days sold and whose sweetness, when sipped along with fowl or gravy, led her sick but conventional over the sill of Christmas or into the first hours of the New Year.

However the first taste of it, as now, always left its port dye in her cheeks and warmed her tongue. Grafton's, unthickened by years of bootlegging, took the Jewish liquor like the Excelsior jams and Delia listening only for a knock at the door, vaguely heard his continuous tone, inquiries and interested laugh. He would have been an ideal son-in-law. Delia sighed. He had the tact that comes with pleasure in the presence of ripe women. Agreeable and loquacious to any not of his sex, he was at his best with those safely over forty.

Openly Delia glanced at her watch. The Excelsior clock stood waiting with the same information on the mantelpiece where the passage of time and the cloistering of heat coincided like modern miracles in the same wall of the low ceilinged room. But the clock seemed part of her childhood. She was no longer used to relying on it. Her own dial, circling her wrist with large but inferior emeralds, seemed to offer keener assurance. Nine o'clock. His train, she had forced Nancy to admit, didn't arrive until ten. Another hour.

She went over in her mind every detail of her attire, selected already from all those better garments housed in her bedroom in the Mews. Nothing was laid out. Delia had not slipped back or so lost her character as to lay

out her clothes, like bridal offerings or tickets
to a first ball, on her bed. But she was managed now by a fastidious sense, almost a personal apprehension which had never marked
her meetings in other years, where a soiled
smock, a torn petticoat or even the mechanical
decoration of a safetypin had not abashed her
or dispirited anyone else. By nature Delia
would have used white thread on the rip of a
sable coat as thoughtlessly as she had yesterday re-touched the faces of the girls, the
tongues of the hounds in her 13th century
studio tapestry, bringing all to a delicate
painted pink in which the imitation of time
they had patiently lost, was freshened again
and the flush of female cheeks, the baying of
young dogs was colored to a fever pitch, satisfying her for a moment that pursuit and charm
never died down. "I think I'll dress," she
murmured.

Her mother glanced up, blankly. "So soon,
dear?" She had not eaten but looked nour-
ished and was not winning but looked victori-

ous over her game of solitaire. From the painted queens, prepared at both ends to smile on the world, and the lonely aces Grafton gazed up, numb witness to Delia's restlessness and his place at her mother's side. Expecting nothing except what he had grown used to in the last few years, his talent for observation gave him the vulnerability usually felt only by one who still has hope. As a selfmade man can watch the mounting success of others, knowing every round of the ladder by sight, or an ex-boxer whose neck is still columnar, whose footwork is still dainty, sits dressed below the ring he is no longer invited to enter half-naked for the fight, so Grafton watched each motion Delia made, richness and strength stirring in him like memories seemingly borrowed from two professions, so dual had his possession of her been. Laughing to Mrs. Poole, counseling the playing of the five instead of the nine of spades, he watched Delia disappear into her room.

Rapidly she stripped, digging among silk

on her shelves, valueing peach lingerie against green. Her naked roccoco figure, long-limbed, long-necked with fluting hips above slim thighs, looked like some baroque statue plucked from the Renaissance—one of those dangerously poised female nudes found on Jesuit tombs in Rome or on livelier cornices of noble country retreats, in which high breasts and a tendril osseous strength, visible beneath stony flesh, marked a sensuous outdoor art which she unwillingly resembled, the regional tanning of her skin, left over from the summer's beach, heightening that weathered indestructible charm that both softens and exaggerates the odd beauty of carved bodies left to sun and rain. Disliking her form, still she accepted it as her domicile in life, covering it when she could against interested eyes whose pleasure only embarrassed her and taught her nothing.

She drew her new gown from its frame on the wall. Ordinarily Delia bought clothes by accident or at the last minute. But this had been a deliberate expensive choice. "Not another gown in town like it," the saleswoman had said. True. Perhaps too true. She slipped it over her head. The black which all other women were wearing existed only at its base and from there by dyes climbing slowly beyond the greying horizon at her waist, evolved to a nacreous pearl at her breast,—a blackish mother-of-pearl like the newel of an abalone shell, above which her face and hair with their yellowing tints, appeared succulent, almost fleshly, like a morsel of what the Italians name fine fresh fruit of the sea.

She was dressed. It had taken only a few minutes. She still had time on her hands. Nervously she sat down on the edge of a chair, incapable of going back in the living room to say "Yes" and "No" and be indifferent to Grafton's eyes. She folded her hands, saw her face in the glass, its eyes questioning the propriety of its overly dark stained mouth. But Delia was too numb to break the clumsy picturesque habits of years. She could only observe now like a new bystander. The telephone rang. Her heart flexed, shrank, distended. She heard Grafton, efficient and jovial as a younger son, laughing "Hello," then, "Mr. WHO?" and adding, "Wrong number but Happy New Year." Then her mother's barely audible smiles, soft words and the silence of cards.

A few moments later she rose to her feet and swung her coat from the bed. She pulled the black pelts high around her head, the skunk skins stiff about her as the collar of a Russian driver. Gloves, money, rouge. There were purses at the studio, odd gauntlets, lipsticks left over from former dinners or nights. But she clutched this special equipment with a sense of starting forth fresh. Nothing touched that had ever been touched before.

"I'll go now." She kissed her mother, slid a kiss even on Grafton's cheek, a gush of nervous generosity warming her now that she was escaping into the cold air. "I don't know when I'll be back. If we're late in coming in,

I think I'll stay in the studio all night so don't worry." She touched her mother's arms.

"Oh, no." Mrs. Poole smiled with uneasy pride.

"Think of me when the band plays and everyone screams at midnight," smiled Grafton. "Your mother and I have reserved our New Year's table here. Smart and select. When the whistles blow we'll drink to you in your awful restaurant. Which one will it be?"

"They're all so jammed, I don't know which one exactly," she said. They were going to none. Alone by the fire, Paul and she, with the sirens and bells of New York clamoring from the outside. She pulled herself loose from her mother's hand, nodded again to the pair by the table, their faces turned up to her like porcelain plates and started with her swift easy speed to the door.

Once in the studio, her anticipations relaxed. Here was where the meeting would be held. And once on its floor, among its tables and chairs, each object was as good as a witness arrived slightly before they would be needed for swearing, but offering authority with their velvet and satin uniforms, that the important interview was scheduled to take place.

A quarter to ten.   She lighted the fire. Delia was artistically competent to know the value of flames couched on flattening embers, —flames licking grey ashes, resuscitating them with their colored tongues rather than leaping with crude newly-lighted energy in a combustive dance from naked unpractised logs.   In a few moments Paul's train would be in.   By the time he arrived at her door, the hearth would make a mature sight, a description in chiraoscuro, in brightness and black, of Delia awaiting him in her room.

It never occurred to her he would not come. She had had no word from him, no cables or telegram.   Living in an age when electricity, first located unamorously on a scholar's kite, had come to be the passionate medium for lovers too impatient to wait and whisper what they had to say, Paul had left her without information. But she took for granted that he would come to see her as she took for granted her own helpless readiness to hear his complaints.

Minutes passed and moulded themselves into the halfhour. As in a crisis, she turned to a book. Delia was far from being an inveterate reader. She took a book as healthy people take medicine—a dose that occurred infrequently and marked only the momentary weakness of a make-up ordinarily sufficient in itself. The words seemed strange as if she were little used to seeing them spread flat with information on the printed page. The Prince Consort, she read, was fond of laying cornerstones and the Queen despite that slanting obstinate profile, liked a strong hand and a firm bed. Disraeli, of course, was having his difficulties. His own novels and Her Majesty's even more novel ideas. Empress of India, indeed! The inspiration of a romantic fictioneer come back on him like a Hindustani boomerang. Delia's eyes wandered. If any, it was the kind of book she would like. It showed steerers of state leading local lives—eating, drinking and ardently quarreling in the imperial privacy of their palace. But Delia couldn't keep her mind on it. Had Victoria been set forth like Queen Elizabeth, as a possible man and the whole sedate epoch been proved as founded on scandalous deceit, still she would have let its history fall from her knees, indifferent to anyone else's human problem, twisted only by her own. For the first time it occurred to Delia to wonder if Nancy really had met Paul's train. She had conceived of it as possible but not that he would be delayed by it.

She dropped her head back onto the lounge. No matter what Nancy would tell him, he would only come to me all the quicker, she thought. Passion first and then jealousy,—those were the emotions that heated the brain until the limbs melted beneath them in maniacal speed. He would come. Be angry. Make scenes. But he would come. What time was it?

Unwilling to look at her watch—it might be

earlier or later than she suspected and each possibility was a separate agony—she closed her eyes. What time was it? She was given her information gratuitously. From a church in the neighborhood came an anticipatory whanging of bells, marking eleven but preparing for midnight. The light dripped through the flesh of her closed lids. Seeing nothing she lay waiting, thinking, listening.

He had missed his train. Those inherited excuses which had never occurred to her before, for no one had ever kept her waiting, now settled into position in Delia's mind like a legacy from all the individuals in her family who had gone before and donated their amatory experience and thoughts. Some one of them, some lovers had been left watching, waiting and disappointed. Old lady Poole perhaps, hot and eager, perspiring for her husband to return from the attractions of the Civil War. Earlier women waiting for news of men in an age when time was slow and excuses or bridegrooms arrived by stage coach, while the

heart ached from tension and the strain of
swelling, without relief like a bud that cannot
burst.   This was what they had felt, Delia
thought—what everyone felt at some time who
went through the operation of love.

With uncertain fingers she lit a cigarette.
Unused to smoking as to suffering, acrid
fumes seeped through her nostrils, biting the
lining of her head as this unaccustomed emotion spiraled through the shape of her heart.
Dressed like an embassadress for a ball, she
sat unattended on a worn beautiful couch, the
bare wall bending without attention over her
yellow lifted head, tobacco smoke and the ashy
black of her gown smouldering, flickering,
seeming finally to be extinguished entirely until nothing was left of them but their inani-
mate shape in the air, like the stale fumes
hanging over a dinner table long after the
diners have staggered away.

As the minutes pattered by, she grew unconscious of the escape of time.   A stiffness sat in
her sensibilities.   Not only were her muscles

cold, but her capacity to feel seemed paralyzed. Her watch rattled on, minute mechan-
isms fitted like heart and liver behind platinum,
all covered by an epidermis of emeralds except
where, like the human countenance left naked
above garments, its little intelligent face
nodded information with a lifted whirling
hand, a creation endowed with pantomime and
energy if not with lips and words.

A few preliminary whistles started practis-
ing on the nearly midnight air. She raised her
head and with wide eyes as if their greyness
and fringed lashes listened, heard the approaching sounds. They began gathering in
a boom, a concentrated frenetic and growing
augury, an overtone of steady whistles, tricked
by the fanciness of strident bells, a roar of
gongs and sirens, barbaric as that which Manchu doctors use to beat off sick spirits from
around a dying man's head, and all aimed in
hearty, semi-christian, prohibition-drunken
human welcome to the fragility, the unstable
newness, the frightened firstness of the New

Year.   One moment out of twelve heavy
months, hanging on the year like twelve
growths on an endless cosmic wall—one moment out of the millions that made weeks and
seasons,—just one moment, this notionate one,
picked from the old pagan solstice and flourishing now with electric exactitude, impaled
between Greenwich and Christianity, and
saluted in synchrony all through Christendom
and drunk in poison in lawless, liberty-loving
New York.

Midnight.   At its height, with the noise
teeming into her room, she heard her bell.
Hers, not a church's, not a boat's in the river,
not a drunken drummer's, swinging up from
the street.   Hers.   She jumped to her feet.
"Come in."   The burst of her voice revived
her.   She ran toward the door.   The entry was
dark and she flung her arms around the black
form she saw there.   From the cold male smell
emanating from heavy wool, she drew a familiar odor and stepped back, sick.

"So this is what he missed, is it?"   She only

smelled the corona-laden voice, seemed not to
hear it. "If you can't speak because it's only
me, you'd have dropped dumb forever if you'd
seen what I just seen. Oh why wasn't you
there to look, to stare, to get your eye full.
You'd hate him now like I hate him. You
would, you poor girl, you would."

She felt his coarse hand on her arm, shaking her as if with a punishment of sympathy.
Then she was pushed into the studio, pulled
under the soft light. They stood there, standing, watching each other without expression
and without words. Goldstein looked as if
midnight had made a clay cartoon of his face
and left it to dry in position above his soiled
collar. "I don't know why it should make me
sore, seeing him there, and with her," he said
at last. He wiped his hand in a circle on his
bald skull. "I hate him and oughta be glad
if you throw him out. Throw him as far as
the East River and leave him sink in it," he
shouted. "What else is he worth? He's just
like all men. Didn't I tell you so the first time

I saw him? And believe me, girl, it certainly showed up tonight. He was—Say, he's rotten." He walked to the couch and sat down. Like an animal whose sensuality leads it to the most protected spot for its sulking or sleeping, he settled between those particular cushions her body had just left warm. And there he heated himself, thinking, considering.

"Well?" she asked at last. "What happened?"

He took one of her cigarettes and spat out his own smoke. "I went over to Ike Jeffrey's place about eleven. You know, over there on 46th, The Berry Bush. Ike asked me. I hate all them damned college boys, yelling and screaming good luck to each other with their hair falling down in their eyes, but I went. And I seen Paul. Him and your Nancy. He was drunk. Boiled. Had that sailor-just-slipped-off-the-ship look in his eyes. Fresh on land and fresh with the first girl. He was mauling her, crying into his flask. They danced like a couple rag dolls with her holding him up,

hanging onto his coat. She wasn't boiled,"
he added impartially. "I could have forgive
her, I guess, if she was. They bitched you."
He sighed and let himself back more easily
against the couch. His personal anger had
left him. He looked only old now, grey and
drawn, cynical with history, memory, faces,
chorus girls' tights and lies. "And they're
bitching you good about now," he augmented,
closing his eyes in his smoke.

"Yes, apparently, they are," she said at last.
She had no thoughts or no surprise. The last
thing she had expected to hear, Goldstein had
just told her. At first his words had dropped
into her ears like hot candlewax, poured in as
old-fashioned healing for some modern pain.
A moment's agony while the heat stung, and
then a coagulation, a cooling, caking numb-
ness that shut out all sound and circulation in
her head except a singing sensation in the center of her drums.

"We might as well have a drink," she heard
him say, indistinctly. She saw him struggling

with his hand in his coat. "Everybody else is tight. Here's how, Delia." He clinked his silver flask against its little cap cup, offering it to her. "Here's to you." His voice sounded thick, sent out through a fog. She saw he had gross tears in his eyes.

"Here's to you." That must be brandy, she thought as it struck her throat. Her palate shuddered, almost regorged. The liquid surged forward into her mouth, then drained down her neck in a burning rill.

Minutes passed. They might have been hours. Without interest, she finally stared at her watch. Five minutes past one o'clock. Everything's changed she thought. Two hours ago a minute was like a week. And now —Before she could finish her thought, they started ticking again, shapelessly, endlessly, amassing themselves in her brain in another empty unbroken pause that numbed her before she realized she had stopped thinking again. With a dull phlegmatic effort she tried to recall what her idea had been. Oh, yes.

That time passed slowly before midnight. Now it ran by and she never saw it go.

"Delia. You ain't the only one that's learned something tonight. I sort of—saw some things clearly myself. One thing. And it's took me years. I been blind. But I was so much in love with you that"—His voice shifted, took a new personal key, one higher, shriller, more raw. "My God. How can a man ever see things straight if he's in love?" He asked himself this, calling for an answer. None came. He did not speak for a moment nor did she. She didn't know what he was talking about, didn't wonder, didn't care.

"You're in love with Paul. I know that now. And were before he went away. But that's not all. It's *that* I found out for myself tonight. That merely being in love with him wasn't all or he—he wasn't all, either. Oh, I was blind, blind. I saw all the rest of them fellas trotting after you all these years but I was so crazy about you I never thought you could have done anything wrong. I—Oh I

didn't know, didn't know." His voice expired.
He found his silk handkerchief and sounded
his nose, a long, brutal masculine blast like a
war trumpet which no female would ever play.
She glanced at him. Only his eyes showed
above white silk and their blue was embroi-
dered with blood-shot veins. "I'm a Jew,
Delia. I guess us Jews got different ideas
from the rest. Though they ain't what they
used to be," he added with listlessness. "It's
all changed. Jewish girls that used to be married to nice young men is out now, leading
what they call their own lives and usually doing the last lap in a hospital. But the men's
ideas is still the same, in a way. Men don't
change as easy as women. They stay—men,"
he said. He accented with his thick hand.
"Rotten, vile, kings of the earth, raping the
chamber-maid in a cheap hotel but thinking it's
all right since she's that kind of girl and nice
girls are—different. There used to be only those
two kinds. A girl would— or she wouldn't.
You either wanted to marry her or you knew

damned well you didn't have to. And until tonight I thought you were—" He flicked his handkerchief, signalling her. Its flash of chaste white apparently indicated the kind of girl he had always thought his Delia was.

"I'm just what I've always been. The same person," she protested without interest. "Your opinion of me may have changed. I've not. I've had lovers. If I'm nice or not nice it has nothing to do with my having been in love."

"Maybe not." He waited. "But don't think you young Americans discovered sex," he scoffed with mounting heat. "Say, it's been heard of thousands of years before your little Christopher Columbus ever thought of being sea-sick. The world's old. Don't forget that. People don't change much. Men like to think the women they love are pure and chaste and the women like to think the men are—well, —strong and brave," he finished with a defiant oriental tip of his hand.

"That doesn't seem to leave much choice. I wager Dante was weak as a cat. However, his Beatrice remained pure. So as usual, the gentlemen were satisfied." She shrugged her shoulders. Above the ashy chiffon of her gown, her bare arm slipped out for a moment's nudity. "Oh, let's not talk."

"All right." His voice was humble and obstinate. "But I'm going to say one thing. I been wanting to for years. And now I know you know—life, as they call it, I'm not going to lose my chances. Delia." He edged forward on the lounge. "I know what I look like," he said with a loud voice. "I know." He stretched his neck. His flabby body stiffened. He sat there making a sacrifice of his appearance, offering her his ugliness for immolation. His nostrils were swelled like an animals, lowing. His visage had the ugliness and pathos of some grey, long-nosed old northern elk who in a scene of classic customs was going to be slain on an Attic altar where the beauty of bulls was more often appropriately seen dying, and where his appearance drew on him the fatality of a monster. "I'm ugly."

His flesh shook. "But I love you. Delia, Delia," he cried. "Could you marry me?"

"Oh, Goldstein. No," she said.

He relaxed, inch by inch, into the lounge. His fingers uncurled. His palms dropped open. "Goldstein! What a name! I don't blame you. I could only understand you a little better if it was Finklebein or Schlossenger. My God," he screamed, "aren't our noses enough? Why did we have to get such names? Ain't the hooked beak sufficient to give the world a laugh? What woman with a Christian name wants to swap it for 'Pleased-to-meet-you,-Mrs.-Baumgartner.' 'Jews not allowed in this apartment house.' Oh sure not. Tie your motor cars and your Jews out on the sidewalk where they belong. The land of the free and the home of the brave. Huh!"

An embarrassed humiliated flush tingled through her skin. She looked at Goldstein passionately, for the first time seeing him as an individual, an alien, a unit from a wandering race apart. As fantastic as he had looked a

moment before, he looked more tragic and isolated now. For the first time, the bitterness
of semiticism sickened her. The Jews. Cursed
by the malignance of a sect whose sweet message had been brotherly love, for twenty centuries Judah had been running before Christianity, those great heroic noses like prows
parting the wind. Love one another. Flee
as a bird to your mountain. All those nobly-
named fighters of the wilderness stories which
her grandmother used to talk about—Nap-
thali, Jethro, Ammiel and Hur,—why had
their lovely titles been lost in flight, why had
each lost his holy name? Sons of Judah.
From the Palestine hills to Riverside Drive,
from the Rose of Sharon to Schmalski's Deli-
catessen on Avenue A, —this had been their
new wilderness, via pogroms, inquisitions, re-
stricted privileges and unrestricted hate, a two
thousand year journey of beards, sheidles, in-
sults and special caps, of new European no-
menclature and fearful Atlantic immigration,
wanderers on the cruel earth, a people spat on,

reviled, burned at the stake until their talent for capitalism finally calmed the Christian heart and a gold standard sweetened the cross of Jesus at last.

"My dear," she said, "I don't love you. Your name could be anything in the alphabet but I wouldn't marry you. Why marry some-one I don't love?"

"Then let me have you anyhow." He threw himself against her chair. "How many men have had you? Why not me along with the rest? My God, don't I ache more than all the rest put together? Once Delia. Once, once. What does it mean to a woman any-how? Something she don't like but can't help, something men have always done while the woman thinks of something else. I'll give you everything on earth I got, if you only will. Delia. I'm crazy, I'm sick for you. Let me, let me." He jerked against her, tried to catch her knee. She saw his hand lift, a flash of fat between her and his face, swollen, grey, decked with streaming blue eyes. She threw him back and pulled herself from her chair. "Don't. How can you humiliate yourself that way, how can you try to buy me, borrow me, like an old hat? Oh, go on home, Goldstein. Go on home. Let me alone."

He sat for a minute then dragged himself away from the couch. She heard his slovenly hunt for his coat and stick. "What are you going to do? About him, I mean?"

She didn't look up. "Get him back if I can. If not—" She didn't know. She had no thoughts. From her bent head, her eyes touched on her new dress, at first aimlessly. Then with amazement she stared at this elaborate scheme of silk, observing it like something she had never seen before. What a needless embellishment of soft dyes. Those stitches there. That luxury of dead color and thread.

"And if you don't get him, then you'll be going after someone else. You will, you will. What'll I do?" He was crying by the door. His muffled pain floated across the stretch of walled space to throw itself into the fire.

"Marry him. Marry someone. Settle down and stick, Delia. Promise it. Promise it," he shouted.

She looked over at him. The shadows blotted out all his face except his protuberant eyes and they had that permanent bereaved curve in their popping arch, that sad circling look of desolation that ornaments a cemetery tomb where, beneath the frippery of carving, the disappointments and the disasters of the dead seem to be seeping through granite joists, and the horror of the defunct gathered in their public place states in final terms, the miserable futility of most of the hopes of human flesh.

"Goodnight." She turned away. She heard the door close. She twisted a scarf over her eyes and with the light still burning in a wasted electric vigil, stretched herself on the couch. Her gown was matting into new chiffon pillows beneath her. In the plaid darkness of the silk binding her head she tried not to think, to feel nothing, to see no images and listen for no sound.

VIII

COMING back into the livingroom again, Delia circled it uncertainly. Then with loose hands braided together like a white buckle against her black dress, she stood for a moment and sat down. The apartment in the Mews was too small. At every turn today she encountered her mother. Or an Excelsior mahagony chair. Or the familiar facet of the room she had just walked out of and now sought again to take her away from the minute bedchamber she had entered as relief. Three rooms, kitchen and bath: all modern comforts except that of privacy. Where in the compressed pyramided dwellings of New York did rent-payers go when their hearts were breaking? Only the rich with their châteaux on state hills or the commuters with their vacant lots had means to hide themselves and secrete their grief, turning it up on a face that lifted to the sky like another new piece of suburban equipment.

She took a deep breath, stood up.

"Are—are you going out, dear?" her mother asked. She suspended her silver pen, looked up from her monogrammed note. She was writing to someone for whom she cared nothing and her child was suffering. The silver pen trembled.

Delia shook her head. "No. No, I'm not going out." No one could have thought she was. Even Delia would not have walked out into the January Sabbath without a hat or coat. Mrs. Poole knew that. But when she looked at her daughter, her heart ached. And sometimes when she could no longer stand the restless silence, it spoke, lifting little phrases to her mouth like gushes of blood that cost suffocation and yet turned to innocuous froth on reaching the air, dissolving into, "Perhaps we would better open the window?" or "Shall we build up the fire again?" Nothings. And always instead of a direct grammatical appeal to Delia's younger strength was substituted that persistent predicating "we" which more than the new logs Delia dropped on to the

coals or the door she set adraft through which
the wind was for a moment allowed to blow,
gave the room its temperature, nervously
warm but with blasts of raw ether in it as if
Mrs. Poole's susceptibility was what alter-
nately chilled or heated the atmosphere with
burning or freezing pain. "If you're not going out—" Her pen still hung in the air. She
looked as if she wished to say more but such
futile attacks on silence were all she dared offer. What she wanted was, abandoning words
entirely, to pull Delia into her arms, strain
her to her breast and, weeping because the
over-grown flesh had come of passionate age,
yet for one minute pretend behind closed eyes
that the dangling legs, the unmanageable
torso, the heavy head had miraculously shrunk
to child's innocent size again and fitted sweetly
onto the maternal lap—the big knowing
bones, the mature extra flesh somehow re-
duced, someway melted by her burning tears
like one of the snow-men of Delia's early days
which, looking from the window years ago,

Mrs. Poole had sometimes watched dwindle to cradle-size under the hot grief of the sun.

Mrs. Poole knew what was wrong. For the first time in her short sojourn with Delia in New York, she had finally got hold of a fact. She had made up her mind, at least, that Delia had been jilted. But she knew nothing of what might have led up to it. Sometimes in the week that had elapsed since New Year's Day, she wished she knew everything about her child. Everything. This was at night when she could not sleep. It had taken her more than a year to get used to sleeping in the house where she had first gone with James Poole and all others in the twenty-five years' subsequence had given shocks to her somnolence. Now this was the last—trying to learn to sleep in New York and with Delia her daughter, the last and most profound link of family life, suffering, the thickness of a thin wall away. And nothing to be done for her. This was what wrapped Mrs. Poole's blue suit in loose dignity upon her dwindling flesh. Incapable of aiding, she could do nothing even to protect herself from the sight she saw for she too was without a haven in the Mews—no garden as in Excelsior where with her mind busily turning problems, her hands churned the heavy earth and decisions were slipped into fertilizer along with seeds which would blossom, like after-thoughts, in the spring, no slow walks on empty suburban side-walks where with domestic property-owning eyes she noted "improvements" on neighboring lots while the marital crises—new maids, old debts or her James' too ardent love —was forgotten for a moment in a nimble calculation of taxes and the increased price the Pooles could get for their own acreage if they sold it now by the foot.

She sealed her letter. She wondered what she had written. There were women in Excelsior—leaders in clubs, a singer or so, a prominent lawyer's wife—to whom, for some reason, she had been a beacon, something superior and refined in the soft-coal smoke of the town. They had, because of their energy, been her friends. But she had left them. What had she written to keep their amity going? "I saw the Ibsen revival. . . . It is cold here. Faithfully, Agatha Poole."

She turned from her uncertain reflection in the mahogany desk and looked across the room at Delia. The disappointment she had always known that her only child was not more grandiosely built, (as if flesh were an assurance against those mistakes in life which slim Mrs. Poole felt slender women inevitably made) struck her now with a heavy accumulation: the black dress she wore narrowed not only Delia's body but her appearance of youth of which, suddenly, nothing, as she stood there, seemed left but her unalterable head, still precociously yellow and young and as signal in its vitality as when Mrs. Poole had first felt it pushing out into the world. "Delia! What *is* the matter? You're thin, darling. Thin. Oh you've eaten nothing for days," Mrs. Poole cried. At her voice, Delia turned, met her mother's eyes and the desire her

mother had momentarily felt to have Delia
tell her everything, dwindled, was silenced in
confusion and reserve of that glance. "Don't
—don't you think we might have a cup of tea?
It—it would only take mother a moment to
make it," Mrs. Poole substituted. Her tone
had changed. She had not dared mention
Paul. But, like a covert reference to him, she
had described the body his absence had altered
and which, all the more because he no longer
cared for it, she guarded. Men's appetites
came and went, she thought, her face tightening bitterly, but she had watched over
Delia's flesh for years and not grown weary,
giving it the meager breast when young, testing on the maternal cheek the heated bottle
during the infantile "second summer," later
forcing carrots and greens on a young Amazon
who preferred meat. Now that routine was
over. Of the long guardianship, nothing but
the pain and anxiety were left. "Let mother
make some tea," she begged.

Delia looked at her mother. When as now,

Mrs. Poole spoke of her maternity in the third person, helplessly referring to it like an identity that demanded a grammar and form apart, —when in her selfless concentration the perpendicular pronoun was lost entirely and if she spoke there was no ego left except the upright loveliness of her voice offering its owner's sacrifice, then, Delia knew, she had reached the limits of her emotional endurance. Only one development lay beyond it—the embarrassment of intimacy. Tea, Delia thought, evading her mother's eyes. Delia disliked tea. But her mother knew that. The familiar Chinese infusion—for the Pooles it was always Oolong with a pinch of hyson buds—was being offered only as a substitute for words, which against her desire, Mrs. Poole was being driven into demanding: instead of "Oh tell mother everything, darling," whispered with embarrassed eyes, if Delia chose there could sound through the room only the tinkle of silver, trembling in her mother's hands and a grateful constrained, "One lump or two, dear?"

"I'll make the tea," said Delia. She even smiled, a heavy labial gesture and saw her mother's eyes, fading from tenseness into a momentary curiosity as she left the room and turned into the pantry beyond. She thinks the tea won't be fit to drink, Delia thought. And she's probably right. But she stumbled resolutely into the kitchen, sick for a moment with the effort she was making and the unfamiliar smell of the room which was scrupulous yet embalmed with all its cold dead Sunday afternoon odors of desertion, resting soap, tinned supplies and unlit gas—a laboratory in tile attempting to make up by modern hygiene for the lost bouquet and charm of immigrant braziers, spicy with garlands of garlic, or the comfortable dirty "range" of earlier western farmwives where, night or day, while females toiled early and late, some stew or mush boiled its inviting hot perfume amid the hanging armoury of copper or feudal black pots.

Someone was at the street door. She heard the bell and faintly, the sound of her mother's inquiring footsteps. Inert on the cook's single chair, as if sharing the social isolation of a domestic to whom guests were only a sound in the front part of the house, she did not even wonder whom it might be. It wouldn't be Paul: so it could be anyone else. She didn't care. All her life luxurious and optimistic by nature, in the last week Delia had forced herself to do without immediate hope, as if it were something she could no longer afford. She had afforded everything else. Gowns. Hats. Furs. As if she had just met Paul, not lost him, she had acquired a fresh chronology of impressive costumes. But beneath their silk and occasional color lay no expectancy, none of that dressing, that timely toilette of the nerves, that gala gayety in their fringed ends to catch at credulity as passementerie catches at light until the scarlet network of embroidery blazes. She had none of that swelling of the flesh until expectancy gives it the thick

erect softness of velour and the body is covered
with an epidermal velvet which, like a last luxury, lines the silk of a sensitive gown. She had
tried to get Paul back and had failed. In
years past, a slow economical stare had
brought men to her door. And to Paul she
had despatched expensive words, had written
them first, had wired them later. Can explain
everything. Stop. Must see you. Stop.
Love as ever. Stop. Delia Poole. But he
had not appeared.

She opened the door to tell her mother that
the tea, such as it was, was ready. Its stewing
leaves made a jet of scented steam in the cold
air of the room. Through the passageway
leading into the front of the house, she heard
the sound of a voice. A male voice. It was
Paul's. For a moment it made no impression.
For a week, every new voice she heard had
numbed her. The first sound of it had been
like a blow on her ear whose disappointment
paralyzed and she had stood each time, unable
to move, her whole body affected by sensation

and excitement that couldn't have been more intense if the emotion forcing it had been ecstasy, the physical ordeal being as keen as if, once set for a manifestation, the nerves patriotically carried it through to a conclusion and defeat afforded the same exhausting result as victory. And now that she really heard him speak, she felt almost nothing. She had repeated her sensations too often. For seven days, waiting for his voice which had never come, her emotions and her straining ears had built up a legend: in her imagination his voice had attained a musicalness which Paul himself would have despised but which, unconsciously improved by longing, had finally come to stand for him and which, as often as she thought of him, she heard like an opera composed of a single sublimated false tenor, performing outside her closed door. Now it would never come again. She turned toward the person who could never repeat it, stumbling with relief to go toward him in the far room.

They were facing away from her. Her
mother was folding and unfolding her hands,
pulling at the flesh, tucking in the lacy fingers
as if working over a mussed handkerchief.
"It's a—a pleasure and gratification finally to
meet my — my daughter's fiancé." Mrs.
Poole's head was balancing in the air. Her
eyes, judged in blackened profile, were apparently aimed at Paul, pinning him down, each
nod tightening him to his place before her, each
word, as if its soft sound were not a conventional blow, a stroke under which he stood
motionless, a silent young man with his hat in
his hand, struck dumb before her dignity and
grey hair. "I had hoped we were going to—
to see you—before this."

The room had probably finally turned cold.
As she listened a chill ran through Delia. It
was like the drafty blast that always eddied
in the wings of a stage in whose center it
seemed to her that her mother at last stood
amateurish, superb, talking with restrained
gestures, amidst a set of Excelsior furniture,

and bringing, with talent that had never been given a showing before, the only emotion she had ever had to the only rôle she had ever known.

"Oh. Yes. I—I couldn't come till today. Until now." Paul answered and then as if he had sensed Delia the way animals sense each other's arrival, he turned. "Delia."

She felt her limbs start and saw him coming toward her, then was touched, not so much by his kiss, as by his effort before her mother as he fumbled near her mouth. "Your mother was just saying—"

On hearing herself mentioned, Mrs. Poole wavered, then moved. "I'll fetch the tea. The maid is—" Paul could barely have heard Mrs. Poole's apologies or the sound of her disappearance. She's throwing out the tea I made, thought Delia. She's starting to boil fresh water. It will boil away to nothing. She's sitting on my chair now, trembling. She won't be in here for half an hour. "You have a new suit," she said. It was brown. Browner even than the dullness of his tanned face. "And you're thin."

"No, I'm not, I'm older. That's all," he said. At first he had been able to keep his eyes from settling on her but now they fell on her with consuming attention. "You look well," he said. It was an accusation.

"I'm not. I feel wretchedly." Yet she had waited so long to see him that relief gave her an involuntary pleasure despite her uncertainty. She realized she should be wondering how she looked—disturbed for fear her black gown lay on her with its customary disorder or that her face, which it seemed to her could at best only be pardoned by saying it was silent and mortal, had any more than a year ago when Paul last saw it that deep-eyed look of porous endurance which afforded its plateaus their curious balance of picturesque recumbent hollows and high lights usually seen, she knew, only in votary effigies. "I have had," she said, "what one might call a bad year."

"So Nancy told me." He laughed with satisfaction. But he did not believe her. His eyes had changed. Delia wondered what he had been doing and thinking on his hemp island. Even without Nancy. And what he had been doing, perhaps under Nancy's guidance, since he had come back to his own land. She would never know. He had changed; that much she saw. Grown thin, she thought. Wise, he said. He was not the same. She still loved him but he was not the same.

"Yes, Nancy told me you'd had—quite a year. She told me that, among other things." This was what he had so wanted to say that he had refused to see her. Now that he had the opportunity, his voice shook with lack of practice. "You might as well know, Delia, that Nancy told me quite a lot. Everything, perhaps. I—I hope so."

"Oh." She sat quiet a moment then in a gesture without defense, she spread out her long hands, each finger naked and elemental like the ribs on a ripped fan. She looked at him without speaking. "If you haven't already done it," she said finally, "you'll have to choose, Paul, between Nancy and me."

She waited. If he had spoken now, his voice would have had on her the effect she had imagined it would have the past weeks when she had been waiting for its sound. In no matter what tone it would have come, it would affect her like an unbearable pleasure. The roaring in her ears, that dullness she had felt when he first walked into the room, was replaced by an acuteness that his faintest whisper could have shocked. But when he said nothing at all, color started spreading under her skin as if, without having uttered a sound, he had been able to burst some vital center of her receptiveness from which her pride, her blood and wounded faculties drained in disorder over her face, swelling her features with scarlet, and loading even her painted lips until they shook, unable to hold so much color and weight.

"Oh, leave Nancy out of it," he cried finally. "Why didn't you ever tell me the truth? Why did you wait to have me hear it from her? You know what I mean. I told you all about myself. But you—"

"You were jealous," she said. "Jealous people are always lied to. And I never tell, anyhow," she added after a pause. She had thought over his demand. Why should she have told him, a year ago, about all the previous elements that had made up her life? Only their result,—what they had made of her —should have concerned or excited Paul. All the subterfuge Nancy had put her to, all the decent criminal shame her mother had forced her to feel, Delia struggled against now. "I told you, that night in my rooms, that I had never loved anyone as I loved you. That was true. It's true now. Nothing else was important. I didn't have anything else to say."

"But since then? What have you to say about what's happened since then? Oh, that's what I can't understand. And didn't I see it coming, too? The night the flowers came I asked what they meant. Now I know." He closed his eyes. He was unwilling to look at her. "Well, what have you to say?"

"Nothing." She tried to move. Any motion in her body would have been a relief. But she could not stir. The self-respect she had built up for herself a moment ago, crumbled. What excuse had she for what she had done to Paul? None. Except that his absence had been too protracted. Time was what she had not been able to manage. It was not her restless body, with its background of free habits, it was the restless months, that had betrayed her. Six months she could have controlled. It was the seventh and eighth that had defeated her. "I'm sorry." Paul's suffering was what was making her suffer now. The wine-soaked night on the Palisades that had been only blurred to her, was a clear event to him. It was the night she had betrayed him. And the night she had gone to his Quaker town and above all, the eve of that departure—that night when Grafton appeared out of the mist—what did those mean to Paul? Or did he know they had taken place? She was ashamed. Even her victories those two evenings were forgotten in this moment when it seemed to her that every human being who lived, lived only to apologize for going through existence housed in the undignity of chemical flesh. "What happened when you were gone will never happen again," she protested. "Believe me, Paul. Oh, I know what I say. It will never happen. Never, never."

He didn't answer for many minutes. There was no sound from beyond the door. Invisible and quiet, her mother too sat waiting. The sound of voices could only be a blurr to her ears. But silence would be acute and even more informing. Quiet, as now, was what would give her agony.

"I believe you," Paul said finally. "Probably it might never happen again. But it's too late now. I know too much about you. Or maybe I don't know enough. When I think of all she told me—But what if there're still things about you I don't know. How will

I ever be sure? Still, I know enough. I know all about you, do you hear?" he cried. "All. All. Do you hear?"

"It isn't how much you know. It's how much you care about me that would have counted. That was important. Now—now nothing is. No, it's finished." She shook her hand at him. She didn't want to hear his voice any more. He had failed her. She had never expected anything of herself but she had expected everything of Paul. She had her weaknesses but so did he. "I would have forgiven you anything," she said. "Anything you might ever have done. What people do is of no importance. It's what one feels for them that counts. Perhaps I regret—some things I did before I met you. But it's for me to regret, not you. It was my life, not yours. What I did since I met you—what I did that one night—that is your affair. I wish it had never happened. It had nothing to do with my caring for you. It would never happen again. It's too late—but it would never happen again." She stopped. "Goodbye." She stood up. She was no connoisseur. She had never known how to prolong pleasures. She didn't know now how to prolong pain. The agony she felt she wanted to cut short. She wanted to go away with it and sit somewhere alone.

"Goodbye?" Paul echoed. "I don't want you to say goodbye. I want you to explain." For each item he had suffered he wanted her now to pay him with a word. For his jealousy, he wanted an inexhaustible flow of soothing phrase. Where she had hurt him by silence he wanted now to be healed by her voice. "Anyhow, it's not for you to say goodbye. That's for me. I'm the one who has that privilege. I'm the one who's been wronged," he cried.

"Yes. But we can't change that. So there's nothing to do." There was a long silence. She heard her watch tick. She wondered if there was a clock in the kitchen for her mother to endure.

"So you think I should forgive you?" he demanded.

"I would forgive you. No matter what you did."

"But I would never do anything."

Probably he wouldn't. "We're different." Emotion wasn't enough to draw people together. They had to be similar, they had probably to act alike. It had never occurred to her before. "We care for each other, but that doesn't help us. So there's nothing more to be done."

"Yes, we care for each other." His admission was almost inaudible. It gave him no pride. And it brought her no result. He did not move. She started toward her room. What was her life going to be like, now? What would she do tomorrow or the day after? Nothing. Nothing. Her future had no more shape than her breath. She would continue moving and breathing but uselessly and without design.

The bell rang. Someone was standing in the Mews at her door. "Ah! That's your latest admirer," jeered Paul. "And I was admitting I loved you! Every man does. Even Uncle Boyd in his way. That's he at the door. Delia, don't you ever let any man alone? Why did he go to see you? I don't know. And understand even less why he made me come this afternoon. Yes, his idea. Not mine. Oh, I never wanted to look at you again. But how could I explain to my family? What could I say to them? They knew everything about us except the truth. And now they'll suffer. Yes and your mother, too."

"Yes," she said with effort. Why need they have known, these older Jarvises and Pooles? She and Paul were young. They belonged in the same decade and could stand what was true. "I don't want to see your uncle." The communizing of private passionate emotion— the rendering of it in terms of family gatherings, public approvals, and the understanding satisfied nods of remote cousins and aunts

—this was what she had always run away from, put to one side.

"Oh, let him come in." Paul threw his arms in the air. "Call your mother, too. How can we get away from our families? What we do they pay for. What they once did, we pay for by being alive. They made us; didn't they? Well, let them stand around and suffer until we all forget and you and I can't feel any more. Or until—" He walked toward her and threw his arms about her. "Delia." Suddenly he kissed her. His mouth touched only the corner of hers. In this unexpected blindness, so he touched her, he didn't care where his embrace fell. The bell rang again. "I'll tell him to come in," he whispered.

Delia wondered how long her mother had been waiting in the door. She had a silver tray in her hand, studded with small offerings in pots. Cream that trembled as she held it and compote of fruits picked and glassed before Mrs. Poole, like another ripe product, had been torn from her familiar suburban vines. Delia tried to speak. She saw her mother was making an effort not to weep. Her soft brown eyes had been set for the pessimistic contortion of middle-aged grief. Now to change from pain to hope was for Mrs. Poole only an added shock.

Sitting a few moments later, her chilling cup in her hand, Delia tried to look about the room. What had altered it so? Paul was by her side. The warmth of his knee shook and pressed against hers. Old Jarvis, paired with her mother's grey hair, leaned over the silver tray, his words and the clatter of his spoon coming across the distant carpet to sound in Delia's ears. What seemed strange as she sat among familiar mahogany objects—polished wood that served only Pooles, chairs that had domiciled and been ignored by her ever since she was a child? These two men were altering an effect she had never even noted before.

Their presence and its circumstance, were making some change. Uncle Boyd's voice had set a new imported note from that lyre-legged table which her mother had used for so many years merely to give her own family tea. The privacy, the close union of the Pooles was gone. One of two women in the room and erect against its background of grey walls, Mrs. Poole facing the elder Jarvis, sat politely listening with the approbation which her generation had always offered the voice of any man.

The moment had come. Delia felt as if she were helplessly drifting into a profession for which she had neither talent nor love. Driven by circumstances and devotion, led by lack of privacy and the exhaustion from suffering, she was closing in on a question that would deprive her of all she wanted except Paul. "Will you marry me?" She did not look at him. He did not answer. But without waiting for them to be alone, his hand covered hers, his fingers clinging, setting her rings deep in the ornament of her flesh. For a moment she tried to think what she had done by her demand. But it was too late. She looked across at her mother. It was the only way.

Slowly Delia closed her eyes, her head sightless, erect, and yellow, holding its distance from the shadows that spread around her in her chair.

FINIS

Afterword

By Janet Flanner

It was on my fifth birthday that I stated I
wanted to be a writer when I grew up. It was
my mother who in a semihumorous adult joke
had asked me at the breakfast table, with its
disorder of my various modest birthday gifts
and their discarded gay paper wrappings, what
my choice of a future profession was going to
be—"to assure for me an interesting fairly
prosperous adult life." Apparently my answer to my mother was immediate, unequivo-
cal, and surprising, even to me. I said that
when I grew up I was going to write books.
"You are going to be an author, darling," my
mother cried with pride. "Do you know how
to spell it?" I made a bad job of it, leaving
out the *u*, the diphthong being beyond me
though my sister Maria, five years my senior,

had supposedly just finished teaching me how to spell even complicated rare words. My first day in public school in Indianapolis where we lived the teacher wrote on the blackboard the word *honor* and asked who could pronounce it. Only I could and did but under questioning I did not know what it meant which was a comedown. When I was in the second grade some school inspectors chanced to visit my classroom and asked me, probably because I sat in the front row, to read aloud to them. Reading aloud was my forte and I dashed through the first page of whatever book they had put in my hand with such speed that the inspectors told my teacher I should at once be promoted to the third grade. I was sent home with a note to my father announcing my promotion.

Next day I returned to class with his note of refusal. He said I was weak in arithmetic which he considered fundamental in education and that I should remain in the primary class, if only to learn to write more legibly. (Today after more than sixty years of penmanship my handwriting is still difficult to decipher, even for me.)

In the sixth grade my father shifted me to a new private school that had just been opened named Tudor Hall which up to a few years ago, at least, was still extant. There I had a wonderful Latin teacher from Cornell named Miss Ann Browning Butler, tall, thin, aristocratic, who had had a carpenter cut a series of wooden blocks for the reconstruction of that famous bridge of Caius Caesar which we read about and which we rebuilt on a large table in the Assembly room while addressing each other in a kind of pig-latin.

It was also at Tudor Hall that I met with the diagramming system for teaching grammar then replacing the old system of oral parsing. Diagrammed sentences looked like beautiful architectural drawings of horizontal, vertical, and angled lines on which the sentences' words roosted like birds perched on various lengths of wire. The diagram lines elucidated the sentences' structure as well as the relations of all its words in a linear system of visible grammatical logic that permanently guided the shaping of my own writing style, such as sufficed to satisfy the strict editor of the *New Yorker,* Harold Ross, and has kept me as a contributor to that magazine for nearly fifty years. Not only did Harold Ross have a passion for grammar, he was also in love with words. We would sometimes see him sitting at his desk in the office reading Webster's dictionary as if it were a novel and he loved to have his secretary read aloud to him from a book of synonyms. Apparently diagramming is no longer taught in American schools judging by the slovenly grammar used by many young writers today.

I am not a first-class fiction writer as this reprinted first novel shows. Writing fiction is not my gift. Writing is but not writing fiction. My best writing about people has been about well-known people who had been public characters and thus had been apt to be already dead or famous as living artists and thus slightly historical rather than ordinary mannerly people struggling with private hopes and dilemmas, such as Henry James dilated upon in the *Golden Bowl* or in that tragic-character novel *The American,* the most interesting to me of all he wrote because I spent much of my adult life in France and thus knew how true it is that humans from differing civilized races

and educations can remain alien to each other,
even in love. Like most authors of a first
novel, in mine I fell back upon the people I
knew best, my family, as my characters. I
recall having noted that Colette always wrote
only what she knew about, including the characters in her novels. She invariably borrowed
them from the limited life she already knew,
mostly in a provincial setting. This left her
free to utilize her literary gift for perfecting
her style of writing rather than in creating
imaginary human beings.

The dramas of reality especially if tragic are
practically always more vivid when related on
the front page of a newspaper, and as fact than
if written even with genius as tragic fiction, as
the Russians with their special racial gift for
mixing blood with their ink customarily write
them, as Dostoievksy did. America has in recent years specialized in fiction dealing with
novels featuring crime: yet what professional
crime-writing expert could have invented a
creation so complicated and involved as Water-
gate, with such a population of participants?
Only men alive, not pens or typewriters could
have produced it as a creation, above all cre-

ated to include the psychology of so variable a President—a President who behind him had in array previous presidents of the type whose visages make a moralistic portrait gallery on our nation's stamps.

For a writer of stature the great need is to have been born gifted. That is the richest, rarest endowment any young ambition can thank its stars for. Talent is a gift of the gods. It is the supreme good fortune in mysterious equipment. Talent is the supreme surprise furnished by nature. Talent is inimitable, being genuine. It is thus the richest of all possessions.

Textual Note: The text of *The Cubical City* published here is a photo-offset reprint of the first printing (New York and London: G. P. Putnam's Sons, 1926). The following six emendations have been made by Janet Flanner.

32.18	beneath [below
51.18	tails, like [tails like
	sailors had [sailors, had
345.6	birth of [birth and death of
394.22	an unit [a unit
415.10	in his [in her

M. J. B.

DATE DUE

WITHDRAWN

PRINTED IN U.S.A.